THE LAUGHING STRANGER

VIÑA DELMAR

The Laughing Stranger

HARCOURT, BRACE AND COMPANY

NEW YORK

Contents

THE *Homecoming*

WITHOUT KNOWING US as we were it would be impossible to appreciate the impact that the woman whose name was Brandon had upon us. And yet I hesitate to describe us as we were. It is so easy to be misunderstood.

I would not have you think that I admired her, for she was wicked. I would not have you think that there was ever a moment in which I liked her. Instead I would have you believe that she came among us and we reacted as we had been destined to react. Or does that sound as though I thought us so important that Fate or perhaps God Himself had troubled to send her to us?

And there I am back again at the beginning, at the realization that none of it makes sense unless we, especially those of us who knew her well, are clear to you. I must take the risk of being misunderstood. Without the risk there is no chance of understanding. It occurs to me that with that comment I have summed up more of the difficulties of living than I had intended.

We were a star-crossed family. Things had happened to us. Tragic things. And here I must beg you to be very sure that you do not identify us with the things of which we were the victims. Do not believe us to be dark and glowering as our misfortunes. If this word of warning offends you please forgive me but I know from experience that there are those who cannot disassociate ill luck from the person whom it has befallen. Thus, in a confused way, the sufferer becomes something to avoid, something from which one shrinks in horror. We, as I said, were a star-crossed family but we remained, I think, in the general pattern of other families. This often surprised people. I remember a new cook who was astonished to find that we intended to celebrate Christmas in the usual way, with gifts and feasting. I presume that she wondered at our having the heart for celebrating. Either that or she thought that we ourselves were the very essence of tragedy and would naturally spend Christmas brewing a poison cup.

I would like to tell about Aunt Laurel first. Aunt Laurel was in her forties at the time of which I write. She was a tall woman with an extraordinarily good figure and a fine complexion. She had an average mind. There were moments however when one was stunned by the shrewdness of her observations. Alas, there were also times when one stood unbelieving at the utter stupidity of her reasoning. Aunt Laurel managed the affairs of our household, my mother having died at my birth. My mother had been a very beautiful woman. All mothers who die young, die beautiful. I think this is a tradition. Or perhaps a plot. The child who has not seen its mother has missed the most heavenly creature who ever trod the earth and must be content to treasure a tintype of a rather commonplace girl with slightly popping eyes and dull, straight hair.

Aunt Laurel was unmarried. Before I was born her evil hour had found her. She had been betrothed to a young man from Boston. It had been the perfect romance. Love, good looks, wealth, the approval of the two families. All these things had existed in abundance. And then on the day before the young man, his family and friends were to set off for New York and the pre-wedding festivities Aunt Laurel's love went boating and was drowned.

I do not think it is a reflection on Aunt Laurel's mental health

to say that she almost went mad with grief. I consider her reaction
to this disaster perfectly normal. She was young and desperately in
love. I would consider her indeed odd had she met the situation
with fortitude or with a philosophical approach. She did neither.
She gave herself up to sorrow and almost died of it but because
she is normal the fundamental soundness of her being would let
her weep only so long. And in time the young man who drowned,
though never forgotten, became someone who had been adored by
a different, happier girl.

There are stories about Aunt Laurel's wedding gown. Yes, it is
true that she saved it. It is as beautiful as moonbeams. What was
she to do with it? Burn it in the parlor stove? Abandon it on a
dust heap? Give it away? To whom? The poor do not marry in
such a gown and any friend of Aunt Laurel's would have under-
standably shuddered at the idea of accepting it as a gift for her
own wedding.

It is a lie that the gown stood upon a dressmaker's figure in
Aunt Laurel's room. It is a lie that she wore it on the anniversary
of the day that should have seen her wedding. The gown rested in
an enameled chest in the storeroom, carefully guarded against the
inroads of time. I do not know why it was not allowed to crumble
away into dust. I do not know why Aunt Laurel preserved it. She
was not saving it for me. Certainly she knew I would never marry.
I admit her careful coddling of the gown was foolishly sentimental
but one would suppose from the stories that were told that every
night as the clock struck twelve Aunt Laurel slipped into her
wedding gown and rode to St. Thomas's church. The stories were
lies circulated in the beginning by servants and carried on by
ladies over their tea cups or in the drawing room while waiting
for the gentlemen to finish their cigars. It is an irresistible story

for it contains all the elements of romance and it suddenly strikes me that perhaps here and now I have given a new credence to the old stories for I am unable to deny the premise. I am unable to say that Aunt Laurel did not save and cherish her wedding gown.

Aunt Laurel's brother, Powell, was my father. I had always called him by his given name. How this came about I do not know. It must have been a whim of mine in the beginning and since all my whims were solemn, if not sacred, considerations in our household I was never compelled to use a conventional form of address. Powell was a lawyer. He was almost *the* lawyer in those days which is now twenty years ago. Surely no legal mind in New York was valued above his. But Powell, though handsome and successful, had withdrawn from social life and there is no deadlier carrier of venom than a disappointed hostess. Powell's brilliance was not in his favor. Indeed it counted against him when the gossip started. All that closing himself away with his books. Dear, dear, no man could do that and have his brain function healthily. Especially when one considered—

As I remarked earlier my mother died when I was born. Powell had loved her well and this in itself was sad but even I, as a child, had seen the deeper sadness, the injustice of the blow he had received. To have exchanged her for me was unthinkable. I did not see how Powell could continue to love God or believe in His fairness or kindness. To have taken my mother and left me seemed both wasteful and cruel. She had a place in life, a reason for being. Yet He had taken her and saddled Powell with me. I had nothing to give, nothing to get. It seemed outrageous. And yet I never knew of Powell to imply in any way that he doubted God's plan.

When I was two he fell in love again. The lady, as I understand it, was lovely and charming and completely fascinated by Powell. She was the daughter of a fine family and the wedding date was named. I hasten to say she was not drowned. Perhaps for Powell that would have been easier.

Instead he brought her to the house one afternoon to visit his children. Brett, who was five, she had seen before and, I am informed, she adored him. She had not seen me. Was it that I was too young to have been awake on the occasions when she had seen Brett? Or had Powell purposely— I don't know so why should I speculate? In any case she saw me that afternoon.

After the engagement was broken Powell never went out again socially and he withdrew from his clubs. His law practice was not neglected and our home life, I assure you, was amiable and wholesome. There was nothing either sinister or morbid about Powell. It was simply that he had had all the heartache he felt able to absorb and he was through. That is all. He devoted himself to us and was an excellent father and an amusing companion. It is not true that he was so steeped in bitterness that he spoke to no one save on business. And it is not true that he hated me and prayed for me to die. He loved me dearly. God knows why.

Now comes the moment I have dreaded. It must be obvious that I have put off the inevitable. Perhaps I can delay it another moment. Perhaps I can first tell of Brett, my brother. But I may as well have it over now as then. Very well. I am named Elizabeth and I have a crooked back. And I never grew very tall and there isn't any doctor anywhere who could do anything about it even though Powell tried everywhere.

There, now I can talk about Brett. Wonderful, handsome Brett who was our joy. He was red-haired, not coarsely, yellowly red-haired but darkly russet except when sunbeams found his hair and turned it into flame. He was tall and straight and gay. His laughter would ring through the house and startle the servants in the basement who were whispering of Aunt Laurel's wedding gown. Brett, my magnificent brother who was not one of us. Brett of whom no peculiar stories were told.

When the war came Powell knew that Brett must go. Young men like Brett must always go. If they do not feel the urge to go then they are not like Brett. Powell debated how Brett should go. And he debated when Brett should go and while he debated Brett went. He enlisted without waiting to find out what Powell had in mind for him. The letters came regularly for a time, then they stopped and we had a communication from the War Department. Brett was dead, they told us. Dead at Fredericksburg. And because we couldn't stand the news there was a second communication. No, wait. Perhaps he isn't dead. Well, where is he? He is missing. Missing? Where? How? Oh, just a minute. We've found him. He's in a hospital. What hospital? We aren't sure. The records, you know, are so jumbled. We do our best but—

Powell sent a hundred letters to the capital, to Mr. Lincoln, to members of the cabinet, but it was many months before we knew that Brett was coming home.

Captain Newland brought him. The Captain had been a young lawyer in Powell's office but he did not linger in Powell's parlor. We had it decked with flowers and the tables were inviting with their trays of wine and fruit and pastries but the Captain stayed but a moment.

"Brett's glad to be home," he said.

We looked at Brett but he did not say that the Captain was right. He did not say that the Captain was wrong. He just stood there looking down at the floral pattern of the carpet. Aunt Laurel took him in her arms and kissed him and then led him toward a large chocolate cake.

"I remembered your favorite," she said.

He did not reply and he did not look at the cake.

"It was bad at Fredericksburg," Captain Newland whispered. "We advanced sometimes stepping on the bleeding bodies of our own men. They screamed and they died but we advanced. It was bad at Fredericksburg."

Powell said, "Have a drink."

The Captain shook his head. "You have one, sir," he said and was gone.

Brett stood in the center of the room gazing about him without pleasure, without interest.

"Sit down, Son," Powell said.

Brett remained standing there in his worn uniform, looking thin and shabby. Our eyes were riveted upon him. He was our love, our hope. Say something, Brett. Say something.

"Your room is ready if you'd like to rest," Aunt Laurel said. "Later Minette is coming over."

Brett walked to the window and stared out through the starched lace curtains into the square where nursemaids sat with their charges in the sun.

"Maybe you'd like to get out of that uniform. It must be heavy."

Brett turned from the window and walked over to the stove and stood with his back to us. There was no fire on this mild day and he seemed slightly incredulous of the bright glass jewels that did not gleam emerald and ruby as he remembered them. He put out his hand and touched the front of the stove experimentally.

"We have roast lamb for dinner," Aunt Laurel said. "Because you always liked roast lamb."

Brett opened the little door of the stove and peered into the blackness.

"But have some chocolate cake now and then get out of that uniform and take a nice bath and a good rest and—"

Brett slammed shut the little door of the stove. It made a ridiculously loud noise considering its size.

"Leave me alone, can't you?" he shouted. "Leave me alone."

Believe it if you can, it wasn't until that moment that we realized that he was one of us now. Someone of whom strange, sad stories could be told over the tea cups or while the gentlemen were having their cigars.

We got through the day. I am not sure how we did it for it was a bad day. I look back upon it and wonder how we managed. And yet I do know how we managed. I know because in the bleakest, the most terrible hours there is always that small, dauntless voice within that keeps piping foolish, cheery little words such as: It will be better when the doctor comes, or The boat will right itself when the storm abates.

For us it was Minette. When Minette comes it will be better. We were all thinking that. Brett had been fond of Minette. Perhaps even in love with her. To us all it had long seemed a certainty that one day Brett and Minette would marry though no one had ever voiced the thought.

And now we waited for her, expecting God knows what magic. Surely there was no wisdom in Minette, no source of calm, sure strength. There was nothing to her save a pink mouth, a cloud of yellow hair and a pair of huge, blue eyes and yet we sat there thinking that things would be better when Minette came. All the logic that abides in a great legal mind did not stay Powell from thinking that things would be better when Minette came.

And so we sat there, at first in silence and then, because each of us was overcome by a desperate yearning to prove to the others that nothing was really amiss, conversation began. You can guess the topics we chose. The weather, of course, to begin with, and from there it is child's play for a really clever conversationalist to introduce the subject of plant life and the birds one has noticed in the square of a morning.

You must understand that Brett took no part in the conversation. He sat staring down at his hands, acknowledging not the words directly addressed to him nor for that matter even our presence. Once he ran his fingers through his hair and Aunt Laurel went to him swiftly as though he had offered her a long-awaited opportunity.

"I always loved the color of your hair," she said. "I wonder if it's darkened any at the roots."

Her hands moved through my brother's hair, making sudden little paths of white scalp. We were mystified for a moment until we realized what she was doing. She was searching for signs of a head wound. When she returned to her chair we could not help but observe that the stricken look in her eyes had deepened. A head wound after all was something that could be understood, treated and prayed over. One scarcely knew how to pray for this other thing—this thing that had happened to Brett.

"Well," Aunt Laurel said briskly, seeing our eyes upon her, "Minette will be here soon."

"Yes," Powell replied and his eyes lighted with hopeful expectancy and one could see that in some curious way Powell had forgotten that Minette was a giddy seventeen. She had become something rather wonderful and vital like the tranquil-eyed miracle woman of fiction who comes down out of the mountains to bring balm and healing to all who suffer.

It is perhaps not necessary to say that only Brett kept his seat when the sound of carriage wheels was heard outside. We hurried to the window.

"That's Minette," Aunt Laurel assured us.

We all recognized the carriage but "That's Minette," Aunt Laurel said again.

Did we think that the sight of the girl would bring Brett back to us? That her soft voice, her small fluttering hands would lure him away from the confused, shadowy world in which he dwelt? Or did we think to lighten our grief by dividing it further? I cannot tell at this late date what we thought or what we hoped. I only know that our disappointment was strong and bitter when we saw the coachman alight and walk toward our door without having turned to give assistance to any passenger.

None of us spoke. We waited and the waiting was very long. It seemed an hour before the parlor maid entered carrying a note.

"For you, Ma'am," she said to Aunt Laurel.

"Have the man wait," Aunt Laurel ordered.

"Yes, Ma'am." The girl hurried to catch Minette's coachman who was already poised to drive away.

"There was no answer requested," Powell said. "Why should the man wait?"

"Why should this come to me?" Aunt Laurel countered and tore open the note.

She was having one of her lightning-swift revelations. I saw it, too, but not as speedily as she.

"Minette cannot come," Aunt Laurel said in tones sharp with the bite of acid. "Her mother writes to say that the child has one of the most devastating headaches possible."

"A pity," Powell said.

"Indeed." Aunt Laurel lowered her voice though such delicacy was not needed. "How could they have been so stupid as to address the apology to me? It was Brett, to all intents and purposes, who was expecting her, was it not? But the note did not come to Brett. And why not? Because they knew he was not—was not likely to read it. *They knew.*"

Powell lowered his gaze before Aunt Laurel's flashing eyes. It was clear, too clear. The waitress at Minette's house was sister to our cook's helper and the girl had visited our kitchen that day. That *could* be the way they knew, for know they assuredly did.

Aunt Laurel stood trembling with rage, her stiff silk skirt making a nervous rustling sound in the silent room. "Stupid. Unfeeling," she murmured. Then suddenly she wheeled and darted away, a fury in a well-fitted, plum-colored dress.

"Laurel!" Powell called after her. "Laurel, for God's sake—"

"This is woman's business," she shot back at him and we could hear her footsteps hurrying toward the hapless coachman.

I do not know what message she gave him to carry to Minette's mother but she came back to the room her color high, her mouth distorted in anger.

"Who are they to do this to Brett? How do they dare?" she demanded.

It struck me that they were not doing it to Brett at all for he alone remained untouched by Minette's defection. He continued to stare at his hands, scuffing occasionally at a loose bit of cuticle.

"Poor boy," Aunt Laurel said. "She'll come. Minette will come. Don't you worry."

"She'll come!" Powell turned in amazement.

"Of course she'll come. Once she knows we're not fooled she'll come. They cannot afford to insult us. Only the chance that Minette will make a moneyed marriage is keeping their credit good. Her mother will make her come!"

Powell said, "If that's the case you are very cruel, Laurel, and so is her mother—if Minette comes."

"I don't mind being called cruel in a case like this." Her eyes went to Brett and they were soft and tender though the rest of her seemed to bristle with fierceness.

It was odd how she did not seem to recognize that Brett, God help him, could not be hurt by Minette's mother or by Minette herself. It must have seemed to Aunt Laurel that he had been deeply cut and I grew frightened at the thought that in time Aunt Laurel would come to believe that it was Minette's desertion that had caused Brett to retreat into darkness.

"When Minette comes," I said, "if she comes, see her alone, Aunt Laurel. Explain that Brett is not well and—"

"She knows Brett is not well," Aunt Laurel snapped.

"But be pleasant to her and perhaps in a few days she will willingly return."

Aunt Laurel's thin black eyebrows came together in a frown. "He's yours," she said to Powell. "Not really mine. But if I have a vote I cast it against permitting Minette to temporize, to wait and see, and then come running back with shouts of blissful welcome the moment Brett is well again."

Powell said, "The whole matter as it concerns the girl is unimportant and I am tired of it."

He looked tired. Did people actually age in a few hours? I had heard that such was possible but I had never believed it—till now. Why wouldn't the evil fates leave him alone? I looked at Brett, Powell's child who had been fine and strong, and I thought about myself, Powell's other child. I thought of my dead mother and of the second woman Powell had loved and I went to him and offered him the comfort of my skinny, undersized hand.

Aunt Laurel said, "Unimportant, did you say, Powell Carpenter? Do you want your son to marry a girl who has not been taught the solemnity of the marriage vow? Brett loves her so I intend to impress upon her the meaning of the pledge which concerns itself with loyalty in sickness and in health. At this stage an afternoon call is even too much to expect of her apparently but after I have—"

"Laurel, Minette hasn't broken any vows to Brett. Do you remember that as yet she has taken no vows with him? My dear sister, I beg of you to be fair. She is not even engaged to him."

"But he has loved her since they were little ones in dancing class. Do you want him to marry a girl who—"

Powell turned wearily away from Aunt Laurel. He said, "I only pray that he will be able to marry someone. Anyone. Now, Laurel, let us be quiet. For the love of God, let us be very quiet."

And so we sat without conversation. No weather. No plants or birds. Just the quiet for which Powell had plead. Outside in the square there were children who raised their voices in song or laughter or simply in a shout, a joyous affirmation that they were alive. Within the room the flowers were already drooping and no one had cut the chocolate cake or chosen one of the shiny, sugary jewels from the pastry tray. We sat in silence.

When the carriage stopped again at our door we did not rush

to the windows. This time we sat rigidly and waited. Only by the twist of Aunt Laurel's lips could it be told that she was satisfied, that come what may she would always believe she had done what was right, what was best for Brett.

We waited till the parlor maid appeared and announced Minette.

"Show her in," Aunt Laurel said, coolly.

Powell rose to his feet and threw an anxious glance toward Brett. It is a strange thing how often custom and habit become our masters. And perhaps it is a good thing, for in that moment Powell was not concerned with the dreadful new misfortune that had befallen him. His mind was busy with one consideration and one only. A lady was entering the room and Brett was still seated. I noticed the tiny scowl that crossed Powell's face. "Damn it," it seemed to say. "The boy knows better. Where are his manners?" Powell slipped his hand beneath Brett's arm and urged him to his feet and the scowl disappeared and one would have thought that all in Powell's world was perfectly right again. In that moment only the insignificant had significance and I thought that perhaps our values were at fault and should be revised. There might be more happiness if we could be taught to regard death and destruction as the little things.

Minette came in moving in the manner of a pink and gold breeze. She always floated through a room. It was her high-arched feet, I supposed, or perhaps her lovely, lovely little figure with its straight back and good shoulders. The parlor maid had taken her bonnet and shawl and she stood facing us in a red challis dress upon which small white stars had been embroidered.

We greeted her cordially and she returned our greetings with polite remarks.

"These must be the things," I thought, "that people say to each other in the first chapter of books for foreigners who wish to learn conversational English."

All references to Minette's headache or to Aunt Laurel's instructions to the coachman were omitted. Everybody was extremely well and as transported with delight at the sight of the visitor as the visitor was with her charming hosts and hostesses.

It was Aunt Laurel who led Minette to the corner of the room where Brett was standing. I will always remember that there was a painting behind him. An Italian lake. I remember because as Minette approached Brett I looked into the blue-violet painted water and I said to God, "Respectfully I mention that You have not done much for this family. May I now suggest that for today we have had about as much as we can bear?"

Minette was not floating as she walked toward Brett. I had never before seen her step so heavy, her shoulders so inclined to droop.

"Here's Minette," Aunt Laurel said.

"Welcome home," Minette said in a thin little voice.

Brett considered her for a long moment. I will not say there was interest in his eyes but he was aware of Minette. And because I knew he was aware of her I was strangely heartened.

"Aren't you going to speak to Minette?" Aunt Laurel begged.

I thought this an exceedingly dangerous approach and wondered at her daring. After all Brett had not taken kindly to Aunt Laurel's prodding. There was no knowing what he might say or do.

No, there was no knowing. No knowing at all. Who could have been expected to remember how he had reached out to the cold, dead jewels in the parlor stove, finding them still colorful, still

reminiscent of other days and other fires? Who could know that
he would wish to touch the bright gold mist that was Minette's
hair?

I remember well for sometimes in the night it comes back to me,
the chilling horror of that awful moment. I had never heard a
woman scream and the terror of it washed my body in sudden
quick sweat. Perhaps as Brett raised his hand she thought that it
was his wish to strangle or strike her. Perhaps. But I do not believe
this is so. I believe Minette's fright was a primitive, unthinking
thing that awakened in hatred and fear at the touch of a man
who, for one reason or another, was not as other men. She
screamed and ran from him, striking out blindly down the considerable length of our parlor. She ran sobbing and babbling to
the hall and straight out the door to her carriage.

Powell said, "Her bonnet and shawl, Laurel. She has forgotten
them."

His voice was very calm and in his eyes there was a curious expression. He walked to the window and watched our parlor maid
carry Minette's belongings to her and I could not help but wonder
if, for him, this painful scene was merely a repetition of something
he had known before. Had another girl, wild with fright and revulsion, once run from this house? A girl who had been expected
to fondle and love a misshapen baby?

I looked at Brett. He was untouched by the scream and by
Minette's headlong flight. He stood motionless in front of the
Italian lake and perhaps it was an indication of our accustoming
ourselves to Brett that no one insisted that he must now seat himself.

It struck me that Minette's story when she reached home would
be an interesting one indeed. And she would not willfully lie. She

need only tell what she thought had occurred. It would be a splendid companion piece to go with Aunt Laurel's mad passion for her wedding gown and with Powell's withdrawal from the company of normal human beings.

Perhaps in Minette's story it would be very clear that Brett had rushed at her reaching for her throat or it might be that he had crushed her savagely in his arms and that only his father's intervention had saved Minette. It was true that there was still quite a lot we had been spared. The stories that had been told of us had never suggested that we were dangerous or violent. Perhaps the time had come for that.

Aunt Laurel went back to her chair and folded her hands. "It will be better after dinner," she said.

And now we sat waiting for dinner though no one could have been hungry. Eternities slid past us as we sat in our parlor and after a thousand years Hendon came in and lighted the gas and the topaz-colored globes gleamed for us and we found no cheer in them. And after awhile when the signal came we went to the dining room and surprisingly enough it was better.

I do not say that Brett ate an enormous dinner or that we all chattered eagerly like the happily-reunited family we had expected to be at this hour. But Brett consumed a fair amount of all that was piled upon his plate and we took a pathetic delight in the fact that his interest had been caught and held by the dumb-waiter which brought our food up from the kitchen.

"You used to ride upon it when you were a little one," Powell said. "Isn't that true, Hendon?"

"Indeed, sir. Many a time I remember my wife would pack Master Brett into it down in the kitchen and me standing right here would open the door and help him out and then he'd yell

until he was put back and received in the kitchen again. At the
end of a rainy day when he couldn't play outdoors my arms would
be ready to drop off with Master Brett's riding up and down."

We smiled. We did not bother to laugh. With some servants it
might have been necessary. But not with Hendon. We had never
been able to fool him and the time had come when we no longer
even tried.

"Your dessert, Master Brett," he said placing a great, over-
sized wedge of apple pie before my brother. And because Hendon
knew we understood him as he understood us he made no attempt
to conceal his own distress as he bent above Brett.

"That's very good pie," Aunt Laurel said, coaxingly.

Brett stood up and walked to the dumb-waiter and opened the
door as he had opened the door of the parlor stove. He felt of the
ropes and I was ashamed that we could not take our eyes from
him. It was as though we were watching a chimpanzee or some
other half-human thing, wondering what next would enter its
strange, subnormal mind.

Brett yanked upon the rope and the dumb-waiter rose. He
stared at it for a moment then closed the door.

"Do you see how it works, Son?" Powell asked.

To our amazement Brett nodded. "I knew," he said.

That was what he said. "I knew." And I can see that there is
no way of writing those two words so that you will be able to grasp
what they meant to us. He knew. A proper answer, properly
placed. We were seized by sudden excitement, even by a feeling
of well-being.

"I think I'll have another piece of pie," Powell said.

"Oh, do," Aunt Laurel begged. "I'll have more coffee." She

was not far from a girlish giggle and I knew how she felt for I, too, was suddenly, foolishly lighthearted.

After dinner we returned briefly to the parlor. We had conversation now. The three of us. It was stilted and meaningless but not so desperate as in the afternoon. Brett answered no questions directed at him and took no further notice of us but we were still beguiled by the memory of his beautiful speech concerning the dumb-waiter.

At length Powell suggested retiring and as sort of a guard of honor we all escorted Brett upstairs to his room. He spoke again at the threshold. He said, "I'm cold."

Aunt Laurel brought two extra blankets and I am sure that only Powell's stern disapproval restrained her from undressing Brett and seeing him safely bedded down.

"Can you manage, Son?" Powell asked.

There was no answer but we pretended that there had been. We said good night and went to our rooms. I did not undress. It was impossible to believe that the night could pass without incident. Brett's room was next to mine. I would be able to hear if he called and so I would stay dressed and ready.

I sat motionless listening and I heard the sound of the servants on the top floor preparing for bed. They walked softly but I fancied that I followed them through the ritual of hanging uniforms carefully upon their rightful hooks, of setting shoes down easily so as not to disturb the family. I even thought I could hear the cook drop to her knees for her nightly prayer. And finally there was silence on the top floor.

But in the room next to mine there was no silence. Brett was walking. I could hear him. Up and down. Up and down. Did he

need me? Did he want me? Or would he resent intrusion? I
stood irresolute and then decision came, for Brett had begun to
weep.

With less stir than a moth would create I went out into the corridor and into Brett's room. He had not taken off his clothes. He
was not really walking. I don't know why it frightened me so to
realize that he was marching.

"Brett."

He did not reply and when he faced me I saw tears streaming
wildly down his face. In his eyes there was a torment I had never
before seen in any eyes.

"Brother, I've come to help you. Tell me what to do."

And I knew that my appeal was childish and unworthy. For it
was I who must think of what there was to be done. The marching man who was my brother had his own concerns.

"You must tell what troubles you, Brett," I said, firmly. "Do
you want to talk?"

He turned from me and broke stride. He leaned against the
walnut chiffonier and gave himself up to his tears.

"Do you want to talk?" I asked again.

And after a bit he answered. "Not to you," he said.

I understood that he did not mean it unkindly. I knew exactly
what he meant. Yes, he wanted to talk, but in mercy he would not
tell me the things he had to say.

Swiftly I ran out again into the corridor. Aunt Laurel's door
flew open and there she was in her plum-colored dress standing
beneath the blue globe where the gas had been lowered for the
night.

"What is it?" she demanded.

"Brett wants Powell," I said. "Go to bed, Aunt Laurel."

And at that moment Powell, still fully dressed, came from his room. "Trouble?" he asked.

"I do not think so, Powell. I think it may be good."

Powell hurried into Brett's room and closed the door. For a long time he stayed there and I could hear the sound of their voices. Powell's infrequently. Brett's high-pitched, breaking, hysterical.

And after awhile there were no more voices and I could hear Brett breathing heavily, noisily in the sleep of utter exhaustion. Powell quietly went out of Brett's room and into his own and all night long I sat in the corridor listening now to Powell walking. Up and down. Up and down.

As I look back I am surprised that it never occurred to us that there would be many nights like that one. In our ignorance we believed that Brett had delivered himself of the memories that twisted and tortured his mind. It seems strange now that we were so simple.

The Battle of Fredericksburg, with all its fearful, useless slaughter, was relived again and again in my brother's room and I do not belittle the bravery of the men who fought there when I say that Powell was worthy of them. I cannot think what it must have taken in quiet courage to arise in the night and to go to Brett's room to behold once more the terrible visions which my brother dredged up from the depths of his bloody memories. To sit there, to listen, to give a steadying word at the right moment, that was Powell's task. No, there was more. There was always the weeping and the hoarse, dreadful shrieks of remembered agony. And on the silent nights there was the waiting, the wondering and the restless half-slumber of those who do not trust the dark hours.

Powell never spoke of the nights. Though they were mentioned.

They were mentioned by the haggardness of Powell's face and the misery in his eyes. They were remarked upon by Powell's clothes that hung now instead of fitting in the manner that one expected of Powell's clothes.

I cannot say the days were bad. By natural impulse we compared them to the nights and so I cannot say the days were bad. After that first day Brett spoke more frequently, though seldom was he part of a conversation and rarely did he give a direct answer. It was his way to speak when moved and it was not often that his desire for speech coincided with another's question or comment.

How did he pass the time? He did not try. Time passed him as he sat in the parlor or upstairs sitting room. Sometimes he sat at the window and watched, with no particular interest, the passers-by. Sometimes he listened as I played for him upon the piano. Aunt Laurel took him for an occasional drive and once or twice he walked with me but it was impossible to tell whether or not he enjoyed these outings. Mostly it was the parlor or the sitting room and Brett far away with his thoughts.

Powell consulted doctors and they suggested many things. Cribbage, cold baths, a lively group of friends. To one who prescribed an evening at the theater Powell said, "Did you ever hear what Fredericksburg was like, Doctor?" And Powell went sadly home.

I do not know how cribbage is played but I brought chess pieces and a board to the sitting room. Brett had forgotten the game though he was attracted by the ivory figures. He picked them up, examined them carefully and arranged them in a semicircle. So much for chess and probably cribbage. Cold baths, Hendon reported, were accepted stolidly without any marked effect, and as for a group of lively friends, we had none. Nor do I believe their contribution would have been great.

We went through the year 1864 scarcely noting the progress of the war. It was never discussed and I cannot tell now whether it was because the war had ended in our house on the day of Brett's return or because we accepted the fact that for us it could never end.

It was the summer of '65, three months after the surrender at Appomattox, that Powell made the decision about moving to the shore. We had not been to the summer house since the war had begun and I had ceased to think of it though in the past it had played a large part in our lives.

He did not ask our advice and it was clear that he had thought the matter over well. He merely stated that in October we would move to the New Jersey house.

"In October?" Aunt Laurel said, her eyebrows high in amazement. "The shore in October?"

"It will take me till then to clear up certain matters in the office. After that I will have things arranged so that my prolonged absences will not disturb the functioning of my practice."

Aunt Laurel was stunned. "Prolonged absences?"

"Yes, my dear. Hasn't it been obvious to you that we can't continue as we are? The boy gets no air or exercise. Let us face with candor the sad situation. Brett is our responsibility now as when he was a child. We must think for him. His body is a magnificent mechanism. It is our duty to see that this at least he retains."

Aunt Laurel nodded slowly. "He certainly can't get air and exercise on these congested streets," she admitted.

Powell's lips thinned as they always did when he braced himself to express a thought either unpleasant or painful. "If he—if he

should find himself during the next year or so we will return to this
house. If by any chance God withholds His blessing then let us
adjust our thinking to being permanent residents at the shore. It
will be easier for us all."

I saw many things that had come into Powell's calculations.
The need for Brett to be formally garbed as became a gentleman
while strolling the streets of the city and conversely how a rough
jacket seized at any odd moment would do for a walk beside the
ocean. And I was sure that Powell had not overlooked the ease of
living among people who considered all city folk odd and we no
more eccentric than the rest.

"We could have gone in June," Aunt Laurel said.

"No. I do not want the shore to burst upon him when it is
busy with summer. I want him to go there while it's deserted and
quiet. By the time the warm weather comes again he'll be accustomed to his surroundings. So we will go in October," Powell
said. "We will go in October."

I remember that I looked long and hard at our New York
house as we drove away from it for I could not help but feel
that I would never see it again. All at once each corner of it was
dear to me and the bright windows seemed to be putting up a
brave front as I looked back at them.

"Never fear," Aunt Laurel said, "we're not going away forever."

I did not answer. I was thinking of the mouse that lived in my
room. Who would ever again bring him crumbs of layer cake or
even of ordinary bread? He must live now in the sunshine of
memory, recalling the days when the world had been a good place
in which to be a mouse.

All of the servants moved with us. None refused, though the

parlor maid was dubious as to how long she would remain in our service.

"The ocean is a wild thing in winter," she said.

"Never mind, my dear, you'll not be asked to swim in it," Aunt Laurel responded. "And contrary to what you're thinking there *are* young men at the shore even in foul weather."

The parlor maid flushed and made her plans to accompany us.

Every ocean town has two faces. In summer it is much like a pretty, foolish girl who wears too many brilliant colors, who laughs loudly to draw attention and who wishes above all things to be admired and loved. When the summer is past, all this is changed. The town is a dour and lonely hag with a fierce temper and a bitter determination to be left in her awful solitude.

We came on a windy day and under a white sky into the town and to our house. It was a very large house for it had been a wedding present to my father and mother from one set of parents. It had been thought at the time that this young couple would have many gay and frolicsome children and great armies of friends. It was a beautiful house, I thought, with an enormous verandah and elegant turrets and towers. I loved its many bay windows and it was my belief that the flutings and scrollwork upon our house were far more elaborate in design—and certainly more abundant—than those on the neighboring houses. And of course in our front yard was the ocean separated from the lawn only by the glistening beach.

Hendon and an assistant had been sent down two weeks earlier and our house was therefore ready for us. It looked rather frivolous awake at this hour, so to speak, for the other fine houses on the ocean front were boarded up and had about them an air of intense melancholy as they stood there lonely in the wind.

Neither Brett nor I had any part in the scramble of unpacking.
Aunt Laurel, an able and experienced captain, had her crew
who knew their duty. I had never been expected to settle my
own belongings and I may say that if there are any advantages
to being undersized and having a crooked back, this is one of
them.

Powell was not due till the evening and I did what I thought
he might do had he arrived with us. I took Brett for a tour of
the house in an attempt to familiarize him with the plan. It was
unsuccessful as tours went, for in the front rooms he was interested
only in the windows that looked out upon the sea, and in the back
rooms he stood transfixed listening for the crash of the waves upon
the deserted beach.

It had been in my mind to take Brett walking beside the ocean
but Mr. Fort came to our kitchen door and changed my plans. As
far back as I could remember Mr. Fort had furnished our summer
household with eggs, milk and butter. He was a small man with
hard, brown skin and black, unsmiling eyes and as a child I had,
as the saying goes, taken to him.

I had regarded his wagon as my own private coach and had
considered my right to ride in it incontestable. Mr. Fort had
seemed to appreciate this peculiar claim I had upon his property
and company and had never challenged it. He had always delivered his dairy products to our kitchen and had then turned a
questioning eye upon me. Sometimes I had been known to shake
my head. More often I had followed him to the wagon and clam-
bered up beside him.

Today there was some uncertainty about my meeting with Mr.
Fort. I had not seen him since before the war. I was eighteen now,
a young lady, as those things are figured by calendar and custom.

If he turned toward me that cool reserve with which he treated Aunt Laurel I thought I might weep. There had been so many things I had lost, so many things that had belonged only to childhood. Should there not be a special dispensation for those who have left the little years behind and yet have nothing to hope for from the others?

I need not have worried about Mr. Fort. I had not changed. Neither had he.

"How are you, Miss Liz?" he asked.

I clasped his tough hand and hoped the slight squeeze I could manage made some impression on its ruggedness.

"How have you been, Mr. Fort?"

"Quite well, Miss Liz. Though we had a bit of trouble. Boy got killed at Gettysburg."

"I'm sorry, Mr. Fort."

"Well, can't tell what would have happened to him if he'd lived. At least we know he's with God now."

I nodded. That was a fine thing to know.

Mr. Fort placed the order upon the kitchen table. Three dozen eggs. A gallon of milk. Six pounds of butter.

The cook said, "I'm not straightened out in my thinking yet. I just got here. Leave that and I'll be able to order proper next time you come."

Mr. Fort said, "That's satisfactory," and turned a questioning eye upon me. Did I want to go riding in his wagon?

I hesitated. "Mr. Fort, there's my brother Brett now. I think he'd like to go, too."

"Well, bring him. Bring him."

It was an odd thing about Mr. Fort. I am positive that no one had spoken to him of Brett and yet Mr. Fort did not seem surprised when no answer was forthcoming to his greeting. Nor did he seek to worry an explanation or apology.

"This is the same horse, isn't it, Mr. Fort? This is Brownie?"

"Oh, yes. Couldn't do without Brownie."

"Where are we going, Mr. Fort?"

It was a question from long ago. I had always wanted to know what our destination was, to whom we were delivering the next batch of butter and eggs.

"Well, now, Miss Liz, I'll tell you," he said. "Fact is in autumn months there ain't no summer people. We're just going for a ride."

To have thanked him would have been to spoil everything. It would have removed me forever from the pleasant little world in which I could sometimes wander with Mr. Fort. The gentle protest that he mustn't waste his time driving us about, even a courteous thank you for such kindness would have signaled my adulthood and the end of gypsy riding in Mr. Fort's old, springless wagon.

Instead I must accept casually what he had to offer, as a child accepts, without lengthy, polite argument and without any show of gratitude.

"Too much blow for the ocean front today," he said. "We'll go inland a ways."

And so we rode back from the ocean, along the river road, toward the bay and the farm lands with the wind clawing at my eyes and hair.

Brownie dreamed as he went his familiar way. There was no hurry. No one was going anywhere. Not Mr. Fort or Brownie. Not Elizabeth Carpenter or her brother Brett. Just going for a ride, Mr. Fort had said. A luxury that could only be afforded when time was of no consequence and surely it was of no consequence to us. How long could a horse live? To whom could you leave a farm when your boy was dead at Gettysburg? What did you do with your life when your back was curved and you'd never grow tall? What was the use of a day when it turned inevitably into night filled with horror? Just going for a ride, Mr. Fort had said, the four of us.

On the wind-blown hill above the bay we paused and looked about us. There was the Coberley house, smaller than ours though almost as lovely. A pity, I had always thought, that it was on the bay rather than the ocean.

"Well, they're different," Aunt Laurel had said. "They're Philadelphians."

I never understood why the Coberleys had preferred the bay to the ocean and I was further baffled by Philadelphia's entering, at all, into their decision.

We sat in silence and looked at the Coberley house. I do not know what Brownie and Mr. Fort thought and I do not know if Brett thought at all. But I know what I thought. I thought that were I straight and strong and beautiful I could not bear it if Conrad Coberley did not love me. This way was easier. This way was without hope and therefore without heartbreak. And I thought of the day during the war that Connie had called upon us.

"Where's my girl?" he had asked.

He had meant me, of course, and I had managed a smile though it was not an easy thing to do. Gentlemen spoke so only in raillery, only when it was a well-known fact that the female in question could under no circumstances possibly be anybody's "girl." I had managed the smile though. I had stood beside Connie and looked up into his gray-blue eyes and I had thought, "Do you know how handsome you are in your uniform, beloved?"

But of course he had known.

He had been a lieutenant and he had laughed to hear that Brett had run off to enlist.

"What did he do that for? The fool! The fellows one meets as a private! You wouldn't believe, Miss Carpenter, the inferior element that finds its way into our army."

Aunt Laurel's eyes had slowly traveled from the shiny, black hair of the young lieutenant all the way down to his shiny, black boots.

"This," she said, "is true in all ranks, I presume."

Had he heard her remark Brett would have applauded Aunt Laurel. He had never liked Connie Coberley. As children on the ocean front they had constantly fought and there had never been any periods of truce in which they had found brief, warm-hearted companionship as children sometimes do between seasons of feud.

The unending conflict was mainly concerned with Connie's shameless passion for victory. There was something within Connie that could not let him accept defeat. He cheated and he lied but he emerged the winner. And Brett, a stern Puritan without humor where the matter of truth was involved, would knock Connie down only to have him rise and report to others that he had whipped Brett Carpenter.

I smiled remembering and the smile was not just for the remembering. It was for that foolish, masculine pride that placed honor above all. It would be impossible for a woman to become so wrought up over whether or not a score had been legitimately won. Only men—boys—could take a lifelong dislike to a fellow who claimed his eyes were closed when they were wide open. Such childishness. And Brett had cherished his low opinion of Connie even after they had ceased to play the games of their boyhood.

"I can't like him. He's a liar," Brett had once said. "I can't like a fellow I can't trust."

Well, I could like Connie Coberley. I could love him. To me it was not of monumental importance that he lied about his swimming prowess or that in a foot race he had never been overtaken without claiming a sudden injury to his ankle or knee.

And I sat there on the wagon and I looked at the blindfolded windows of the Coberley house. I thought that if I lived long enough I would see the house inhabited by Connie and his wife and children and I wondered how much pain that would bring to me.

"Too bad," Mr. Fort said.

I was startled but he pointed to the Spurney farm and I understood what he meant.

"Oh, yes," I said. "It is too bad."

Beyond the Coberley property, bordering upon it in fact, was a wasteland of wild neglect. Years ago when the Coberleys had bought their place, the Spurneys had had a fine, prosperous acreage to offer the view of a neighbor. Now the place was abandoned and had gone to ruin. Trees blossomed and bore unnoticed and untended and the buildings sagged and rotted and the odd thing was that one looked at the farmhouse itself and got no feeling that it was a farmhouse. It did not appear to be wood and nails but flesh and blood and it seemed to be suffering, dying in agony. And the whine of the wind searching, seeking out the weaknesses of the old house could surely have been moans of anguish.

"Let's shoot it," I said.

And I was pleased that Mr. Fort was not amused.

"Pity something isn't done about it," he said.

We stared at the hanging shutters and the roof that had once known its function but in its misery had forgotten and cared no more. I turned my eyes from the dismal, brooding landscape and toward the splendor of the Coberley house with its carefully boarded windows and its smug air that comes with the certainty that one is very precious.

Mr. Fort motioned toward the house.

"That boy was in the—"

"I know," I interrupted. I had become adept at fending off that terrible word.

"Wonder how he made out."

"He's home safe," I said.

If I was sure of nothing else, I was sure of that. Right up to the surrender at Appomattox I had been a subscriber to three Philadelphia newspapers.

All my life I had played a secret game and now I tried to share it with Brett. It was a splendid game and it was called "You Amuse Me." It sounds unkind but it was not. The victims were unaware of the game and indeed it was a score against me if I became careless enough to arouse suspicion.

The game itself was very simple, the rules uncomplicated, the object only to find the ridiculous something that exists in every human. I had played first against my tutors, experiencing boundless enjoyment in discovering their foibles which they thought so well concealed. Miss Canby's inordinate pride in her great mountain of fine, blond hair. Professor Doyle's too intense humility. Mademoiselle's depressing daintiness. It was a delight to me when at the age of eight I found that the game need not be confined to tutors. It could be played against anyone and if interest did not slacken, if one persisted, there was always a score made against the opponent. An expert player would always find something foolish or contemptible at which to laugh. And I played this game for years without knowing why it was a matter of utmost importance to me that my fellow man should be someone at whom I could be amused.

Here at the beach town the game could be played with tremendous success. The horse and the small light carriage which Powell bought for us made us free to roam the countryside in search of players for the game. We called on the Brooktons who were almost too easy because Mrs. Brookton was a glutton and Mr. Brookton a stingy man. The Robertsons were fault finders. They couldn't understand how it had happened but their children, their animals, their house, their lives, everything had turned out downright disappointing. There were others. But Mrs. Daniels was perhaps my favorite. She was the soft-hearted one. She had a habit of looking first at me and then at Brett and suddenly turning away to weep softly. She was the best, I thought.

We did not always ride but walked, too, in the damp autumn air. I would have preferred the sitting-room fireplace and a book but I did not forget why we had come to the shore and so we walked for some part of every day. Brett liked the beach best but to me it had a forbidding aspect at this time of the year. Under a sunless sky the water was neither blue nor green but only a sulky, grayish color like tarnished silverware. In the summer the ocean was a gay monster, rolling and roaring like a fat man overcome by mirth. But now to look at it was to think dismally of drownings and of the poor, lonely dead that lay within that sullen sea, perhaps not far from one's own verandah.

I remember that we had come in from a walk along the beach

and that Brett was carrying a salt-encrusted log which he meant
to burn in his bedroom fireplace. I remember that we walked
to the kitchen to beg a bowl of hot soup from the cook. Mr. Fort
was there displaying a half-dozen mallards that he had killed
that morning in the hope that they would please Aunt Laurel.
I did not look at the ducks for I have not the kind of appetite
that is sharpened by the sight of a plucked bird and I did not
thank Mr. Fort either for the information that he was passing on
to the cook. It concerned some hog slaughtering in which he
would shortly be engaged and I felt that I would be happier
without the pork he was promising our kitchen and without the
conversation that touched upon it. Strange how I recall all that
now and how I have never forgotten any detail of that day.

I tried to close Mr. Fort's remarks out of my consciousness but
I heard him when he said, "Oh, I got a little news. The Coberley
house is open."

The hammering began in my temples and I felt it travel down
through my arms and I could hear my heart pound and my body
became one great throb of excitement.

"Seems strange, don't it? I'm going over there tomorrow to see
if they want their deliveries same as usual. It's open all right."

"Eat your soup, Brett," I said. "Go ahead. Eat your soup."

And as my brother ate I plotted ways in which I might leave
him home and ride fast and free all by myself to the house on
the bay. Connie might be there, I thought, and Brett had never
liked Connie. He should stay home. Moreover the weather was
lowering and Brett need not be out in it though anyone of sense
could see that I must go.

But when we had finished our soup Brett followed me to the
little carriage and I had not the heart to do other than smile

at him and take him with me. And so we rode inland toward
the bay and the house that stood upon the hill above it and
as we rode the bare trees watched us and the sky darkened and
made ready for a storm.

I must tell you that I never approached a house in the ordinary
way. It had long been my custom to call a lady's name from her
front steps for I had learned much in my lifetime. I had learned
how to benefit from affliction. I had discovered that one can
be forgiven for eccentricities if only one has had the forethought
to be born misshapen. I had found how to dispense with the
stupid ritual of servants and "Who shall I say is calling" and
"Will you please step in here, Miss." Just call loudly enough and
the mistress herself will come to the door. I must add one word
of caution however. Be certain that you were poorly put together
by Nature. Then your strange behavior will be quite acceptable,
as it stands to reason, does it not, that with such a body your
mind, too, must be slightly twisted?

I hitched our horse to the iron serving-boy who stood eternally
waiting and I called. I remember how I stood under the dark
sky that day and called, "Mrs. Co-ber-ley" and how the wind
picked up my voice and carried it in a circle over the dying house
on the Spurney farm and back again to me. "Mrs. Co-ber-ley."

And as I waited I had a presentiment. Suddenly I knew that
something unusual was about to happen. Something that had
never happened before. The door would be opened. Yes, it would
be opened, but nothing would be as I had expected it.

And the door did open and my brother Brett and I saw her
for the first time. Brandon.

I would have you know that I had never seen anything like her
nor had I believed that such existed. I had thought beauty was

something all pink and gold like Minette or dark curls and the sparkling eyes of an actress I had seen at the theater. True, the Bible hinted that once there had been beauty so overwhelming, so breath-taking that even to gaze upon it was danger. I thought that like many things mentioned in the Bible it had gone from the face of our earth. But it was here. Here on the Coberleys' verandah. The lips like a thread of scarlet and the hair silken black or perhaps grape-purple as the Bible says. We stared at gardenia-white skin and at eyes that flashed a peculiar amethyst shade beneath thick, dark lashes. And I who am designed for no man's pleasure gazed upon the full, swelling hips, the tiny waist and the generously proportioned breasts that almost burst in their eagerness from the tight, black basque she wore.

I found my voice at last. "Sorry to have troubled you," I said, uncertainly.

She smiled a lazy, friendly smile at us. "Why, you didn't trouble me none," she said. "Mighty glad to have someone call."

And only the way she spoke could have stunned me more than her beauty. For there was no doubt about it; this was a secesh woman. It was impossible for her to be anything else. I had heard that easy, drifting talk before, that affectation of poor English that somehow strikes Southerners as being the last word in charm. I remembered secessionists from the old days when one met them here at the beach or even sometimes at church.

I glanced uneasily at Brett for it was not a far cry in the matter of thought association from this careless, slurred speech to a rebel yell on the bloody field of Fredericksburg.

"Excuse us, I beg of you. We had heard that Mrs. Coberley was here."

The secesh woman laughed. "Why then I guess you're right in a way, seeing as that's who I am. Mrs. Connie Coberley."

I do not think that my expression changed or that I paled. We only believe there are things that cannot be endured. Actually when the moment comes, when the worst happens, there we are saying the right thing, doing what we have been taught to do as though all our lives had been merely a rehearsal for disaster. And perhaps that is what it comes down to in the end.

"A pleasure, Mrs. Coberley," I said. "I am—"

"You are Elizabeth Carpenter," she interrupted, "and this is your brother, Brett."

And she did not have the grace to look away from me. She did not have the tact to pretend that Brett's red hair, rather than my crooked back, had identified us.

"Come in, won't you? Got nothing to offer you except a little conversation."

"I don't think so, thank you. My brother isn't well and I think it might rain."

She turned her strange eyes upon Brett and laughed at him. "Not well? Why, I never saw a man look so good in my whole life. Stop fooling me, will you? Walk in."

Without downright rudeness I could protest no further. I entered and behind me the secesh woman came, urging Brett by clinging to his arm.

"Don't you want to come with me?" she asked him. "If you don't, honey, then you're a new kind of man." And she tossed her head and opened her beautiful mouth wide to roar with laughter.

I cannot explain why I felt sick at that moment. I am not certain that it was because Connie Coberley had married a coarse woman. It may have been only that the artist that lurks in all of us was pained by this desecration of such heavenly beauty.

The secesh woman looked at me and saw something in my face that hushed her laughter. She said, "Isn't it awful how I go on? No harm in me, you know. Just high spirits."

We were in the parlor of the Coberley place and even the flaming brightness of the woman's beauty did not dispel the funereal air of the room. The mirrors were shrouded and the chilliness of the place suggested that it was being kept cool for a rather unpleasant reason. But there was no casket. There was only the secesh woman and we Carpenters in the Coberley parlor. There was something else, too. Six apples, an agate saucepan half-full of milk and a piece of common kitchen cheese from which a bite had been taken. I will admit that these things in themselves are not unusual. It was only their presence in the Coberley parlor that made them seem so.

"You'll have to excuse the way the place looks. Haven't done a thing yet. Don't plan on using the whole house of course. I'll just live in here and in one bedroom."

"You're here alone?"

"Why, of course, honey, except for my baby. I didn't tell you I had a baby, did I? I sure got one. Want to see her?"

I shook my head. "No," I said. "No."

"No?" She looked at me unbelievingly. "What's the matter? Don't you like babies?"

It seemed to me that it didn't matter what I said. This was a dream. It couldn't be other than a dream. How could it be reality when I was standing in the Coberley parlor with a secesh woman who was Connie's wife and the mother of his child?

"No, I don't like babies."

She shrugged. "Some women don't. Come to think of it, what are you anyhow? Are you a woman or a little girl? Can't tell for the life of me by just looking at you."

"I'm nine years old," I said.

"Oh. Is that all? Well, I couldn't tell." She studied me with a deep frown for a moment and then smiled. "No, you don't," she said. "You don't fool me like that. Nine years old! I bet you're old as I am."

"Maybe." I had already made my guess as to her age. Twenty-four or five seemed likely.

I was grateful that she had forgotten about the baby. I would have to see it of course. Sometime. But for the moment it was enough to see her, this woman who was Connie Coberley's wife.

"I don't think I even told you my name, did I? It's Brandon. Folks call me Brandy of course. Connie and I were married down home during the war."

"That was romantic," I said. "Where is he now?"

I had to ask though somehow it hurt to seek news of Connie from this laughing stranger.

"He's in Europe," she said. "Can you imagine?"

"No." I turned toward her startled and interested.

She said, "Oh, it's a pretty bad thing. His folks, you know. They don't like his marrying me. The war is over but they don't want to believe it. They're still mad at people born south."

I was not sure of that. It was possible, of course, but there was the great probability that the Coberleys had hoped for something more cultivated in the way of a daughter-in-law.

"Have they met you?"

"Met me! Honey, I've been in Philadelphia for months in that clammy old museum they call a home. I just couldn't stand it no more, especially after they all went off to Europe and left me and the baby alone with Grandpa Perry."

There was a ray of humor in the thought. Wispy, little Grandpa Perry closed up in a house with this Brandon whom Connie had married.

"You see, honey, they had planned on taking Connie on the grand tour when the war was over. Way back before he met me they planned it and they were right disappointed when he came home married. They said the tour was off and they said it just broke their poor hearts 'cause they'd so planned on it and I just sat Connie down and I said to him, 'Now, honey, I don't want you disappointing your folks. You go just like I never happened and I'll wait right here for you.' "

That had been decent of the girl. No one could ask more of her than that. And Connie had gone to Europe and left her alone. Speaking generally it was not a nice thing for a man to do, but Connie Coberley had done it and so I thought it would be unfair to judge without knowing all the facts.

"But Grandpa Perry got so disagreeable after they was all gone that I just said to him that I was going to come here. You know what he said? He said, 'The key's at the livery stable in the village and you can run a bill at the farms for all the food you need.' Seems like he was right glad to have me go, don't it?"

That was like Grandpa Perry. I could picture the satisfaction and relief upon his thin, white face when his grandson's wife had departed.

"So that's the whole story. Say, don't your brother never say nothing?"

"He's thinking about building a fire in here," I said. "Aren't you, Brett?"

"Yes," he said but he did not move. He stood as he had stood from the beginning, watching the secesh woman, never taking his eyes from her wonderful face.

"I'll show you where the wood is," she said.

"He knows how to find it," I told her but she went with him. I had wanted her to remain. I had longed for a word alone with her. Never before had I felt it necessary to explain to anyone that something had happened to Brett, something that had left him defenseless and in need of protection and understanding. In an odd, chilling way it came to me that I must tell the secesh woman what I had never brought myself to tell another soul. But she had not remained to listen and I was disturbed to hear her laughter ring out from the far corner of the basement where they had gone together.

When they came back Brett built the fire and I told her that Mr. Fort would be along tomorrow and I asked if she needed anything.

"You don't happen to have a candle with you, do you? Seems like I can't find none and there's not a drop of oil for the lamps."

We had no candle with us but she waved aside my offer to drive to the store for her.

"I'll go to bed as soon as it's dark," she said. "Thanks for stopping by."

"It was a pleasure," I said, stiffly.

"Come again, won't you?"

"Why, of course."

"Come tomorrow. Say you'll come tomorrow, honey."

I was about to reply but fortunately I caught myself in time. She had not been speaking to me. She had been speaking to Brett and the amethyst eyes were alight with a curious fire that I did not understand but only feared.

And as we drove away from her she found something—God knows what—at which to laugh and the laughter traveled with the wind and followed us down the slope of the hill and homeward through the bare trees. I thought her very brave to stand there laughing all alone without a candle to turn back the night and nothing but the sight of the deserted Spurney land and the death throes of the suffering old farmhouse for company.

The storm broke that night with a fury that let no one rest. The wind screamed and the ocean flung itself about in the frenzied motions of a maniac who destroys himself. The house seemed to shiver and cringe with fear as the howling voices of the storm mounted and the rain fell in torrents.

I stood in the bay window on the second floor and watched the great waves, fearsome in their might, as they thundered toward the beach and died there in frothing rage. And I watched others come, stronger and noisier. And the whole world was savage and brutal and filled with peril.

In the room behind me my brother's mind had gone back to Fredericksburg and once more he marched through the blood of men who had been his comrades. And sometimes I could not distinguish whether the eerie cries in the night were born of the storm or of the battle my brother fought.

I looked out upon the threatening sea and watched the gigantic beast thrashing in its torment and I listened to the sound of weeping and howling and I was afraid of a world in which even black water knew no peace. Its suffering, as I watched, seemed to increase and the night was wet with tears and rain and the wildness of the sea. The sounds in those hours of tumult were all ill and ominous and it seemed a certainty that tonight the earth would crack and crumble away and only the screaming, howling wind would endure. It would go its way forever more, shrieking through empty blackness, on its way to nothingness.

And the wind did not slacken and the wind did not still but from my brother's room there was a sudden pause in his battle and a half-sleepy murmur as though he must now rest and perhaps even dream for a time.

Powell came into the corridor and hurried downstairs. He did not speak to me but as I turned I saw upon his face a look of puzzlement.

When he returned he carried a tray, and the puzzlement had not left him.

"This never happened before, Liz," he whispered, "but it can't do any harm and he asked for it."

I looked down at the tray. Powell was saying more but I could not hear him for the wind had set up a demoniac, ear-splitting outcry and the ocean responded with a mighty roar and I stood trembling there in the bay window. For Powell had understood Brett's murmured yearning and yet had not understood it. On the tray was what Brett had asked for and yet had not asked for. On the tray was a bottle of brandy.

THE *Invaders*

*T*HERE IS A KNOWLEDGE shared by all women who have been acquainted with well-equipped homes. A navigating sense one might call it by which it is possible to actually feel where one will find the linen room and to know what will be upon the shelves and in the drawers. These small pieces of comprehension come naturally and lead a woman to conclusions so infallible and mysterious that she will know by the size of a silver chest how to estimate the contents of the preserves closet.

Brandy had no such knowledge. She had not even known where to seek out the things she needed. The night of the northeaster she had slept with only her cloak for cover and had wrapped the baby in a heavy table pad she had found in the dining-room sideboard.

I asked her if the storm had frightened her and I drew scornful laughter for my question.

"I don't scare, honey," she said. "Don't know what the feeling's like. Wouldn't recognize it if I got it."

"You'd recognize it."

"Tell you one thing I know—I know when I'm cold. Guess this house being just a summer place they don't have no covers."

I led the way upstairs. I may tell you that never before had I opened a door in the Coberley house but unerringly I walked directly to the linen room and pointed out a tremendous stock of blankets, quilts and comforters.

"Well, for Heaven's sake," she said, "what do they do with all them? Seems like they're in the cover business."

"There are a great many beds in this house," I explained, "and even in the summer it sometimes turns cool."

She had spent the night in the main bedroom, having chosen it because it was the largest and most elegantly furnished. I made a suggestion now and saw a shadow of disappointment cross her face.

"Why should I sleep in that itty-bitty old room, honey, when nobody's here and I can have the great big—"

"I mentioned the itty-bitty old room because it's easier to heat," I said. "However, please suit yourself."

She stood irresolute, looking sullen and hurt, but she dragged three blankets down from the shelf and threw them on the bed in the small room at the end of the hall.

"The sheets and pillow slips are here, too," I said.

Never in my life had I raised a hand to help with the making of a bed but I can tell you that I knew how the task was accomplished and I stood amazed, watching her as she dealt awkwardly with the fine bed linen that I had found for her. The bottom sheet never came straight and smooth, the far side of the top one lay dragging on the floor and the blankets were not tucked under the mattress but simply left loosely on the bed. The pillow slips she disregarded completely.

"I always had servants to do these things for me," she said.

I nodded gravely.

Of course it would have been good sense for her to have settled on the kitchen wing as her living quarters, using the servants' sitting room as her own. I did not voice the suggestion for it seemed clear that she would not relish it. Instead, like a miniature

Aunt Laurel, I proceeded to give the orders that would restore the parlor to a state of comfort and attractiveness.

Under my directions Brandy and Brett set to work stripping the dust sheets from the furniture and the cheesecloth from the mirrors. When the coarse runners were removed from the carpet Brandy flung herself upon the deep, silky pile and lay stretched full length at our feet.

"I'm sure tired," she said. I turned my eyes away from the tousled, black hair, the flushed cheeks and the rounded, heaving bosom, but I knew that Brett had not turned away. No man could. And I was relieved when I heard the baby wailing in the room upstairs.

Brandy looked at me in mock despair. "Just when I'm so tired. Go shake the rocking chair a bit, will you, honey? That'll put her back to sleep."

I smiled down into the amethyst eyes. "You know I'm not really nine years old," I said, "and, if you recall, I don't like babies."

"Don't like 'em much myself when I'm this tired," she said. But she scrambled to her feet and ran lightly up the stairs.

She brought the baby with her when she returned. It was a very damp baby and it occurred to me that the fine pillow slips that belonged to the senior Mrs. Coberley might discover themselves in strange service. Nowhere had I sighted a trace of luggage or even a single object apart from Brandy's cloak that was not being worn at this moment by the child or its mother.

"Well, this is the baby," she announced.

Politeness demanded my inspection. She lowered the child to the level of my glance and I saw—or perhaps imagined that I saw—Connie Coberley's eyes looking up into mine.

And I turned away suddenly tired, too, though I had done no more than supervise the work that the others had done.

When we left that day I had the feeling that we had been as neighborly as anyone could reasonably expect. The larder was stocked and Mr. Fort had the Coberley house under his regular care now. There was kerosene in ample quantity and Brett had carried a small mountain of wood into the house. For my part I was finished with Brandon. Although no one of startling beauty can be completely without distinction, she came depressingly close, I thought.

I remember that it rained very hard that night and that within our sitting room there was an atmosphere of great coziness and charm. Aunt Laurel knitted, the firelight edging the darkness of her skirt, and Brett sprawled on the floor beside her chair staring into the flames. Powell and I sat close to the table where the lamp burned strong and yellow, glinting upon his burnished beard and heavy gold watch chain. He was studying some impressive-looking papers that had come that day from the office. I was deep in a Scott romance and I was startled when I heard Brett speak into the warm silence.

"She's Connie Coberley's wife," he said.

"Who is, darling?" Aunt Laurel asked, gently. "Is Connie Coberley married?"

"Yes," Brett said. "She's his wife."

Aunt Laurel put down her knitting and turned to me questioningly.

"He's right," I said. "Connie's married."

My aunt sat there with a temporizing expression upon her face as though it were up to her to decide whether or not Connie's marriage was an actuality. It was perfectly ridiculous, the manner in which she seemed to be weighing the matter.

"How do you know?" she asked.

"We saw her," I said, impatiently. "She's here in the Coberley house. We've visited her."

"Really?" Aunt Laurel went back to her knitting. "Strange that I never read that he had married." And then with one of her flashes of insight she added, "I suppose his parents kept it out of the papers. What is the girl like?"

Powell looked up from his work. "You seem to have decided what she's like, Laurel."

"Well, when an item like that doesn't get into the papers—" Aunt Laurel broke off and looked irritatingly knowing. "Is the girl pretty?" she asked after a moment.

"Oh, I suppose you'd say so," I said. It amused me to voice so gigantic an understatement.

"She has a baby," Brett said. "A very little one."

"Oh?" Aunt Laurel again turned to me for confirmation and I nodded. "How long have they been married?"

I saw Powell's lips twitch in a quick smile which swiftly vanished. I knew he was aching to say something ungentlemanly and I wished that I could have heard his thought expressed.

"I don't know, Aunt Laurel," I responded. "It was sometime during the—the last few years."

"A Philadelphia girl?"

"She's a Southerner," Brett said, unexpectedly.

For a moment no one spoke a word. We glanced uneasily at each other and waited and then felt like fools for nothing momentous occurred. There was only Brett looking at Aunt Laurel, wondering why she did not remark on this piece of news.

"A—a Southerner," she said, rather weakly long after the need for comment had gone.

"Yes," I said, "she's a Southerner."

Aunt Laurel gazed into the fire and mentioned that there certainly must have been nice Philadelphia or New York girls that Connie could have married and then her voice trailed off and for a time there was silence.

No one spoke until Brett pulled himself off the floor and went to the kitchen in search of something to munch. Then Aunt Laurel spoke again.

"What is she doing here, Elizabeth, at this time of year?"

I yawned. "A long story, Aunt Laurel. And please don't fret about inviting her over. She's a boresome female being both stupid and coarse."

And I could feel Powell's wise, sorrowing eyes upon me and I wanted to say to him, "That happens to be the truth," but I held my tongue for he cherished the belief that his pity for me was a carefully hidden secret.

"Well," Aunt Laurel said, "if she is coarse I certainly hope that you won't call on her again."

Brett returned to the room carrying a handful of cookies. He took his place again beside Aunt Laurel and we resumed the form of our former tableau, Powell and I reading, Brett and my aunt at the fireplace. I regretted that Brandon had been brought into the conversation. Lamplight and firelight conspired to make even the Carpenter family circle seem cheery and snug and there was no room within it for the secesh woman.

I have stated my reflections on that day as I remember them. And now as I reread what I have written of all that was said and done I am tempted to a few embellishments, to claim for instance a wondrous omniscience and a compelling force that drew me back again to the house on the bay. But I shall remain firm. The truth is that I only returned because my brother made it impossible for me to do otherwise.

When I was young I had enjoyed the kitchen. I do not mean that I had ever cajoled the cook into letting me bake a cake or that I had a yearning to contribute in any way to the never-ending business of feeding us. I had never begged permission to beat eggs or whip cream and am still at a loss as to what pleasure children find in such activity.

I had only wanted to sit near the stove with the kitchen cat upon my lap. To me there was nothing in life that matched the beauty of the colors that leaped from coals upon which a steak was broiling. I realize that this sounds like the paean of a gourmand but I must add that I did not care to eat the steak. I only cared for the scarlet and orange and unearthly blue lights that sprang into life as the fat dripped upon the coals. There was a sense of well-being in the kitchen, for it was populated by healthy, brisk people whose standards of disaster were so different from ours that a scorched pan was a matter of grave concern and sometimes tears. I would sit silently with the kitchen cat in my lap and admire the goldenness of a cheese wedge upon a crimson plate or speculate on why a pickle appears humorous and a stalk of asparagus has the look of a beaten, defenseless creature ready for surrender.

I had not sat in the kitchen for some time because it was a pleasure that belonged to childhood and was not mine any more.

Servants were self-conscious with a young lady about and I knew
that Aunt Laurel thought it added to our "oddness" for it to be
said that I sought my company below stairs.

But one day in the middle of the following week I awakened to
a raw, wild wind blowing from the sea and I thought that it would
be a fine day to stay home, to read and perhaps to doze a little
beside the sitting-room fire. I did not even think of the kitchen
until there arose from it a fragrance that intrigued me. The cook
was baking ginger bread and at the same time something heavy
with cinnamon was boiling upon the stove and filling the air with
delight. And it seemed to me that God had created this bleak day
only for it to be forgotten in the warm brightness of a kitchen. I
looked for Brett but he was not about and I guessed he might be
with Powell in the den. I picked up my copy of Scott and made
for the kitchen. There I found my brother.

He was bending over the table watching with deep concentration as the cook filled a basket. I had no way of knowing what she
had already packed but as I arrived she added a jar of preserves
and a small poundcake to whatever else the basket contained.

"What's this?" I asked.

"Well, in a way it's cookies," the cook said.

"Really? In what way is it cookies?" I spoke sharply because I
was displeased. It was clear that somehow the cook had known
that my approval would be lacking and she had simply, emotion-
ally dedicated herself to pleasing Brett.

"The young man likes my cookies. He wanted some for a friend
so I just put in a few extra little things we don't need, Miss."

"Mr. Brett's friend is not in want."

"But I didn't think there was any harm—"

I turned to Brett. "The weather is vile," I said.

He threw a disinterested glance toward the window.

"I'm not going to get la grippe," I said, irritably, "just to bring cookies to—"

Brett picked up the basket from the kitchen table and walked toward the back door and I realized for the first time that he intended to go without me.

I put my book aside and got my weather cloak and followed Brett out to the stable. He was angry at me. I had come to understand him well and I could feel his resentment though his silence was no deeper than usual, his gaze no more shadowed.

We followed the muddy road inland and the wind blew across us with its penetrating chill and all the way to the Coberley house I thought of the warmth of the kitchen I had left behind.

Brandy had built no fire. She was wearing her cloak. The baby, lying upon a velvet sofa in the parlor, was wrapped in the table pad.

"Will you build a fire, honey?" she asked Brett.

She thanked us for the basket and wondered if it would be safe to feed the preserves to the baby. When she stared speculatively at the poundcake I felt constrained to say that it did not seem logical baby food to me. This was an excuse for her laughter that was always so ready, so anxious to be heard.

When the fire burned brightly she took the baby from the sofa and cradled it in a chair close to the hearth. I could not help but notice, as she lifted the child, that the sofa had suffered and that Mrs. Coberley, Senior, was going to be annoyed.

Brandy put her cloak aside and seated herself on the floor. She broke off a piece of poundcake and popped it into her mouth.

"Glad you came," she said. "It gets lonesome."

I had no doubt that she did indeed find time weighing heavily, for it is always the shallow mind that experiences boredom. Here in the Coberley house there were books and certainly sewing material but I had a strong suspicion that her own insufficiencies would withhold these pleasures from her.

We sat in silence and Brandy sighed and I could see that she ached for entertainment and I wondered what would amuse her. Surely not conversation. Had she ever played games? I supposed not. I could not picture Brandy taking part in charades or bothering her pretty head over a riddle.

"Let's sing," she said, suddenly.

Why, of course. She would like singing and she would like dancing even better, but she had come to the wrong place, the wrong people and at the wrong time of year.

"Down home we always sing," she said, "when we're sitting around with nothing to do."

I compared our more formal use of song. The evening, guests, a lady in a low-cut gown standing beside the piano nodding encouragement to her well-tailored accompanist.

Brandy popped another piece of cake into her mouth and looked expectantly at Brett. "Go ahead, honey, sing something," she said.

He did not reply and she was disappointed.

"Tell a story then," she urged him, and when he still did not answer she was at a loss to understand. And I must tell you that her bewilderment was natural, for my brother had developed a protective device which deceived many. He had a way of appearing to listen when he was not listening at all, of turning his eyes upon one and seeming to follow a train of thought when within him all was confusion and uncertainty. We who were close to him knew when the mists were heaviest and we had learned, too, that they lifted from time to time and gave a hazy view of the harbor. These things Brandy did not know so she sat staring at him a little hurt, a little angry.

"We don't know any songs or stories," I said. "We are woefully dull."

"Everybody knows a song or a story," she said, sulkily. "Down home we got people who just make up a song and sing it without even thinking twice. Maybe just an old owl screeches in a tree and someone will have a song fast as lightning. Why, I know a little girl down home—" She broke off and her eyes clouded. "Well, anyway, I bet you just couldn't mention nothing that she wouldn't have a song about right that minute." Her eyes went back to Brett and the strange color of them deepened till they were almost purple and she said to him, "What's the matter with you?"

I could see that no man had ever puzzled her before. She moved closer to him across the silky carpet and looked up into his face and when he did not smile she placed her hand upon his knee to draw attention. And he reached out and covered her hand with his.

"I thought you were mad at me," she said.

He still did not answer but he looked down at her hand and then into those curious eyes of hers, and I knew he was conscious of her and of all the pleasure and beauty of her for their glances held as though a spell had been cast upon them.

"The wind has died down," I said and they became aware of me. Brandy took her hand from Brett's and she laughed but there was a new quality in her laughter. It sounded self-conscious and slightly apologetic and when I looked at her she flushed and turned from me.

"Shall we go for a ride?" I asked. "Would you like that, Brandy?"

"I sure would. I haven't been out of this old house since I got into it."

It seemed a good idea to me for it would get us away without our visit seeming to end too abruptly. After the ride we had only to drop her at the door without re-entering.

"Of course the weather is not perfect by any means but still—"

"I'll just be glad, honey, to get out for awhile." She reached for her cloak and flung it about her shoulders. "This is really right nice of you." The gaze she turned upon me was one of gentle surprise as though she had not expected any kindness from me.

"The baby?" I asked. "Does she stay here?"

"Why, sure. Nothing here to hurt her."

Brandy went to Brett and linked her arm through his. "Come on, honey, I'm just dying for a little air."

She hurried him out the door and as I lingered behind I could hear her whispering to him. I did not know what she said nor what he responded but she laughed. And her laughter was ill-timed, I thought, for I was gazing down at her baby who was a forlorn-looking little thing. Not clean, not chubby, not pretty, and I looked at the walls of the Coberley house and I said to them, "You be standing when we get back." And I looked sternly at the leaping flames and to them I said, "No tricks now." And the baby woke up and I saw Connie Coberley's eyes and I said to them, "Don't look at me that way. None of this is my fault."

I went out then and followed my brother and Brandy toward the carriage. Her laughter rode upon the wind but even so I heard the voice when it spoke.

"How are you, Brandy?"

I looked about me and saw no one but I knew that I had not imagined the voice for I saw Brett's back stiffen and I saw his head lift as though to give greater range to sight and hearing. There was no indication that Brandon had heard and yet I knew that she had.

"How are you, Brandy?"

The voice was male but it was twin in accent to Brandy's own. A secesh voice. Another one. Here in our midst.

"How are you, Brandy?"

And now I located it. It was coming from the stand of trees just beyond the curve of the Coberley property line. The trees were on Spurney farm land and they were ill-fated, tragic trees and propped up against one of them was an ill-fated, tragic boy. He had the look of a hound dog, sharp, bright but sorrowful. His hair, light brown in color, was longish and it spilled over his forehead and into his eyes. He was shabbily dressed but someone had furnished a rough blanket for him to rest upon. They had pitied him, I supposed, and well they might for the boy was missing an arm and a leg.

As I walked toward him he changed his tune. "How are you, Billy?" he called. This was directed at Brett and I knew that in all good nature it should have been answered by a careless, "How are you, Johnny?" but Brett gave him no more notice than Brandy had given. I let them go ahead of me to the carriage and I spoke to the boy for no one else had done so.

"Why wouldn't he answer me?" the boy asked in an injured tone. "The war is over."

I thought it odd that Brett's silence rather than Brandy's had nettled him.

"He was a soldier," the boy went on. "You can always tell the way a fellow walks whether he was in the army or not and I can tell that fellow was in the army. Why wouldn't he answer me?"

I said, "He meant no harm. Perhaps he didn't hear you."

"He heard me all right. Who is he anyway?"

"He's my brother. Who are you?"

"I'm a fellow that got an arm and a leg shot off."

"I'm sorry."

"Like hell you are. Yankee, ain'tcha?"

He had a point there which I could not argue. I remembered
nights when I had gone to bed comforted by newspaper reports
of fearful injuries to the enemy. And this boy was the enemy in
whose maiming I had once rejoiced.

"Yes, I'm a Yankee," I said. "Brandy an old friend of yours?"

He studied me with a hard, blue gaze. "You didn't hear her
answer, did you?" he asked.

"That's right. I didn't."

"Well, then I guess we're not old friends. I guess she don't know
me."

"But you called her by name."

He raised his eyes to the baleful sky above us. "Lord Jesus," he
demanded, "do I gotta lay out in this filthy wind and get pestered
besides by every crazy, nosey Yankee brat who's got a question?"

I was accustomed to being mistaken for a child but it pleased
me that in his appeal to the Lord he had not called attention to my
crooked back. I was grateful to him for that.

"I'll go if I annoy you."

"Go then."

"Can I give Brandy a message for you?"

"Tell her I said 'How are you.' That's all."

I walked away leaving him out there in the cold wind beneath
the naked, tragic trees. The Spurney farm never seemed more
haunted, more forbidding than when I looked back at it that day

and saw the broken boy lying against the tree staring after us.

How had he gotten there? And why? As I drew near the carriage I could hear Brandy's whisper and then her laugh.

I said to her, "Who is that boy?"

"How should I know?"

"He knows you," I said.

"Does he?" She eyed me with amusement.

"What's funny?"

"Oh, you kind of are," she said. "Little old maid. Don't know nothing about love."

"Granted."

"That boy followed me here. Sits out there like that every day. Disappointed lover, that's all. He's just wild for me and what can I do? I'm married." She faced me, her eyes wide with what she hoped was a reflection of her virtue and innocence. "I have a husband. I can't be nice to just anybody who happens to fall in love with me. Now can I?"

I picked up the reins and bade our horse to take us away from here, to take us somewhere else, anywhere. But I knew that wherever we went we were taking danger with us for Brandy was beside me, her arm still linked through Brett's.

"You must have known that boy before you knew Connie," I said.

"Oh, I sure did."

"And he was in love with you?"

"Don't sound so surprised. I had quite a few fellows in love with me."

"No doubt, but this one must have been about twelve."

The laughter again. "Don't let him fool you. He ain't so young. He only looks young."

"That's because life's been so kind to him," I said, grimly.

"Well, I couldn't marry everybody who wanted me. Wouldn't you rather have Connie Coberley?"

Rather than what? Than my eyes or my ears? Yes, I'd rather have Connie Coberley.

"Oh, maybe," I said. "It's possible."

"Sure you would, honey. Anyhow who'd want that raggle-taggle little nothing? He ain't even a whole person any more."

I turned to look at her for I did not believe that ever again would I hear so callous a remark. I thought to see upon her face an expression of coldness, of wanton cruelty and I was amazed to find nothing there but a childish interest in the scenery.

"Oh, it's sure good to be out again," she said. "But it's real cold and mean." And she moved closer to my brother.

I thought that there were two things I knew now about Brandy. She was without fear and that no doubt was admirable though in some circles even this could be debated. And she was without pity. This was not admirable at all. I looked at my brother but he did not look at me. He was lost once more in the light of those peculiar amethyst eyes.

All through the evening I was troubled by the memory of the boy who had lain under the windy sky on the Spurney farm land. I was disturbed by the thought that there was something I should have done for him. How had he gotten there? Who cared for him? Was he alone in the world? I thought that perhaps I should not have taken his dismissal so docilely. Was I at fault? Should I have told him straightforwardly that I was not a child and that I stood ready to offer food and shelter if such were needed? It was possible that he was homeless and hungry and I knew that if this was the case Powell would not even notice that the lad had been a rebel soldier. I should not have turned my back upon the boy. I should have made certain that he was not in need.

I could barely wait for morning to come and after a hurried breakfast I set out alone. I told myself that later I could explain why I had not waited for Brett, why I had not informed Aunt Laurel or even a servant that I was leaving. Now it was only important to me to find the boy and to know whether or not he required assistance.

As I took the road toward the bay I wondered, and I wonder now after all these years, how it happened that I had walked away from the shattered boy. True, my mind had been with Brett and, too, I had been shaken by the sight of the boy and the odd manner in which his greeting to Brandy had been given and received. But it was no excuse for having left him without knowing that somewhere, close by, someone was interested in his welfare.

I passed the Coberley house without pausing and turned in at the old Spurney road. There had been a gate there once. Now it no longer swung upon its hinges but lay rotting away on a bed of weeds. The wind had dried the road but the going was rough for it had dried stiffly, hardening into a miniature terrain of mountains and deep valleys with an occasional wide fill of muddy water. My horse, I thought, harbored a dislike of the whole project for he looked about him from time to time with what seemed like a curious awareness of the desolation.

"It's all right now, fellow," I said to him. "It's all right."

But I was not certain for here on Spurney land nothing had prospered. There had been only failure, death and the withering away of all things that seem good and wholesome.

And I said to my horse, "Now you say something to comfort me."

I would have been amazed had he complied but perhaps only a shade less than I became in the next moment, for I heard music. Music here on the deserted Spurney farm land.

There was a meager girl sitting upon a log at the side of the road. She was playing upon a banjo, and I would have you know that until that moment I had thought a banjo the boisterous, happy instrument of a Negro minstrel. I did not know that a banjo was capable of expressing itself in soft, low chords that spoke of grief and troubled dreams. She did not pause at sight of me. I stopped and the horse and I stared at her though she gave us no such attention but bent her concentration upon her music and her song. She was the palest girl I had ever seen, for her hair and brows and lashes were almost white, her eyes a faded blue, and she was dressed in a colorless cotton with a tattered, grayish shawl about her shoulders.

"Good morning," I said.

Her glance was a rebuke. It told me to be quiet. And the banjo sounded a chord and her song rose on the morning air.

> "The moon is pure silver,
>   The sun is pure gold,
>   The flowers are jewels, all dew-pearled,
>   And I know a woman
>   Who doesn't deserve
>   To live in this beautiful world."

I waited politely for perhaps she was not finished, and in truth she was not. Though what came next was very brief.

> "Heart of stone, heart of stone,
>   I'm watching you,
>   Heart of stone."

She did not lay aside the banjo nor did she look up at me but
the music ceased and she sat in silence and I guessed that she was
willing for conversation if such could not be avoided. But I was
not ready now. I was thinking of her song, of the quaint words
and the mournful melody.

She raised her head and looked at me. "Well? Got something
you want to say?"

Of course I was not surprised to find that she was a Southerner.
I think I had known it from the moment I had heard the first note
of the banjo.

"You sang a very pretty song," I said.

She squinted her pale eyes at me. "You think that was pretty,
do you?"

"Very. Play it again."

She looked at the banjo as one might gaze at an understanding
friend when a particularly stupid remark has been made by an
outsider.

"I only sing a song once and then only 'cause the situation calls
for it. Like if all of a sudden a goose flew by or something."

I remembered Brandy, sitting before the fire, recalling how the
people "down home" made up songs and sang them without even
thinking twice.

"I imagine you know," I said, "about a young man I saw
yesterday. Perhaps he is your brother. He—"

"I ain't got no kin," she said.

"Well, in any case, you probably know him. He had lost an
arm and a leg in the war and he was lying over there close to the
other property line."

She gave me a frozen stare though nothing in the world was

more positive than that she was thoroughly acquainted with the
boy.

"You don't know of whom I'm speaking?" I asked, impatiently.

She nodded. "I know. What you want with him?"

"Well, I assure you that I don't want to hurt him."

She smiled. It was a cold smile and in its coldness was a guarantee that I need not worry about the boy. For the smile said
that not I, not anyone, not anything would be permitted to hurt
him. She reached for the banjo again and I gathered that she was
finished with me but she did not play. She sat gazing ruefully
down at her fingers. I have my share of curiosity.

"What's the matter?" I asked.

"Fingers chilled," she said. "Mighty mean weather you Yankees
got. Might be I won't be able to play all winter."

"Are you planning on staying all winter?"

She shrugged. "As soon as I get a song about it I'll know," she
said, cryptically. "But my fingers hurt from the cold."

"That's a shame," I said.

"Yeh, sure is. And you know what? You're trespassing. You're
on our property."

I eyed her steadily. "Whose property?" I asked. "I'll just wager
this horse against your banjo that I have more right here than
you have."

She dropped her glance. "What I want with a horse?" she
asked. She sat upon the log then in silence for a moment. I
watched her wondering what was coming next but I was not prepared for the smile she flashed at me. It was friendly now, warm
and rather sweet. "His name is Tippy," she said.

"Whose name?"

"The boy you were asking about."

This was all very puzzling and I decided to be puzzling, too. "I'm not interested in him. I don't care what his name is."

"Well, you asked about him, didn't you?"

"I don't remember," I said.

She glared at me and jumped to her feet and I could not tell whether accident or design released the harsh, discordant noise that came from the banjo. "Honest," she said, "I've tried everything with you. I've tried being like I didn't care and I tried being nasty and I tried being nice but you're just so plain old stuck-up, cat-mean that there's no—"

"That will do," I said hoping that my tone had the coolness and authority of Aunt Laurel's. "Now just what is it you want?"

"Your gloves," she said in a small, wheedling voice. "Could you just let me have your gloves? Honest, my fingers is freezing."

I stripped off the gloves and gave them to her. They had been made to order for me and I knew they would not fit her. I watched her as she tried to work them down over her large, bony hands and I sat there in my carriage suffering for her disappointment.

And after a moment she stopped trying and returned the gloves. "They come in sizes, don't they?" she asked, wonderingly. "Just like shoes. I didn't know."

I nodded. "Yes, they come in sizes."

She thought that over for a moment. Then:

> "Things come in sizes,
>   That's how the world's made,
>   It's full of surprises
>   And I'm sure afraid
>   That though there is something
>   For each she and he,
>   There'll never be nothing
>   That's just right for me."

It wasn't magnificent poetry nor was the music memorable and stirring. Still when I considered that she had simply touched a fount of imagination within herself and that the little song had emerged appropriate to the occasion, I confess that I was impressed.

"You have amazing talent," I said.

She grinned. "But no gloves."

"You'll have gloves," I promised.

"You're not fooling me?"

"I'm not fooling. Now tell me something. Where do you and Tippy live?"

She gestured toward the old farmhouse. "In there."

Could people actually live within that frail shell? How it had survived the northeaster was a mystery to me.

"Do you live there alone?"

She shook her head.

"Are you hungry?"

"Course I'm not hungry. What do you think I am? Do you think I'm a beggar just because I asked for your dirty old beautiful gloves?"

This was a strange child, I thought. A genuine curio of nature. It amused me that I, with my dull mind and routine way of thinking, seemed to others as this one seemed to me.

"How old are you?" I asked.

"Fifteen. How old are you?"

"Eighteen."

"Were you always like that or did you have an accident?"

"I was always like this."

"A real shame, I say. A real shame."

"Well, we won't talk about it."

"Shucks, no. I should say not. Ain't worth even thinkin' about when a girl's got a sweet little face like you got and all that nice brown hair."

I felt suddenly dizzy and I clung to the reins, for I had never before heard a compliment that had not come pityingly from a member of my own family. I felt tears on my cheeks and I leaned over and squeezed the arm of the girl with the white eyelashes. She said nothing because she was strange and like no one I had ever met before. She simply picked up her banjo and fingered the strings and her eyes and her thoughts seemed far away.

And after a time I said to her, "I suppose you know Brandon from down home."

She would not bring her eyes and her thoughts back to me. "Brandon?" she questioned, blankly.

"You must know her."

She shrugged. "I must know a lot of people. Feel I ought to tell you something. It's gonna rain. Best you get going."

"But do you know Brandon? Brandy, I suppose you call her. Do you know her?"

"It'll just come teeming down."

"All right," I said. I signaled to the horse and we went our way leaving the girl behind us standing on the Spurney farm land staring up at the threatening sky. And her voice followed us as we went. She would not speak of Brandy but she would sing and I could not help but hear her song.

> "I met a rabbit and I had my gun.
> The rabbit he said, 'Well, I guess I am done,'
> I said, 'Cease your weeping, your freedom I give.
> Why should I kill you and let that gal live?'
>> Heart of stone, heart of stone,
>> I'm watching you,
>> Heart of stone."

"It's all right, fellow," I said once more to the horse. "Really, it's quite all right." I said it several times because it was my impression that he had shivered.

There were four of them living in the Spurney farmhouse and if I told you that I came to know them then I would be lying. I never came to know them. There was a fifth but he did not live with them nor did I see him till later, so perhaps I will wait to tell you what he was like. Of the four in the farmhouse there was Tippy, the maimed boy, and there was the girl who could make a song of anything under the sun. The other two were older and seemed to know each other no better than they knew me. It was an impression, you understand, nothing more, for never did I know what they thought or what they were inside themselves.

When I reached home that day no one asked where I had been or why I had gone alone. It was even possible that I had not been missed. Powell and Brett were in the morning room before a bright fire and Powell was trying to teach Brett to play checkers, a game that Brett had once known well. Aunt Laurel was busy with the maids, unpacking a crate of fancy foods that had come from our grocer in New York. I observed that Aunt Laurel was very busy indeed so I went to her room and examined the contents of her glove box. Fortunately Aunt Laurel had nice large hands and kept a very poor count on her personal possessions. One pair of gloves was prettily edged in rich, dark fur but regretfully I returned them to the box. It seemed to me that even Aunt Laurel might notice the absence of such handsome fellows. I shopped carefully and finally settled upon a splendid pair of fleece-lined gauntlets and took them to my room.

It seemed probable that after lunch, weather permitting, I

would drive out with Brett but I was determined that we would not call on Brandy. Surely I had some rights in the carriage, too, and I was prepared to argue my side of the case. Though I was not prepared to be wholly honest. I knew that to make an issue of Brandon would be a mistake so I intended to argue on the premise that I simply had to visit the Snyders today. I knew exactly what I would say and I was left with a rather foolish feeling when Brett retired to his room after luncheon and went to sleep.

"This is new," I remarked to Powell.

He nodded. "I'm afraid I tired him but he was beginning to remember. Perhaps I should not have pushed him." Powell shook his head in weary discouragement. "It's so hard to know whether one is doing right or wrong."

It always amused me when Powell mouthed a homely phrase and sounded for all the world like his sister, Laurel. At such moments I could not refrain from thinking of the things that were said of Powell's brilliance, his masterful use of language, his talent for original forms of expression. Were all famous people pretty plain when you knew them well? Perhaps they were and perhaps it was a little gift that God gave along with the large one, for never did Powell draw my love and sympathy more surely than when he spoke a humdrum, hackneyed phrase.

"Are you going out, Liz?"

"Not if you need me."

"I always need you but I shall be busy all day and I just wondered if you would be lonely."

"No, I shan't be lonely."

I did not tell you why I had driven past the Coberley house that morning and directly to the Spurney place. I thought it unnecessary, for you must understand by now that I did not like

Brandy and would never have visited her of my own volition. That afternoon when I drove out to deliver the gloves it had been my intention to by-pass Brandy again. I was not successful, for she was walking on the bayside road and she waved to me as I approached. I stopped for her and she came toward me so swiftly that her hair blew in the wind and her cloak billowed out behind her and she looked so wild and magnificent that I was moved, despite myself, by her rare beauty.

"Just taking a ride, honey?"

"No, I am on an errand."

She was downcast by my words. "I thought maybe you'd take me out a bit. Seems like I'll die being alone."

I could have pointed out that both the house and the baby had need of the time that lay so heavily upon her but I restrained myself.

"You don't have to be alone," I said. "The clever little girl from your home place who makes up songs is here, isn't she?"

Brandy laughed. "I declare, honey, you just know everything, don't you? Yes, she's here."

"Well, she'll entertain you."

"Entertain me? That dirty little draggle-tail? I wouldn't let her in the house. Why, she'd steal something, I'll bet you."

"Maybe she would," I said. The idea was not too fantastic. "What is she doing here, Brandy?"

Brandy's eyes opened wide at my question. "Why, I don't know, honey. She got a right to come here if she wants to, I reckon, only I don't have to be friends with her, do I?"

"Where does she come from, Brandy? Where do you come from?"

"North Carolina."

"What's it like in North Carolina?"

Brandy shook her head. "I wouldn't know how to tell you. It's a ordinary place. Houses, people, animals, smoke."

"Smoke?" It was a curious thing for her to have said. Houses, people, animals, yes. But smoke?

"I always think of the smoke. It has a friendly look. People cooking supper. You look out across a valley and you see smoke and you know that people over there are cooking supper and you know that nothing's wrong. When something's wrong you don't see the smoke 'cause when something's wrong people ain't cooking supper."

And I sat in my carriage on the bayshore in New Jersey and I looked at North Carolina, saw the blue smoke rising from the cabins, saw the great, white face of the Southern moon. And the cabins were rough hewn inside and out but I saw beds covered with bright patchwork quilting and heard the singing and smelled the hot, wild odor that rose from the swinging pots above the fire.

"Oh, yes, smoke," I said.

But she was not listening to me. She was looking out across the bay and her eyes were filled with remembering.

"Homesick?" I asked.

"Homesick? Me?" She threw back her head and howled with laughter. "For what? For working like a nigger and for wearing a stringy cotton dress and going to bed with a man who smells of hard work and sweat? Not me, honey. Not me."

Her laughter was very loud and it grated upon me and I turned from her and saw coming toward us an aging man with a shotgun on his shoulder. He was seventy, I thought, though he carried himself erect and proud and as he came close to us he spoke.

"How are you, Brandy?" he said.

And her laughter never ceased nor did she trouble to even cast a glance at the old man. He kept walking and paid us no further attention.

"A former admirer?" I asked. "Who was he?"

"Oh, honey, quit bothering your head about them people. They're nobodies. You don't gotta be worried with them no more than I do. After all, they're trash and I'm Mrs. Conrad Coberley and you're Miss Elizabeth Carpenter. Now let's forget 'em."

"It seems you could answer when they speak to you."

"Why should I? They ain't no friends of mine. Down home I never spoke to them. They're trash I tell you. My folks were high-toned people. Real ladies and gentlemen just like your folks."

"That's obvious," I said.

And at that moment I heard something that was not Brandy's laughter but sounded surprisingly like it. It was a ringing chord struck upon a banjo. Brandy stood impassive, staring out across the bay. She showed no sign of hearing even when the voice of the white-haired girl came to us from somewhere calling, "How are you, Brandy?"

There was a slight scratching sound from the nearest tree as though a squirrel was descending and I knew that the girl was gone. I squinted my eyes for a sign that she was streaking toward the farmhouse but I saw nothing.

"Well, I must go," I said.

Brandy shrugged. "All right. If you can't take me for a ride then go ahead." She waited, looking hopefully up at me. Then, "Where's your brother?"

"Home."

"Oh. Tell him I miss him."

"Very well. I will."

"Tell him I miss him something awful."

I nodded shortly and she began to laugh and I suspected that there was something genuinely amusing here that I had not the wit to see nor the courage to question.

I do not believe that I would ever have approached the sagging old farmhouse without an excuse. I do not believe that I would have dared to face with a limp answer the question of what I was doing there. The invaders had taken over the Spurney land and, though it was my guess that they had no legal right to tenancy, I was not prepared to argue the matter. This was a strange family, if family it was, and I had no reason to think that they would welcome a caller.

Still it was unlikely that I would encounter anything more devastating than a rebuff and it would be interesting to know how life was lived in the deserted farmhouse.

Nothing stirred as I left the carriage and walked toward the splintered door. I was conscious as I walked that I was being watched and I took Aunt Laurel's gloves from my pocket and made elaborate show of them.

The door swung open leaving in mid-air my hand that had been poised for knocking. Within, the room was dim. The windows that long ago had lost their panes were sealed against the wind by rough boarding and the blaze on the hearth furnished all the illumination there was.

"Come in," a voice said. And I was in with the door closed behind me. For a moment I stood almost without vision and then I began to see. Stretched out before the fire lay the boy, Tippy. His eyes were closed and he did not open them. He lay there as though asleep but such was not the case for I knew, as one sometimes knows these things, that only a moment before there had been talk in this room. The banjo sounded and I raised my eyes to see the girl perched a-top the ladder that reached toward the sleeping quarters above.

"There you are," I said and the banjo spoke again in answer.

My eyes became aware of the broken floor boards and the dangerous decay of the walls. There was nothing here in the room that could be correctly classed as furniture. Blankets and barrels seemed to take the place of couches, tables and chairs. There were a few cooking pots, a kettle and various oddments that I supposed were the complete representation of the kitchen department.

"I brought the gloves," I said.

"That was extremely thoughtful of you." It was the voice that had bade me enter. I turned and saw who had spoken. She was a woman of middle age, tall and slender with stony, gray eyes. Her hair was also gray and she was dressed in plain, dull black. Her figure had the look of soft pliancy about it and I realized that she was not corseted and that her trim shapeliness was utterly natural. She eyed me unsmilingly. "May we know who you are?"

"Elizabeth Carpenter," I said and waited but there was only silence.

I looked up at the girl in some annoyance. "Shall I throw them to you?" I asked.

The woman with the stony, gray eyes said, "A proper question indeed. Cannot you bother to descend when a lady has brought you a present?"

The girl scrambled down from her perch, grabbed the gloves

and flew back again to the top of the ladder. I was reminded of
a monkey venturing forth to accept a proffered peanut.

"And have you no word of thanks?" the quiet voice demanded.

The banjo announced that a proper acceptance was on its way.

> "Thank you, oh, thank you for your kindness to me.
>   If you're ever a-freezing I hope you'll feel free
>   To sit by my fire or borrow my shawl.
>   If you're ever in trouble you know who to call."

"No, I don't know who to call," I said. "I haven't the slightest
idea what your name is."

"Mockingbird," she said.

"Mockingbird!"

"Sure. What's the matter? Sound funny to you?"

"Of course it does," the older woman said. "It would sound
funny to anyone so do not make yourself absurd by acting as
though your name was an ordinary one."

The girl did not reply. She was occupied with the business of
working her hands into Aunt Laurel's gloves. We watched her
as she frowned and struggled and finally with pride mastered
the situation.

"Splendid," the woman observed.

I had no excuse to linger now. I had delivered the gloves and
I had been thanked. I had seen the interior of the crumbling farmhouse and I had encountered a woman who spoke in cultured
words and tone, a woman who could not possibly be related to
Tippy or Mockingbird.

I was about to take my departure when the old man with the
shotgun pushed open the door and came into the dark room. He
had killed a rabbit and it was interesting to me to observe that

the woman turned her eyes from the dead little furry thing in much the same way that I did myself.

Tippy looked around at the old man. "Waste," he said. "Who in this here world wastes powder on rabbits? Can't you set a snare? Or was you raised rich and don't know nothing but shooting?"

The woman said, "You know I will not have snares set. We either kill them swiftly and decently or not at all." She looked at the old man and then at me and I knew that she was troubled by a problem of etiquette. It was then I got the impression that she either did not know his name or that he was perhaps a social inferior whom one did not introduce. I must tell you that her perplexity was apparent and that it was an odd thing to come upon in the dim room of a dilapidated farmhouse.

I smiled at the old man and I said, "We almost met a little while ago when I was talking to Brandy and you passed by."

I must say in all honesty that I did not speak so in an effort to relieve the woman's uncertainty. It was an opportunity to mention Brandy's name, to watch, I hoped, a reaction. But there was no reaction at all and the old man did not even bother to reply.

"You must know Brandy," I said to the stony-eyed woman.

She said, "We all know her, my dear, and you know full well that we do. And when you speak to me pray remember that I am not simple-minded. If you have a sensible question that would not be an impertinence put it to me. But do not believe that I will be fooled by an oblique attack."

I am sure I turned crimson. "I do apologize."

She nodded graciously. "I am sure we pique your curiosity. I regret this deeply. Do put a question if you wish."

I shook my head. "When one considers the rules, Madame, I have none that would qualify. Any question that comes to mind would be an impertinence. Thank you very much for admitting me."

"You were kind to bring Mockingbird the gloves."

I looked at the others but to bid them good day would have been slightly foolish. One could feel a curious withdrawal in them all as though they had learned to compensate for the proximity in which they lived by building imaginary chambers of privacy into which they retreated.

It will not be hard for you to believe that I thought of these strange people all that evening and that my Scott romance lay open and unread before me. The woman could be related to none of the other three. Tippy's words to the old man did not suggest a family connection. Mockingbird had said that she had no relatives. And what were these people to Brandon?

As I sat by the cheerful lamp I listened to the wind howling and I thought that soon the autumn would be gone and I wondered what comfort gloves would be to a girl in a tattered shawl. And I thought of the boy, Tippy, and his rough, worn blanket and of the woman who would not have snares set and of an old man who must be the hunter and whose powder and shot were not plentiful. And I tried to remember that they had probably brought all their suffering upon themselves by being secessionists and rebels but nothing helped for I knew that the woman, the old man and Mockingbird had no more power to make war than I myself and that if Tippy had done wrong, he had paid for it.

I felt that I must assist them somehow but I would not have you believe that mine is a beautiful soul dedicated to aiding the needy. I am only one who wishes to enjoy her fine, soft bed and warm hearth without being nagged by the thought that others are in want. I trust you can recognize the fine distinction that exists between the true yearning to succor the unfortunate and the really very selfish desire to feel that one has done all that can be expected and is now free to forget the whole unpleasant business. It seems to me that it is only fair to explain this.

I planned as I sat there that night in the lamplight. It seemed sensible to first offer a roast or a pudding or something and then if that were accepted it would indicate that I had not pride or stubbornness to fight against. In that case I would then take the matter to Powell—perhaps. I remembered all the beautiful blankets in the Coberley linen room. Why couldn't Mrs. Conrad Coberley share with her fellow Carolinians? And why couldn't she, who had unlimited credit at the farms, offer an occasional sack of potatoes? Why indeed? What was between her and those who came from "down home"? I did not know but instinctively I felt that if they would accept charity at all, it would not be from Brandy.

Aunt Laurel raised her eyes from the eternal knitting. "It seems to be blowing much harder tonight," she said.

Brett stirred at the sound of her voice and smiled up at her.

"What did you say?" he asked.

"The wind. Blowing hard tonight."

"Oh, yes. Last night, too."

Powell did not move but I knew that he was listening in that strained, anxious way of his. Always when Brett spoke Powell was aware of every word, of every intonation.

"I know," Aunt Laurel said. "I heard it."

"You did?"

"Of course. Didn't everybody?"

She turned to us and we agreed that we had. The conversation was at an end but it had been fine evidence that things were going

well. Some day we would once again be able to accept incon-
sequential observations for what they were. Some day Brett would
be himself, willing to remain full time in our world instead of coming only as a visitor. The time was not now but it would come,
we told ourselves. It would come.

I would say that it was a little after ten when we retired that
night. I would say so because at the shore that was our usual bed-
time. I am more certain of the fact that at midnight I was still
awake. My mind was running on at a great rate and giving me no
chance to relax and find peaceful sleep. The woman with the stony
eyes. Mockingbird. Cabins. And supper smoke. It was impossible
to sleep.

The wind howled and a shutter slapped dismally somewhere in
the back of our house. I hoped it would not awaken Brett. I
hoped that if it did he would not awaken in terror facing again
the terrible march at Fredericksburg. We had been so fortunate of
late. Not since the night of the northeaster had he gone back to
the war. I had more than half expected it last night but it had
not come. And not so far tonight. Perhaps it would never come
again.

The shutter banged and the house creaked and somewhere
down the ocean front the wind was tearing at the defenses of
the boarded-up houses. The noise was worse here than in the city,
I thought. And it occurred to me that if a troop of robbers burst
in to relieve us of our silverware they need not tiptoe nor whisper.
They could slam cabinet doors or rip up the carpets if they chose
and we, lying in our beds, would blame all peculiar sounds in the
night upon the wind.

I lay there thinking again of many things. I thought of Brandy,
for sooner or later my mind always turned to her. I thought of

how she laughed when we had parted that afternoon. I tried to remember just what particular thing had given the excuse for
laughter. And after awhile I remembered. I remembered what she
had said and how she had said it. And all the memories of the day
came flooding back to me and some adjusted themselves in perfect counterpoint to the howling wind, the wind whose noisy roar
would reduce to nothingness a light and hurried footstep on the
stair.

I did not rise immediately. I would not have you think that one
rushes into such a matter. One does not. For there is always the
possibility that one would be better for not knowing.

But in time I lit my candle and ventured out into the corridor
and now that my mind was made up I did not hesitate at Brett's
door. I walked directly into his room and I stood beside his empty
bed and I had no thought of waking Powell for I knew where my
brother was. I knew where he was tonight and I knew where he
had been the night before.

It will be easy to understand why I could not discuss this matter
with my brother. But perhaps explanation is needed for my silence
to Powell or Aunt Laurel. In regard to my aunt I need only say
that from her no words of wisdom would have been forthcoming.
She would have been conscious only of Brett's wickedness and of
the sad fact that his soul was imperiled. After that, whether I
would or no, the information would have been taken to Powell.

To me it seemed that Powell could do without this additional
worry. There was no doubt that Brett had embarked upon an
amorous adventure that could bring great distress. I knew that the
woman, Brandy, was dangerous. I had known it from the start
and there was the likelihood that to possess her was to breed

violence and ruin. Still when I thought of burdening Powell with the unpleasant knowledge that was mine I hesitated. I did not tell myself that I would never reveal the dark truth to Powell but I decided to ponder and reflect.

For several days I did not drive out to the bay. Brett made no request to drive that way and I wondered at his artlessness. Was it a symptom of his mental illness or had he always been a poor dissembler? I, in his position, would have made a great point of remarking on how long it had been since a visit to Brandon. But my brother said nothing. He did not mention her or the Coberley house.

It was a Sunday morning upon which we had our first fine day. It was cold but clear and the ocean glittered like carved ice in silvery sunlight. I rose early and went down to the kitchen. There I found a ham and a rice pudding. Carefully I took them out to the carriage and drove with them to the Spurney farmhouse.

I cannot say that having met the invaders face to face bestowed a new feeling of assurance. The brooding atmosphere of the farm still hung thick and forbidding and as on the occasion of my first visit I was not certain of my reception.

This time I did not even make the effort to knock upon the door. I simply waited and the door opened. The stony-eyed woman looked down upon me from her great height.

"This is an interruption," she said. "We are at prayer."

There was no invitation to enter and I felt extremely awkward. Still I had come as a friend and there was no cause for anything beyond a simple apology.

I rallied and spoke directly up into those hard eyes.

"I regret, Madame, that I have chosen an inopportune mo-

ment to call but you may be interested in accepting a small gift
which I have brought you."

"A gift?" Her tone did not suggest a quickening interest but
only a shocked disbelief as though my presumption was thoroughly
incredible.

"It is for Mockingbird, too, and Tippy and the—"

"We are at prayer," she said again.

I decided that I had better dispense with the wordy effusions
reserved for drawing rooms and decaying farmhouses.

"I have brought a ham and a pudding," I said, bluntly. "Do
you want them?"

She stared down at me for a long moment. Then she said,
"No," and closed the door.

I had blundered badly. It would have been wiser to have
negotiated with Mockingbird. The feeling was strong within me
that the woman would not have refused that which Mockingbird
had already accepted. There had been no quarrel about the
gloves. But perhaps the gloves were different. To accept a gift
of food is always considered degrading to the foolishly proud
and it had long been my observation that the more badly needed
the food is, the more fiercely it is rejected. It was clear that my
help was not wanted and that the invaders would starve and
freeze before they would falter in their determination to sustain
themselves. Or at least the woman who was apparently the head
of that weird household would prefer disaster to charity.

I drove away considering the situation. Deep in thought as I
was I still did not miss the sight of Brandy on the bay road. I
could see her in the distance and while I was still beyond the
sound of her shout I made a decision to circle the Spurney farm
and the Coberley house from the rear and thus avoid her. Surely

it is plain why I could scarcely bring myself to look at the woman. To drive an unnecessary three miles was preferable to listening to the sound of her laughter.

So I turned right instead of left as I came through the gap where a decent, self-respecting gate had once swung upon decent, self-respecting hinges. It was a quiet world through which my horse and I moved. A silent, Sunday world and we thought our thoughts and traveled the narrow road under stark, leafless trees. There was no sight of the bay now, no sound of the ocean. This was the country that never saw summer people but instead sent to them its eggs and butter and luscious blueberries. Only I of the summer crowds was no stranger here. There was the farmhouse of the Lanktons. I played with the idea of dropping in but it came to me with a sense of shock that I had indeed been shattered by the woman with the stony eyes. If by any chance I was greeted at the door with news that the Lanktons were at prayer it would be too much.

So I went on till I was stopped. Stopped by a voice from the roadside.

"Little girl! Hey, little girl."

He was a man I had never seen before and he was sitting on a tree stump. It surprised me that on this cold morning his shoes were off, till I realized that he had been rubbing his feet. He was a young man—twenty-eight I guessed—and he was slim in that certain way that never suggests feebleness but instead a terrible, muscular strength. His face was ruggedly handsome, his eyes keen and sharp. The clothes he wore were threadbare and in need of cleaning and they were of military origin though there was nothing spruce or trim in their appearance.

"What place is this here place I'm in, little girl?"

I told him and his face lighted with satisfaction and he pulled on one of his rough, worn shoes and laced it while I watched. He paused as he reached for the other to give me a brief, flashing smile.

"You can go along now," he said amiably. "I just wanted to make right sure this was the place."

I returned his smile but held my horse motionless in the road. If this continued, I thought, our ocean town would have more secessionists in residence than Yankees. Who was he? What connection did he have with the odd ones already nesting on the Spurney farm land?

"You come a long way?" I asked him.

"A long way?" He shook his head wearily. "You've got no idea how far I've walked. Maybe ten thousand, maybe twelve thousand miles."

I studied his expression and saw that this was not a casual exaggeration. He believed it himself.

"Where did you come from, Mister?"

"Oh, lots of places. Just now from North Carolina." He laced his shoe and looked pensive. "But I had another long walk first. I walked all the way to North Carolina from Illinois."

"What?"

"Why, sure. Once in awhile I got a little tiny ride on a wagon but it never lasted no time at all and then I was a-walking again. Took me one long time, I can tell you, to cover all that ground with just these two tired feet."

"Your home in Illinois, Mister?" What a question!

It brought forth the bitter grin I had expected. "Not by a damn sight it ain't. I was in a stinking, filthy Yankee prison out there."

"Prison? What did you do bad?"

"Bad? I didn't do nothing bad. I was a soldier in the best army this world ever seen. I was a prisoner of war, that's all."

"Oh, did they treat you nice?"

He gritted his teeth and his jaw whitened. "Little girl, you go home and tell your father that I wouldn't treat a snake that bit my Ma like them—" He broke off. "It was sure uncomfortable," he finished.

"And then you had to walk all the way to North Carolina."

He nodded. "And when I get there what happens? I have to light out for this Lord-forgotten place."

"Why?"

He shrugged and looked puzzled. "Ain't sure yet myself. People wouldn't answer no questions. They just told me to come here."

"That sounds exciting."

"Oh, sure. Nice pleasant walk. Especially when a man's hungry."

"Are you hungry?"

"Sure am. Nothing much left to eat anywhere down home and you don't get nothing to amount to nothing along the road and before that I want to tell you that we didn't get fed proper in prison."

"You didn't?"

"Sure not. You don't expect no Yankee to feed us, do you?"

"It could happen," I said. "Come here."

"You want me to come over there? What for?"

"Well, you've walked twelve thousand miles, a few steps more won't kill you."

He gave me a sudden, startled look and blushed furiously. Then he reached for his cap and removed it.

"I just now catch on you ain't no little girl. I'm sorry, Miss."
I thought him rather simple not to have observed that I, myself,
had fostered his false impression.

"That's all right. Come here."

He came at once and I pointed to the towel-wrapped articles
beside me. "There's a ham and a rice pudding," I said. "Don't
say that no Yankee ever fed you."

"Well, God love you, Miss." He wasted no time in taking
what the woman had refused. His knife flashed in the pale sunlight and he was at work on the ham. I waited in silence for
several minutes. I waited till he looked up at me from his perch
on the stump.

"Maybe you could help me, Miss." He smiled and added,
"Not that you ain't already but I mean this way, for instance—
you know a lot of people around here?"

"Quite a few."

"Know any new people who might have just come lately?"

I considered the matter with a suggestion of doubt in my
expression. One could always change a no to a yes. The reverse
was more difficult.

"I'm looking for a girl. A mighty pretty girl. Hair black as
night and funny eyes. I don't mean they're *funny* but they have
a different kind of color."

"Brown?" I asked.

"Oh, no, Miss. They're real purple kind of color. You know
anyone like that?"

I continued considering the matter.

"I sure would like to find her. They tell me she's here."

"Who tells you?"

"People down home. I gotta find her."

"You sound as though you're in love with her."

He grinned. "I sure am, Miss. Got every right to be, too." He chewed comfortably. "She's my wife."

I did not answer. I sat numb and silent in my carriage looking at the wiry, steel-spring build of the man from North Carolina.

"Just gotta find that gal," he said. "I love her to pieces and I can't stand much more of this yearning for her."

"How long since you have seen her?"

He shook his head sorrowfully. "Three years. Three terrible, lonesome years but I'll find her," he said. "I'll find her."

THE *Candlelight*

I WILL NOT SAY that I should have held myself aloof from the situation. Indeed I do not believe that I could have done so but as I look back upon that Sunday morning I am tempted to pass over it swiftly. However, I will not yield to the small voice that tells me there is no need for me to recount those details which will present me in an unfavorable light and give me pain in the telling. I will not yield because I know that if once I flinch there will be no end to the small dishonesties, the slight omissions, the pretty embroideries that so gracefully suggest themselves. I will not weaken and since that is my chosen course I cannot do other than say that I handled myself in sorry style that morning.

It was my advice that directed the man from North Carolina toward the ocean front. This was a calculated play for time on my part. I feared that he would ask his questions at a nearby farmhouse and that he would thus find Brandy before I had an opportunity to face her with the truth. And I wanted to face her with it. And that is one of the things I did not wish to say of myself but I have said it.

All the way back to the house on the bay my thoughts ran wildly from one phase to another of the curious tangle. She was not Connie Coberley's wife and if my heart did not actually sing then it hummed a small, muffled tune. I cannot say why it was happy for how could it matter whom Connie married when it never could be me?

I thought of Brett and I was bloated with pride that I rode

armed with his salvation. The woman would leave now and he
would forget that he had ever known her. And my brother's soul
would be saved.

That Sunday morning was very long ago but I have not forgotten how my thoughts ran and I have not forgotten that in
my mind I described my aim with pretentious words and that
suddenly I was ashamed. I was ashamed, for there was no denying that I was beginning to see myself as a brave and righteous
defender of the pious and of the afflicted. I was making a crusade
of it and this was no crusade. This was only Elizabeth Carpenter
with the crooked back taking a great deal of vindictive pleasure
in the prospect of striking a blow at a beautiful woman who had
known Connie Coberley too well.

I had played my secret game of "You Amuse Me" so long and
so skillfully that I was able to recognize a weakness when I saw
one. And once again I had scored. This time it was against myself but it was a score nevertheless and somewhat drearily I recorded it.

"You amuse me, Elizabeth Carpenter," I whispered. That was
the ritual by which the score became official.

Brandon was still at the bayside when I came full circle. Strictly
speaking she was not alone, for the woman with the stony eyes
was also there, standing motionless, looking out at the bay. It
occurred to me that these Carolinians were indeed a different
breed for they seemed to require more air than we did. Powell
went to the post office every day and took an occasional walk
with Brett but beyond that he kept to the house. Aunt Laurel,
to my knowledge, had not been outdoors since our arrival at the
shore, yet these people seemed to live most of their lives away
from their natural shelters. The stony-eyed woman, for instance,

was doing nothing. Simply standing in the frosty air with a black shawl tucked snugly about her. She did not appear to feel foolish or self-conscious but instead stood calmly as though there was purpose and reason in her performance. She nodded to me and I acknowledged the greeting coolly.

Brandon made quite a show of welcoming me.

"Why, honey, it's sure nice to see you. I'm so tired of just being here alone surrounded by nothing but trees and water and old trash."

I said, "Come in the carriage. I'll drive you up to the house."

"I wasn't thinking of going in," she said. "I like it here even if I do have to put up with—"

"Please come with me, Brandy."

She tilted her head to one side and looked at me appealingly. "Now what do you want in the house?" she asked. "It's real nice here if a person's got someone decent to talk to and walk around with."

I did not answer her. I knew that in a moment she would cease this nonsense and step into the carriage. The exhibition was not for me. It was for the stony-eyed woman and though I did not understand it, I realized it must have some significance. I waited while Brandy took a leisurely turn or two. Then as I had expected she joined me in the carriage and we started up the slope to the house.

"I just wouldn't give her the satisfaction, you know," she whispered to me.

"Satisfaction of what?"

"Of thinking she was spoiling all outdoors for me."

"Oh. Is that what she was trying to do?"

"Sure thing. Couldn't you tell?"

"Who is she?"

"That woman?"

"Certainly that woman. Who is she?"

"Mrs. Shieldstone. She's a witch."

I could not help but stare. "A witch? You're joking."

Brandy shrugged. "You asked and I told you, honey."

I said, "You don't believe it yourself. Anyone who believed in witches wouldn't dare insult one. You would be afraid to speak as you—"

"I told you once I'm not afraid of anything, didn't I?"

I nodded. "That's right. You did."

"And I'm telling you now that Mrs. Shieldstone is a witch."

And I wondered if my horse had fear of witches for a strange tremor seemed to pass through him as though he had swiftly caught his breath or missed a heart beat. But it was not witches that had shaken him. It was only that he had noticed Tippy, lying back against the tree. Today there was a blanket wrapped Indian fashion about the boy as well as one between his body and the cold earth.

"How are you, Brandy?"

She gave him no notice but instead muttered impatiently, for even here, a hundred feet from the doorway, we could hear the baby crying.

"Does that all the time," Brandy complained.

I suggested that the child might be hungry.

"Sure enough she ain't. She just hates food. Gets sick every time I give her some."

"Then there must be something serious wrong with her."

"No. She's just like all babies. They make it a business, honey, to see if they can't drive you just crazy mad with their crying and their carrying-on."

We left the carriage and walked past Tippy who looked at me soberly and asked, "Have you still got it?"

"No," I said. "I'm sorry." And I thought that I would indeed astound him if I mentioned to whom I had given the ham and the rice pudding. There could be no doubt but that all these people were acquainted.

"What's he mean?" Brandy asked. "Have you still got what?"

The boy laughed a thin, piping laugh. "Roused your curiosity that time, didn't I, Brandy?"

"What's he talking about?" she demanded. "What did you have that you ain't got now?"

I shook my head. I would not tell her, for it was obvious that Tippy had been disappointed. Brandy would laugh if she knew and a person with a full stomach and a whole body had no right to laugh at Tippy.

She looked at me sulkily. "I thought you were my friend," she said. "I didn't know you were theirs." She pushed open the front door and we walked into the parlor. There was a fire glowing dully on the hearth. The room was in a disgraceful condition and I thought it odd that she did not seem to need clean air indoors. I observed that she had no liking for the lamps and perhaps no understanding of them for she had been using candles. They stood in pools of their own grease atop the mantel and upon the piano and she had ignored the holders and their underplates.

"Sit down," she said.

"Where?"

The question was not honestly in order. There was a chair or two that I could have used but in truth most of them had blankets on them. She and the baby had been sleeping around in the chairs it seemed. Undoubtedly to keep blankets handy in the parlor was sometimes easier than building a fire. There were unwashed dishes on the tables and even on the seat of a straight-backed chair. And somehow she had managed to burn a hole in the carpet. When she saw that I had noticed, she explained.

"A flaming hunk of wood rolled right out. Lucky I just didn't go up in a blaze myself." She tossed her cloak aside and turned to me. "Did you want to see me about something private?"

"Yes," I said, "but go get the baby first."

"Well, she'll just cry here same as she's doing upstairs. She cries all the time wherever she is."

"I don't care," I said, stubbornly. "Go get her."

She gave me an uneasy glance and the sulkiness deepened. "Riding a pretty high horse, ain't you?"

I said nothing. I waited in silence and she waited, too, but she had not my calm and patience. There was a thing in the air that put her at a disadvantage and of this she was well aware. From under her long lashes she studied me slyly but was unable to perceive a sign of weakening. At length she turned and went upstairs and we both knew that I had conquered and my victory felt warm and comfortable within me. And I will not bother to apologize for having experienced joy in the winning of my small battle for though the foe was unworthy, the taste of triumph was new and distinctly piquant.

She came back to the room carrying the baby whose cries had diminished to a faint whimper. The heat and strength of human arms had eased the wretched loneliness, I thought, for to me it seemed possible that even a baby could know despair.

Brandy sat down on a huddled blanket and asked quite meekly, "What was it you wanted, Elizabeth?"

It was not my wish to be dramatic. I may say that I detest

in others any penchant for the brief, explosive sentence and do not excuse this affectation even in myself. The technique of reporting an occurrence in that manner has always seemed cheap and theatrical to me. I abhor people who, under the guise of keeping everything simple and straightforward, deliver themselves of tragic, earth-shaking news in a terse, well-considered word or two. This to my way of thinking is extremely histrionic and therefore ill-bred. That is why I stood there before the fading fire considering, summoning the words with which I would inform her of my discovery. In my mind I ran over the entire adventure in which I had encountered a strange man upon the roadside. When I had it all properly assembled in decent, coherent order I turned to her.

And I was thunderstruck at what I said and how I said it. "Your husband is here."

The amethyst eyes flashed complete bewilderment and then she smiled. "You're fooling me," she said.

"No. Indeed I am not."

"You mean Connie? He's here? When did he come?"

"I do not mean Connie," I said. "I mean your husband."

She sat quietly with the baby in her arms but I knew that her mind was racing, casting about for the words that would extricate her from the trap in which she found herself. I pitied the effort and was more than half inclined to tell her that there were no words which could possibly help her, that she might as well desist from the strain that mental exercise must cause her. I was conscious of the smug, cozy feeling it was to hold, for once, all the weapons against an unarmed foe. And I liked myself less, for I must tell you that the feeling was pure ecstasy.

Brandy shifted the baby about from one arm to the other and

she said, "I don't know what you're talking about. I guess you're just making up a story."

"You think so? He's here, I tell you. I left him within the hour."

"You just ran into some no-account who gave you a great big lie and you're willing to believe him. If that's being a friend then I don't—" She paused and her eyes narrowed. "Oh, I see. They've been telling stories, haven't they? Them dirty, trashy rats roosting in that old—"

"Listen," I said, "you're a fool. Talk isn't going to melt the man I met on the road. He's here and he's your husband. I know he is, for he had no reason to lie. He'll be here. He'll find you. Don't you think you'd like to leave before—"

"Leave?" She looked at me as though my suggestion was quite mad. "I'm not going to leave."

"I think you are," I said. "You have no right here, you know."

She said, "Just the same I'm gonna stay." Her cheeks were suddenly flushed and the purple glow of her eyes was deep and dark with brazen defiance.

"I don't think so," I said. "You won't fool everyone as you fooled Connie. You tricked him into a bigamous marriage, didn't you?"

"I don't know what that means."

"You didn't tell him you had a husband."

"I did so tell him. He knew. I never lied to Connie about nothing. Right from the start he knew—"

She stopped talking, aware that she had already talked too much.

I said, "Then you did not go through a wedding ceremony with Connie?"

"Course not," she said. "That ain't allowed."

"No," I said. I was beginning to feel a little sick. For the first time I sat down, dropping into a chair without even bothering to examine the blanket. It did not matter whether or not the poor, damp baby had been there before me. I was thinking of Connie and how it had never mattered to me that he cheated at games and had not seemed to value honor as others did, but he had brought a woman into his parents' home and had lived there with her in intimacy. That was not easy to accept.

I said, "His mother and father—" And I could say no more.

She looked away from me. "You got everything so wrong," she said, "I don't even know where to begin setting you straight. His father and mother don't know about me."

"But you were in Philadelphia, in his home. You were—"

"See? You're willing to believe anything anybody tells you. I never was in Philadelphia in my whole life. I don't even know where it is. I just know Connie, that's all. He told me about the house and about his folks and I just remembered everything he told me. Like when he talked about people he knew. I remembered everything. I knew you when I seen you, didn't I?"

I nodded. And I think I could have smiled for he had not taken her to his home after all. He had not done the awful, unforgivable thing of which I had suspected him. Where was my faith in Connie's basic fineness and decency, the faith that had made me wise enough to overlook his small imperfections? And I can tell you it is no pleasure to see oneself too clearly for as I stood there thrilled with the splendid news that he had not violated the sanctity of his parents' home I kept thinking of something else. I kept thinking that it was odd indeed that a girl of my upbringing should find Connie's behavior so satisfyingly ex-

emplary simply because he had restrained himself from bringing
his woman into his parents' home. "If I were truly a girl of lofty,
Christian principles," I thought, "I would quite properly faint
at the mere idea of his having had so sordid a relationship as this
one with Brandy." Instead I was quite content that he had con-
ducted himself with propriety and a very touching regard for the
niceties. For the second time that day I found myself amused
at Elizabeth Carpenter. But I had no time for her. My business
was with Brandy, the woman who dared call herself Mrs. Conrad
Coberley. "What are you doing here?" I asked her.

"Living."

"Well, you can't live here any longer."

"Why not?"

"Because I won't let you."

She managed to laugh. "How are you going to chase me?"

"It wouldn't be too difficult. First I will tell Mr. Fort and other
farmers if necessary that you are not Mrs. Coberley and your
credit will be terminated. Then I will have whoever is responsible
for Coberley property turn you out as a common housebreaker.
So you see you had better go."

"I am not going," she said, flatly. "I am going to stay right
here."

"Your husband is coming."

"Let him come. Go find him if you want. Bring him here.
What do I care? He don't mean nothing to me. He's a man I used
to know. That's all he is to me now. Bring him here and I'll tell
him so. I always knew I'd have to tell him some day if he didn't
rot in your filthy, Yankee prison."

"You're a dreadful woman," I said.

"Why? Because I want Connie Coberley? Who with good sense wouldn't want Connie Coberley?"

I was a poor one to answer that question so I did not try.

"I love Connie," she went on. "I loved him from the first moment I ever seen him and he loved me, too, that same way. I never stop thinking of him, of wanting him, every moment I live, I'm living for Connie. Everything I do, I do for Connie."

I must tell you that I was fascinated by her outrageous dishonesty. I stared at her, unable to take my eyes from her lying, red mouth. It seemed to me that she should be struck dead on the spot, that it was intolerable that a woman should speak such evil, lying words with such terrible force and sincerity. I thought of how I had stood in my brother's room and had looked down at his empty bed. And I made it a point to bear this well in mind, for her performance was frighteningly convincing and I might come to believe her. I might begin to remember that human impulses were not always simple to understand and that life was not truly the way it seemed when one first began it.

I said, "You have nothing to pack. Why don't you come with me now? I'll drive you to the station at Seaverne and we'll see what time you can—"

She threw her head back and roared with laughter. "Honey, you sure are a troublesome little fusspot. You're not going to get me out of here that easy. You want me out, you go ahead and wear yourself to pieces doing it. You go ahead and get the farmers to stop feeding me and you go ahead and find a sheriff or whatever they have around here to put me out. Go ahead. I'll sit here and let you scurry around. You prove I'm not Mrs. Coberley."

"The proof will be here soon, I can assure you."

"Oh, him. He looks hard, don't he? Well, let me tell you something, Liz Carpenter, he's a baby. He'll just stand here and cry when I tell him I don't want him no more. That fellow's just so crazy about me he'll wind up swearing he was a witness when I married Connie Coberley. He'll do anything I ask him to do. So you go ahead, prove I don't belong in this house."

"I'll prove it."

"How? Nobody can reach the Coberleys to ask them. Right now they're in Europe and after that they're going to France and Italy."

I let that pass. It did not seem quite the right moment for a geography lesson.

I said, "If you come with me now it will be simpler for you, Brandon."

She did not reply but her silence did not signify that she was considering the matter. She was looking at me with coldness in her eyes.

"I won't go," she said.

The baby wailed and I looked at it speculatively.

"Is she really Connie's?"

"She sure is."

"Does he know about her?"

"Course he knows about her. She's his. His and mine. Whose did you think she was?"

I shook my head. "How would I know?"

"Well, I'm telling you. She's Connie's. Wait. You just wait." She stood up and dropped the baby into the folds of the blanket and ran up the stairs. I stayed alone in the dusty, dirty parlor, listening to the crying baby and breathing the reek of the heavy, stale candle grease and feeling deep within me a sad conviction that somehow the chance to save Brett had slipped away, that somehow I had blundered.

Brandy came back down the stairs. "Here," she said, "read this."

I accepted the letter which she offered me. At a glance I recognized Connie's handwriting and it is a foolish thing to record but my heart beat faster at sight of it. I remembered a letter he had written me during the war. It had come in reply to a question I had asked him. What was his sock size? He had responded so sweetly, declining my offer to knit for him, explaining that his mother was a veritable knitting machine but thanking me sincerely for my kind thought. He had closed by expressing hope for my continued good health and by warmly assuring me that he was forever my friend. I still had the letter. Now I looked down at this one that had come to Brandy and I wished that I need not read it but there was no escape.

My darling, my beautiful:

There is no way to avoid it. I will have to go with my folks as I had feared. I hate to go without seeing the baby but tell her that her father is busy at the moment trying to be a good son. Tell her that when I return we will never again be separated.

Honestly, my love, I would not take this trip to Europe except that I know I am going to break my mother's heart and I want her to have these few months of pleasure before the blow falls. It will not be easy for her to reconcile herself to the fact that I want you even though it is wicked to want you. I will take you, my wonderful one, any way at all and if we must live as outcasts forever then I am not only willing but eager for that adventure. I do not believe that any man has a better right to you than I, for no one could love you as I do. Beloved, when I think of you I grow weak with desire to hold you in my arms again, to feel your mouth upon mine, to know the joy of having you, all of you.

My sweet one, never forget that I love you and do not subject yourself to any hardships but go at once to the house in New Jersey if you feel the need of a haven. Remember the instructions I gave you about where to find the key and how to run a bill with the local farmers. I will look first for you there when I return. If the house is closed I will continue on to North Carolina. Remember to say in New Jersey that you are Mrs. Coberley as that is the way you will get credit. When I come for you I will be proud to tell everyone that you have a full right to the name for you are the only woman I will ever want and the only one who can ever bear that name other than my mother.

And now, my precious, good-by for a little while. It is only a little while though to me it will seem an eternity. I love you. I love you. I love you. A kiss for the baby and, my adored one, a million kisses for you, each carrying the love of a man who worships you.

Your ever constant,
CONNIE

I must tell you that I did not look up from this letter with a brisk nod and a quick reassembling of the pages. Instead I sat as though reading it, long after the words were deeply etched upon my brain. I could not surrender the letter so easily. He had written it. What was the harm in pretending for a small moment that he had written it to me?

"My darling, my beautiful." To me he had written those words. And observe that in another place I was "beloved" and still somewhere else "precious." He was not only forever my friend but a man who worshiped me, a man who sent to me a million kisses. For a long while I sat there with the letter in my hand, the letter he had written to me, and then I folded it very carefully and handed it to Brandon and now it was my letter no more and I was no longer beloved or precious.

"You see?" she demanded.

"I see." And my voice sounded strange. It was very low and it did not seem like my voice at all.

"You wanted to know if he knew about the baby, didn't you?"

"Yes. I wanted to know."

"Are you satisfied?"

It was a fair question. She had every right to ask it.

"Well," she prodded me. "Are you satisfied?"

"Yes, I'm satisfied."

"Do you see now why I'm going to stay here? I'll tell you fair and honest that I can't go back to North Carolina and if I don't wait here Connie won't know where to find me."

"He'd find you," I said. "He'd always find you."

"But I gotta wait for him here."

"Yes," I said. "You'll have to wait for him here."

I could not conceive of her leaving. She had to be here waiting for his anxious arms to embrace her. Whatever else was false, this much was true. Connie loved her. And I would not have him know the ache of searching and not finding.

And I thought it astonishing that she had drawn from Connie this deep and ardent love. And it occurred to me that the things that one is taught are cheerful, pleasant lies and that it was high time that someone had the fortitude to admit it. Why did we bother ourselves with such nonsense as principles and graces and ideals? Why did we not face life realistically? Why should not such as I be told in the beginning that without beauty there is nothing? Why had I been taught that knowledge was finer than beauty, and goodness better than all? Why had I been furnished with spiritual tools for the cultivation of my soul? Why in God's name did the world continue to mouth such banalities regarding the unimportance of beauty and the inevitable victory of goodness

over evil? Why instead were we not taught strength so that we
might bear the brutal truth which is simply that physical beauty
is the greatest gift that God can bestow?

I pulled myself away from the nest of blankets into which I
had fallen. If I had come there giddy with power, I was leaving
weak with defeat. I had followed a vixen into her den. I had
come to torment and destroy her and she had retaliated by tearing out my heart.

My darling, my beautiful.

And Brandy stood watching me weep and she did not know
the bitter taste of my tears but she knew that somehow she had
beaten me.

"Are you going out to get the sheriff, honey?" she laughed.

I moved blindly across the room toward the door and there
I stopped.

"Brandy, will you do something for me? Will you—will you
leave my brother Brett alone?"

I could not meet her eyes as I asked the favor for I was no
longer bloated with pride or riding courageously to a crusade
which would free my brother from the toils of sin. I must tell
you that I was not pleading for my brother's soul and that I was
not even thinking of it. I was only begging the woman, Brandon,
to be faithful to Connie Coberley and that is why I did not wish
to write this sequence of events into the narrative.

After I had relinquished my horse to the coachman I entered
the house very quietly. It was my desire to go to my bed and to lie
there for the rest of the day or perhaps for the rest of my life,
alone with my misery. This I could not do for I knew the anxiety
I would rouse. Never in my life had I feigned illness, indeed often

denying a genuine indisposition in order to spare Powell and
Aunt Laurel any unnecessary alarm. However, no one would
think it odd if I retreated to my room with a book and this I
did, sitting all that Sunday afternoon before the fire with *Lass
of Kinsloe* in my lap and never a page turned. When I sent word
that I had had my midday meal at the Lankton farm this was
accepted without question as during the summer months such
was frequently the case.

I would not like you to believe that I sat before my fire weeping. I have no patience with those who are unable to put an
end to tears and it was with the greatest reluctance that I was
forced to report that there had been tears at all. I would like
to say that I had conquered the impulse to weep before I reached
home that day but this is not entirely true. I had conquered only
the weeping.

As I sat there with my vision dazzled by the leaping flames I
made an effort to understand the sorrow within me. What sort
of unreasonable mind was mine? First I had been pained by the
sight of a woman who was represented to me as Connie's wife.
Then, common sense reminding me that it would be this one or
another, I had accustomed myself to the idea of his being married. Now Brandy had been revealed to me as an impostor and
my heart was heavier than ever. Why?

It may be difficult to credit but it took me hours to solve the
puzzle. Perhaps I was suffering from honest confusion or it may
be that I was avoiding the truth. But in the end I knew the
answer. It was a simple answer and it spoke but meanly of the
spirit of this creature I was. I had accepted Brandy as his wife,
knowing full well her unworthiness and I had taken comfort
from the fact that she was not his mental or social equal. I had

adjusted myself to a marriage in which I might pity him for his mistake, a marriage that he had doubtless made in the hectic, devil-may-care mood of wartime. This I had accepted. Perhaps I had even come to rejoice in the situation for truly it offered to me the promise of a lifetime in which I could dream, in my most romantic moments, that he regretted his hasty marriage. I could spin away the empty years of my youth pretending that he had come to know the worth of my faithful heart only when it was too late. And I could play that between us lay the unspoken promise that on the other side of the grave we would find the love that had been denied us here.

Then I had been faced with the letter he had written to Brandon. Even as I sat there in my analytical mood I was almost unable to bear the memory of that letter for even the most absurd of girlish daydreams could no longer find anything upon which to feed. He had not made a youthful, ill-considered marriage. He had made no marriage at all. Instead he had taken another man's wife and was prepared to face the world with her, gladly exchanging his family and all they represented for a life spent with her. And I had not known how much he loved her but I knew now and it was the knowing that I found so hard to bear.

And I stared into the flames and I thought that I must take heart and find a measure of delight in the fact that I loved a man who was capable of such devotion. There was a certain splendor within him, a courage that cannot be revealed or even tested in those whose weddings are reported in routine manner upon the society page. Connie was not frightened. He would consider the world well lost for his love and it must be enough that I had chosen, above all others, Connie to adore forever. And I will tell you that I sat there hoping to match his great soul, to equal, if I could, his nobleness of nature, but I was too small-minded, too pettily carping. For all my efforts I could not help but feel that she was nothing but a slovenly, ignorant wench, no worthy beneficiary of so genuine and unselfish a love. But I must accept things as they were. Those who refused to do so were fools and perhaps ingrates, for in the darkest hours, when nothing else offers release, we always have our tears.

I walked to the window. Down on the beach Powell was strolling with Brett. They seemed to be having a rather animated conversation. I rested my hands on the sill and stared out at them. It was true that Powell was doing most of the talking but Brett appeared to listen and when he spoke he seemed to be in opposition to Powell. I did not care what their subject was. It was enough that Powell had caught Brett's interest. My poor brother, Brett. If today I had been able to win for him his freedom from Brandon— But I had failed him. She had not promised anything. She had only laughed at me. And I would be no further help to Brett, for I was on the woman's side now. From this day forward I would live with new and different loyalties, and those who sought me would find me busy at a strange work. They would find me guarding the position and security of the woman whom Connie Coberley loved. And I could not help it that he came first in my heart and that I could only pray now for the brother whom I had abandoned.

But at the dinner hour I found one thing I could do for Brett. A thing of which I had not thought, for I had considered the day already filled to the brim with events and had not looked for more.

We gathered at the table in the large dining room that differed so from any in the city. Here there was white woodwork and wallpaper of bright green leaves, a compliment to the summer season.

"It will look queer at Christmas," Aunt Laurel had said.

It looked queer now, I thought, for the room had a decidedly lighthearted, informal look quite at variance with the early darkness.

"Well," Powell smiled at me, "did you finish your book?"

"Not completely."

He said, "You can finish it tomorrow. You and your aunt will have the house all to yourselves. We men are going up to the city."

I was very surprised and I am sure rudely open-mouthed as I turned to Powell.

"You and Brett?"

"And Hendon. I'll have to be up there two or three days. An inconsiderate but important corporation demands that I represent them in person and I have decided to favor them. Mainly, my dear, because their insistence sets so well upon my vanity. In any case I refuse to go without company."

I looked down at my plate thinking how selfless Powell, my father, was. He would not permit us to face Brett's nightmares alone. If his work made it necessary for him to leave, it would only be with Brett beside him.

"Anything I can do for you in the house, Liz?"

There was the mouse. Perhaps he would still be coming hopefully every night to my room. I would tell Powell but not now, not with Aunt Laurel listening. She had never understood about the mouse.

"Maybe," I said. "I'll be thinking."

"Very well, dear." Powell turned and grinned at Brett. "We

may never get this red-haired fellow to like New York again," he said.

Aunt Laurel looked pained and I thought how odd it was that she preferred the city to the shore. I could not see an iota of difference between her life here or there. It was identical in every respect and yet there was evidently, for Aunt Laurel, a very obvious advantage to living in the city.

Now she asked sadly, "Why do you say that, Powell?"

"Well, there's a train going through Seaverne just about now. We could have been on it, but the young master here said no. I tried to convince him that it would be fine to get the trip over tonight but he's in no hurry to get to New York. He wants to wait till tomorrow to go and he won the argument."

I sat very quietly. On this I had not figured. I studied my brother's face but it betrayed nothing. I could not even tell whether or not he was listening. I had not thought about the night but I was thinking of it now. I was thinking of the man from North Carolina, Brandy's husband. A dozen possibilities came to mind, all of which might spell danger to my brother. There was nothing one could rely on where the woman was concerned. I had no doubt but that the man who was her husband, if only he spoke fairly, could find his way into her bed once more. And if Brett arrived I did not question but that she'd lie and have him murdered if it served her purpose. And I took no comfort from the thought that it could be Brett who would fight and kill at a word from her. And I would have you understand that in the past my mind had not been given to the painting of lurid pictures. It seemed very odd that I, who had never quite believed the violence one read in the daily prints, was now sitting at my dinner thinking of adultery and murder. And it occurred to me that

at least one of the things I had been taught was true. Bad asso-
ciates are a corrupting influence. Formerly my thoughts had dealt
with matters of an uplifting nature but that was before I had
known an evil woman.

"You must have eaten hugely at the Lanktons'," Aunt Laurel
said to me and I smiled apologetically for the poor reception I
had given the fine dinner.

"I—I was wondering," I began and looked from her to Powell
and back again, "would anyone mind if I spent the night at the
Coberley house?"

Powell and my aunt were gazing at me in surprise. If only, I
prayed, if only I might rivet Brett's attention as well as theirs.

"She—that is Brandon, of course, is so lonely and she's asked
me to spend a night with her. Today I said that I would do so
this week but I would not leave Aunt Laurel alone, Powell, and
since you'll be away—" I let my questioning eyes finish the sentence for me. Would my father and my aunt consent?

Aunt Laurel said, "I thought Connie's wife was too coarse to
be suitable as a companion."

"I am afraid I was harsh in my judgment. I did not understand at first the high spirits and lack of reticence of Southern
girls."

My aunt was unimpressed by this explanation. "In my youth,"
she said, "I was well acquainted with young ladies of Atlanta,
Charleston, Richmond and many other Southern cities. I did
not observe the standards by which their well-bred people lived
were less strict than our own."

"Your youth, my dear sister, was some years ago," Powell said,
ungallantly. "The rules may be less rigid today. What does it

matter if this young wife of Connie's did not immediately win Liz's affection? Liz likes her now."

"It is entirely up to you, Powell," Aunt Laurel said. "I was not offering an objection really. I was only rather taken aback that—"

Powell said, "It is a good thing for Liz to leave her books occasionally and to chatter with another girl."

"Then I may go?" I asked. "I may spend the night at the Coberley house?" I raised my voice slightly, hoping to draw Brett's interest. "Really? You mean I may stay all night at the Coberley house?"

Aunt Laurel smiled. "Goodness, what excitement over nothing." She stared at me. "I'm sorry I even uttered a mild protest, my dear. I had no idea you were so anxious to—"

"To spend the night at the Coberley house? Oh, yes. I would love it. And I'm going to do it tonight."

"Well, keep your voice down, child." She rose and walked to my side. "Are you feverish?" She laid her hand upon my forehead and looked at me in puzzlement.

I was watching Brett and I saw him turn his eyes upon me as Aunt Laurel considered the state of my health. He was watching. But was he listening?

"I will be at the Coberley house all night tonight," I said and I could only hope that he was drinking in my meaning for I could not prolong this silly performance beyond the point I had now reached.

I knew that if he had absorbed the content of my words he was damning the misfortune that had caused me to choose tonight to visit Brandy. He would be furious to be bilked of his opportunity to see her before leaving but I was not concerned with his disappointment. It would be plain to him that he could not meet with his love if his sister was to be present and that was all that concerned me at the moment.

"May I go directly after dinner?" I asked. "The moment we rise from the table?"

"Of course," Aunt Laurel said. "But you may not go alone. It's dark as pitch out. McDonald will drive you there and call for you sometime tomorrow."

The other preparations for my visit contained certain elements of humor. My aunt ordered a small bag packed with my night clothes and toilet articles and I was amused as nothing could be more incongruous for the night's work than my very proper little overnight case all neatly and tidily packed. My hostess neither expected nor desired my company and I wondered what I would do if I were refused admittance to the house. It occurred to me that I might be seeking shelter with a farm family before the night was over but it did not matter. My purpose would have been served. Brett would believe me to be with Brandon. That was the important thing.

I found a moment in which to brief Powell on the mouse's habits and preferences and then I was ready to depart. I executed my kisses and good-bys with so great a flourish that they would not have seemed cool had I been leaving for Tasmania. I do not believe that I neglected any device which seemed likely to stamp upon my brother's mind the memory of my departure and my destination. When I left him it was with one of those overcasual remarks that rang very falsely in my own ears.

"Well, I'm off to spend the night at the Coberley house." And I made my exit feeling like an actor who has been forced to speak so hollow a line that he has been unable to do it with naturalness and conviction. I could only hope that, artistic or not, my performance had been successful.

McDonald was a silent man and we went forth without more than a courteous acknowledgment of each other's presence. Behind us the ocean tossed and in the night a lonesome bell sounded from a village church and a wild creature in a tree saw us and told his companions that we were harmless. And I had time for my thoughts as I rode that night and I would like to tell you the things I thought, for there is a great probability that at this point you do not find my course illuminated with wisdom or even common sense. It may seem to you that with a father such as mine I had only to go to him, explain the problem and have it solved with sympathy and understanding. This is not the truth. I knew it when I was eighteen and I know it now for although Powell was both kind and brilliant he was also fifty years of age.

Could I go to Powell and tell him why I rode tonight through the dark to the house of the woman, Brandon? I could not do so, for knowing her story he would not suffer the woman to live another day in our midst. I tell you in the event you are not of an age to know that there is a grand union of older people. Sometimes they speak in uncomplimentary ways of each other and lead the unsuspecting young to think that there are some who know the faults of their own generation, but never be misled. Always in the end they stand together against youth. Thus, though not overly partial to the Coberleys in the past, my father would suddenly become mightily zealous in behalf of their property and their good name. He would not weaken as I had weakened. He would not care that Connie loved the woman. Upon learning of Connie's devotion Powell would feel doubly justified in ridding the Coberleys of her. He was fifty, remember, and when one is fifty any love that is not suitable or convenient can be brushed aside as infatuation. And I would not have you think that Powell could ever be cruel. Very sweetly, very tenderly he would assure me that I was not to be concerned, that everything was being handled sensibly and fairly and he would not fail to add that when I was older I would realize and appreciate how fully he had acted in Connie's best interests.

Could I tell Powell of Brett's secret visits to the woman? I knew now that I could never tell him for it was a shame upon Connie and I would breathe the word to no one. Moreover such knowledge would incite Powell to act in wrath against Brandy and this I would not have for, God help me, I was in her service now. My brother would have to do with whatever small crumbs of protection I could spare him and even this he would receive only when it did not threaten the woman's safety.

And I rode along beside the river and I thought that if things were difficult I had made them so. For it was I who had walked willingly into my brother's empty room and it was I who had read the letter that Connie had written. It would be simpler if I did not know my brother left his bed at night. And simpler still if I had never learned the depth of Connie's love for Brandon.

The horse came to a stop and McDonald said, "Here we are, Miss Elizabeth." He lifted my small case from the floor of the carriage and I took it, unwilling to have McDonald gain the verandah. There was no telling how I might be greeted and our coachman was thoroughly capable of carrying me back to the carriage and into my own house if Brandon made it apparent that I was unexpected and unwelcome.

"It's very light in weight, McDonald. Thank you."

"But I will walk you to the door, Miss. I may just as well be carrying your—"

"No. No, McDonald, I know the house well. Good night."

I hurried away from him. I heard him grunt his disapproval but he turned and headed the horse for home and, relieved, I continued on to the verandah. I had stepped very quietly for I did not want Brandy to appear before McDonald was beyond earshot. I stood waiting for him to be well on his way and I used the moment to peer into the blackness that surrounded me. I had often wondered if Tippy or any of the others were nocturnal wanderers, but I was alone in the dark outside world. All alone now, for McDonald was gone and all was silence. I stood on the verandah of the Coberley house readying myself for the foolish thing I must now do. What were the proper words to employ when one came uninvited to spend the night?

And suddenly as I stood there I became aware of something that was almost like muted thunder and I was surprised when I recognized it as a human voice. It was a man's voice thick with rage and it came from within the house. I ran to the north side where the windows reached from floor to ceiling and I looked into the Coberley parlor and caught my breath. There, by candlelight, I saw the man from North Carolina and he was murdering Brandon. You may be sure I have not forgotten the weirdness of that scene. I still remember the dim, yellow glow of the candles, the grotesque shadows that made great, frightening monsters of the man and his faithless wife. I stood frozen, unable to move or breathe, and then his large hands wrapped themselves about her throat and I saw her body that had strained against him go suddenly still. And at last I was able to move and to think and

I thought well enough to remember that I could do no more against that man than Brandy's wailing child.

And I dropped my silly little overnight case and flung aside my cloak and I ran from there screaming for help as I ran. Across the Coberley property and down the slope to the Spurney farm and all the while I ran I shouted. And I did not know whether the strange people who lived in the crumbling farmhouse would even answer, but I called their names though my breath was nearly gone. I shrieked for Mrs. Shieldstone and for Mockingbird and for Tippy and though I did not know the name of the strong old man I trusted that he would come. Once I fell and I thought I would never rise again but I rose and went on running and screaming till I stood at last before the splintered door and it flew open and past me rushed Mrs. Shieldstone and the old man on their way to the Coberley house. And I sank to the ground for there was no strength left in me.

Mockingbird emerged with Tippy leaning upon her and because she could not hurry she spoke to me as they passed in the dark.

"We were all asleep. We couldn't get going no faster."

I had not the breath with which to make reply.

"Why don't you go in? You'll freeze just lying there. Get under my blanket. It's the one nearest the door."

But I could not move and I lay there on the chilled ground, grateful that Brandy's neighbors had not refused their help. I thought of Connie and I prayed that Brandy still lived and it was a long while, despite my shivering discomfort, before I could pull myself to my feet and walk back to the Coberley house.

One of the long windows was open and I walked through that into the parlor. Brandon lay upon the floor and Mrs. Shieldstone, on her knees beside her, was vigorously chafing her wrists. I observed that Brandy's tight basque had been opened and that someone had already brought a bowl of water and that a wet cloth had been placed on Brandy's throat.

"Is she alive?" I whispered.

Tippy nodded. "Seems like." He looked about him with an expression of disappointment in his blue eyes. "Beats me where he got to so fast."

"Who?" I asked.

"Gilly. Sure would have liked to have saw Gilly."

The boy's attitude was that of one who has missed a friend at a church social or perhaps in a railway station. He seemed quite bewildered that a man would strangle his wife and not wait about to shake hands with a few old friends.

"Was it Gilly who did this?" I asked.

"Must have been him. Who else?" He scowled out into the darkness. "Now where do you think that fellow got to?"

"I'll find him," Mockingbird said. Her voice drew my attention. I had not looked at her before this and I was touched to see that she was wearing Aunt Laurel's gloves. Perhaps she slept with them upon her hands.

Mrs. Shieldstone raised her head imperiously. "Leave him alone," she ordered. "He left her for dead. Let the deception continue. It is as I desire it."

Mockingbird stood still and silent for so long a time that one would have been justified in supposing the subject closed but I was watching Mockingbird. I could see that rebellion flamed within her and because I understood nothing of these people I could not guess why she wished to oppose Mrs. Shieldstone and yet stood tongue-tied.

At last she spoke. "I can't let him spend the rest of his life thinking he's done murder. She ain't dead but he'll be haunted and
he'll be just ready to die himself. I don't want Gilly to go around
miserable."

Mrs. Shieldstone forced Brandy's eyes open, stared into their
depths and then permitted them to close again. She said to the
old man, "We'll carry her upstairs shortly. For the nonce I dare
not relax my touch upon her pulse. And as for you, my Mockingbird, I want no emotionalism or— Oh, dear, you don't even know
the words which describe your aberrations, do you? Well, just
listen and I will put it simply. If he knows she lives he may return. I want him to think he's done his work. I don't want Brandy
murdered, do you?"

Mockingbird's pale eyes flashed to the corner where Brandy
lay and the expression that crossed her face left me in doubt as
to what her reply might be. But when she spoke it was with conviction. "No, I don't want Brandy murdered but I don't want
Gilly to have to go around thinking that he murdered her. That's
a terrible feeling."

"How could you possibly know, you foolish child? He's probably exultant and full of a deep and abiding satisfaction." Her
hard eyes left Mockingbird and went to the lovely, limp body of
Brandon and I have never in my life seen such contempt, such
loathing in a human gaze. And my confusion was great, for they
had raced, these people, to rescue Brandon and I had thought
that the thing that lay between them was, after all, not so savage,
not so deep, but I knew that I would not soon forget the cold
hatred I had seen in those stony eyes.

And the small yellow flames of the candles fluttered and swayed
and the corners of the room were dark and the figures of the

Carolinians were distorted and sinister in the capricious light. I longed for the steady, hot shine of a kerosene lamp so that I might see clearly, and it came to me that within my mind I had lived in candlelight since first I had glimpsed the woman, Brandon. I had seen nothing plainly but had groped in semidarkness, perceiving little and understanding naught of even the things I saw. And I knew that the time had not yet come for the lamp to be lighted so that in its strong, unwavering glow I would be able to say, "Oh, yes. I see." The time had not come yet and I must continue to move half-dazed in the vague, yellow candlelight.

Mrs. Shieldstone tossed her head in sudden annoyance and said, "I have pity for the baby. I can tell it is sick but its mewling is nonetheless unbearable and I must have quiet. Go fetch the brat."

She spoke to Mockingbird but the girl did not move. She stood staring at Mrs. Shieldstone and her eyes were sad and pleading but yet she held her skinny body with the stiff determination of one who will not yield.

Mrs. Shieldstone's mouth curled in a chill smile. "A child may be excused for acting childishly," she said. "Tippy, you couldn't negotiate stairs and carry a baby, too, could you? No, of course not." She turned to the old man. "Only my hand upon this woman's pulse keeps her living so you must fetch that baby for me."

And now there were three of them looking at Mrs. Shieldstone sadly and pleadingly. Three of them who would not do her bidding. She kept her position kneeling beside Brandy on the floor but the power of her eyes created the illusion that she towered above us all. "I must remind you," she said to the three, "that it was you—not I—who claimed to find in me a talent for com-

mand. Now you wish to flout the authority you forced upon me.
I think it only proper to warn you that once confidence in a leader
is lost defeat follows without delay."

So that they might remain firm they lowered their eyes against
the attack of her steely stare.

"But if Gilly thinks he—"

"Damn your Gilly. I don't care what he thinks. He's unimportant."

Tippy said, "We don't feel that way, Mrs. Shieldstone."

The stony eyes traveled over each in turn and did not misinterpret what they saw. Mrs. Shieldstone sighed and surrendered.
"Very well. Go find him. Bring him here to me." Mockingbird
moved so swiftly toward her quest that the woman was obliged
to raise her voice to reach her. "Don't forget. Bring him here.
I must speak to him. It is the only way I can counteract your
foolishness." She sighed again and turned her attention back to
Brandy, speaking quietly to the old man as she did so. "Now perhaps you will fetch the baby."

"Where is it?" the old man asked.

Mrs. Shieldstone raised her eyes pleadingly toward Heaven
then lowered them and replied evenly, "I would think it wise to
follow the sound of the crying. It could quite possibly lead you
directly to the child."

And when the old man had left the room she addressed a remark to me, and I was startled for I had come to think of myself
as a spectator at a play.

"Ignorant people," she said, "are invincible because they are
always in the majority."

Outside in the night we could hear Mockingbird calling. Her
voice was high and penetrating and it had a melancholy note.

Somehow I was saddened by the sound of it and I had a sudden desire to weep though I knew not why. And I can tell you that I never hear a voice calling in the darkness that I do not go back to the time that I sat in the candlelight and listened to Mockingbird search the night for a man who believed he had murdered his wife.

"Gilly! Gill-y! Gill-y!"

And then after awhile she sang to him and her voice came back to us and it was part of the night sounds and I could not find the key to the heart-soreness and the feeling of unrest that her song inspired. But I knew that she sang so that he would say to himself, "It is someone from home. Someone I can trust."

"Gilly! Gill-y! Gill-y!"

Her voice was sometimes near and sometimes far as she covered every inch of Coberley property and ranged far into the wild, neglected places of the Spurney farm and it must have come to her as she searched that she had been a child when he had seen her last and that he would wonder who called.

> "I was very young when you went to war,
> The motherless daughter of Samuel Moore.
> You gave me a puppy. You sold us a cow.
> Oh, Gilly, you must remember me now.
> I am your friend, Gilly, come out.
> Come out, Gilly, I beg you come out."

The old man had returned to the room and he was standing with Brandy's baby in his arms waiting for Mrs. Shieldstone's notice. I saw that she was not apt to give it at once for a noisy, drawn-out breath had escaped Brandy and Mrs. Shieldstone was finding some significance here. She listened to the beat of her patient's heart, examined the eyes again and seemed satisfied.

"Place it on the floor beside me," she ordered and when this was done she stared long and hard at the baby. Then she said tersely, "It will not live."

And I can tell you that her pronouncement turned my bones to water for I had not dreamed that the baby was so badly off. This was Connie's baby and he had never seen it. He had sent it a kiss and it must not die. "It has to live," I cried.

Mrs. Shieldstone looked at me gravely. "Really," she said. "How will you arrange that?"

"I don't know but—"

"My hands are busy. You come here and undress the child."

I knew nothing of how an infant was handled and I hesitated. She misread me and looked at me with scorn.

"The child's condition seemed to wring your heart," she said, "and since there are no nursemaids about it appeared logical that you would assist. However, let the child lie as it is."

"It is only that I never touched a baby before."

"My fine lady," Mrs. Shieldstone said, "I never touched a slut before but I'm doing it now. Of course it's up to you. I do not mind if the child dies. It was you who seemed disturbed at the thought."

I knelt down upon the floor and removed the baby's blanket which was soiled and wet. Underneath there was a woolen garment of some sort and I was shocked and sickened at sight of it. I paused in my work and the woman said, "I must look upon the child naked. Please continue the undressing."

And when I had done so she gazed upon the wretched, wasted body of the baby and she said, "Dress it again. I can do nothing. Death is on the way."

But this was Connie's baby and I could not be a party to its degradation. I could not replace the dreadful garments I had taken from the pitiful little body. And if death must come I would not let it find Connie's baby disgracefully clothed. And I wept for the sorrow that must come to Connie for his firstborn and I dipped my handkerchief into the bowl of water and I gently patted the inflamed skin of the poor infant.

Mrs. Shieldstone said, "That water's cold, you silly goose."

And my tears flowed more swiftly for I had wanted to help the poor little thing and I had been so stupid that I had only brought further discomfort. I remembered my overnight case then and fetched it from the verandah. Within it I had a flannel nightgown and this I wrapped about the baby and then I chose a warm, dry blanket from one of the chairs and cuddled the baby into it. After that I raised it from the floor and held it in my arms and it was quiet. So quiet that I feared.

"Is it dead?" I asked and I held it so that the woman could look at its pinched little face.

She shook her head. "Not yet."

"But it must—it must die?"

"I am busy," she said. "Ask me again when I am free of its mother."

And I sat in the candlelight with the sick baby in my arms and after awhile Mockingbird stepped through the window and behind her walked Brandy's husband.

Mrs. Shieldstone did not look at him. She only said, "Sit down. I am not ready for you."

He sat down. He looked pale but I cannot be sure that he was, for the small, flickering flames cast a most deceptive light. His glance went to Brandon's still figure and his eyes burned fiercely and it seemed to me that Mrs. Shieldstone had been right and

that he was not finished with his wife. Upon his face there were
bloody, parallel lines that ran from temples to chin, evidence
that Brandon had fought hard against him. His eyes fell upon me
and the fierceness faded and bewilderment came in its place. I
knew that for him it was all a matter of living through a bad, confused dream in which all sorts of unaccountable people appear
and must be accepted without reason or explanation.

Tippy leaned forward and his eyes were shining. "Gilly," he
said.

The man turned to him and spoke. "Good to see you, fellow,"
he said but it was clear to me that he did not know Tippy. "What
happened to you?"

"What? Oh. Oh, that. Just the war, Gilly." He was not concerned with the lost arm and leg. He was only anxious that Gilly
should know him and I was anxious, too, for the shining eyes of
the boy were heart-breaking to see. "You don't recognize me,
do you, Gilly?"

"Oh, sure I do. I don't rightly recall your name but I know
you. Sure I do." And Gilly was striving to wipe out the disappointment in the boy's eyes and he said, "You were a great
one for fishing and you had a wonderful ma and let's see—"

"That's right." Tippy was breathing easier now, the eyes alight
with pride, the bitter young mouth smiling in innocent pleasure.

"But you were only a little one when I left."

"I must have anyway been fourteen," Tippy said.

Gilly nodded. "And the best of the whole bunch, too. I always
said so. I always said, 'They ain't gonna keep that boy out of
this war. He'll be with us.' I always said that."

"Did you, Gilly?" And I thought that Tippy might die here
and now of his delight and I thought that it would be a fine

thing if he did. Surely for this boy Fate had no moment in store that would glow as brightly.

And I looked at the man who knew nothing of Christian principles concerning forgiveness, the man who had tried to murder his wife, and I was not concerned for him. God would forgive him.

The old man came out of the shadows and he and Gilly clasped hands solemnly.

Mrs. Shieldstone looked up at them. "Are you congratulating Gilly upon his night's work?" she asked.

"No, Mrs. Shieldstone, I'm just right glad to see him."

"Are you? How touching. If you are ready you can help me bear this one upstairs." She favored Gilly with a glance. "You are of a strength that could spare us the effort," she said, "but I do not trust you." And she bent her firm, well-shaped body to the task of lifting Brandon.

Mockingbird hurried after them with a candle, receiving orders from Mrs. Shieldstone as they climbed the stairs. The girl was to build three fires, undress Brandy, heat water, heat milk and find a brick or an iron or something else that would serve as a bed-warmer.

We waited in the parlor and I thought that Gilly and I were like people waiting in a tribunal chamber for the authorities to deal out justice or aid. I with Connie's baby and he with the scratches on his face. We waited, neither of us comfortable or at ease. I wondered if she would attend to him first. It seemed unlikely since he would accept postponement and Death would not, but the woman was not predictable and I held the baby tightly, hoping to defeat Death with the warmth of my body and the strength of my will.

Gilly sought Tippy's eyes in the shadows and he whispered, "Is it true that she's a witch?" and he asked the question in the only way a man could ask it, jestingly, as though the idea amused him.

Tippy said, "People sure say so."

"I know. I heard but course I never knew her well."

"Me neither till—till not so long ago. She's smart and she can sure do things."

"Like what?"

"Oh, finding out things. I could tell you lots but—" He broke off and directed his gaze to me and it was the same as a pointed finger. "I'll tell you later maybe."

Gilly nodded. "Sure. You can tell me later." And he half-smiled at me and his glance was not unfriendly and we were both remembering the ham and the rice pudding. And I must say that I wanted no particular kindness shown me for my gifts to him. They were things that represented no sacrifice on my part, and I do not consider gratitude an essential where the favor has been no more than a careless whim on the part of the giver.

"I cannot walk through dark rooms with the baby," I said, "or I would leave. Why don't you two go somewhere else to talk?"

Gilly shook his head. "I was told to wait," he said. And I could not tell whether it was Mrs. Shieldstone's reputation for witchcraft or her cultural superiority that bound him to her order.

We sat without further conversation. Once the baby whimpered and Gilly looked toward it and then away. And because I have read too much I am imaginative and I thought that I knew how a man would feel about a baby who had been given to his wife by another man.

Mrs. Shieldstone came into the room and she said to Gilly,

"My heart goes out to you in your great trouble," and her voice was strangely ironic. "Your wife was unfaithful. What a terrible thing. How sad. How tragic. Come, I want to talk to you." She snatched from the mantel the one remaining candle and walked off followed by Gilly.

Tippy said, "Wake me when Gilly comes back."

I was already on my feet. I put the baby down carefully on the chair and departed for the kitchen. There would surely be candles there which I would somehow locate.

Perhaps it will not be believed but I did go in search of candles. It had not been my original intention to spy upon Mrs. Shieldstone and Gilly. I am only explaining this because it is the way things truly were. Certainly I am not mentioning it to establish the fine, high quality of my character, for spy upon them I did.

Mrs. Shieldstone had led the way to the dining room and I passed it on the way to the kitchen. There were sliding doors to the Coberleys' dining room and Mrs. Shieldstone had closed them. The top halves of the doors were frosted glass and there were twin designs—knights in armor, I recall. To achieve definition of shading and form the glass had been left clear in places and so upon the shields of the knights there were, for instance, a few narrow lines completely transparent and at eye level.

Mrs. Shieldstone had taken a saucer from the china closet and was setting the candle upon it. She then placed the light in the center of the table and she and Gilly seated themselves. They spoke very quietly. I heard no word.

At first she seemed to be taunting him for he looked sullen and he stared into the candle flame with resentment in his eyes. And then quite suddenly she changed and she began to speak to him in swift, low words that caused his jaw to drop and his eyes to

bulge with astonishment. He kept shaking his head in disbelief
and she rose from her chair and bent close to him talking, talking,
and after awhile he seemed not to disbelieve her any more. He sat
with his head bowed listening and even before I saw his tears
glitter in the candlelight I knew from the slope of his shoulders
that he was filled with grief. And when I turned my eyes upon
the woman she was crying, too, and it is hard to say why I was
shocked and startled but it was rather like seeing tears roll down
the cold, hard face of a statue in the park. And now he sat there
nodding in full and sad agreement and he wiped his tears away
with the back of his large, rough hand. They got up from the table
and Mrs. Shieldstone took the candle and I scurried back to the
parlor where I was sitting quietly with the baby in my arms when
they entered.

Gilly did not intend to pause a moment in the room. He walked
directly to the long window. "Good-by, Ma'am," he said. "I'm
sorry for the extra trouble I've put you to."

I could not keep silent. "Wait," I begged, "just a second. The
boy—his name is Tippy—wanted a word with you."

He turned from the window and walked to the sofa upon which
Tippy lay.

"Tippy," he said, "I'm leaving now."

Tippy awakened and looked up into the face of the man. "You
got around to remembering my name," he said in happy wonderment.

"Sure. I never really forgot it. It was just pushed in back of
a lot of things and I couldn't find it right away. I gotta say good-
by now."

"Well, good-by, Gilly. Good luck to you. Mighty fine seeing
you."

The man patted Tippy and disappeared into the night. Tippy lay staring after him, his eyes still bright, his lips still smiling.

Mrs. Shieldstone said, "The others will be resentful that he had no good-by for them." I saw that she had purposely heightened the boy's pride and happiness and I was pleased with her.

"Madame," I begged, "will you look at the child?"

"I must first see that its mother still lives," she said and hurried away. And in a moment I heard her scolding Mockingbird and the old man and again I sat quietly waiting with the sick baby in my arms.

Mockingbird came down the stairs and in the dimness I had the fantastic impression that without the slightest exertion the wraithlike child was carrying Brandon in her arms but it was only Brandon's black dress. Mockingbird flashed by the parlor door and when she came back she brought firewood and she knelt at the hearth and she sang as she worked.

> "Burn, fire, burn, chase the shadows away,
> Chase from his heart a love that's all pain,
> Give this dark night the brightness of day
> And let Gilly know gladness again."

I did not see what future happiness there could be for Gilly nor for any of us there in the glow of the candlelight. And I thought that some day the Coberleys would return to this room and they would find it strangely restless and unlike itself. The room would not forget what had happened here and the curtains would rustle, mentioning to each other the curious things they had seen and the oddness of the people who had used this room. The very walls would recall and gossip of a gray-haired woman with stony eyes, a girl who sang as easily as she breathed and a man who had tried to do murder.

Mrs. Shieldstone walked down the stairs and over to me. She held out her arms for the child and she placed it close to the prospering flames and took the wrappings from about it. She shook her head and I watched her, searching her face for a clue to what she saw. And after awhile she spoke.

"The child has been badly fed and underfed," she said. "It has skin poison and disorder of the eyes. Moreover there is a digestive malfunction and a lack of liquid in the system."

"Can—can anything be done?"

Her mouth twisted sourly. "Why should I bother? As soon as the woman returns to health and vigor she will once again reduce the child to a sorry state through cruel neglect and ignorance."

"I do not think so," I said. "I think I can prevail upon Brandon to—"

"To act human? Not possible."

The woman's doubt was regrettably valid but I had my secrets and my methods, too. It seemed to me that I might influence Brandy, for surely she would not wish it said to Connie that she had killed their child. The threat that I would not hesitate to tell him could not fail to impress her. She had no way of knowing that I would never burden Connie with such dreadful knowledge.

"I beg of you, Madame, do what you can."

And she asked Mockingbird about the water and the milk that she had ordered to be heated and she wrapped the child once more in my flannel gown. She called the old man and sent him to the farmhouse for a thing which she called her herb case and she said to me, "Everyone will have to help if I am to save this child."

"What must I do?" I asked her.

She said to me, "You must pray," and, though I have abiding faith in prayer and hold it in proper respect, I know no deeper insult had ever been dealt me. She had accurately and pitilessly gauged my value as a practical assistant and as though to underline the measure she had taken of me she said to Tippy, "Come, you must watch the milk and remember that it cannot cool and it cannot boil and you must count the drops of water."

I do not know how I will be judged but I must confess that I hoped she was a witch and that she could produce a magic that would heal Connie's baby. My education had not conditioned me for belief in witches but it had always seemed to me that there was cause for regret that such wonderful creatures did not really exist. I think I yearned toward fantasy because reality was not completely pleasing and it occurs to me now in passing that it is not only the ignorant and uneducated who recount strange, supernatural tales. And there are those who, of a Hallowe'en night, gaze upon the white face of the moon longing for the sight of a broomstick and though they turn away laughing at themselves they are not really amused, for they were straining toward hope. If one could see a witch, if one had proof that such existed, then anything, anything at all could be possible and it would be so much easier to live in a world where that were so.

And the strange people hovered over Connie's baby before the fire. I could see nothing but I could hear the brisk orders of the woman and I could hear the baby cry. And there was the rattle of basins and saucepans that had been brought from the kitchen and the acrid odors of things that came out of the herb case. After awhile the child ceased to cry and the woman spoke no more and it was so warm and silent in the room I must have slept. For I do not know where the night went.

Suddenly the sky was streaked with light and in the room about me the Carolinians were asleep on the chairs and sofa. Only Mrs. Shieldstone was still awake. She stood before me with Connie's baby in her arms.

"Take it. I am tired."

"Is it—is it well again?"

"It will need till sunrise of the third day."

I held the baby and looked down at it in wonderment. Its cheeks were faintly pink and from the small body rose a fragrance of pure delight. It was only the mingled odors of sweet milk, cleanliness and warmth but it was more exciting than perfume.

I said, "You are very wonderful, Mrs. Shieldstone."

She did not answer. She sat down and closed her eyes and in a moment she was asleep. I looked about me at the weary figures of these strange wanderers and, though I knew them not, I felt a curious tenderness toward them. I asked myself what I could give as a token of my friendliness and my mind busied itself with thoughts of what I could buy that would find favor with the Carolinians. But all the while I knew that I could buy them nothing that they wanted, nothing that they would accept. And I knew that it was because I was a poor, shallow thing indeed that I could reveal my liking only in terms of what could be bought in the shops. There was not one among them who would have expressed admiration in so facile a manner.

And sometimes the things one can do are very great and important and sometimes these things are very small. I nestled the baby upon a chair and went to the kitchen. There I found coffee and I made it ready against the time when they would awaken. I had never before done such a thing but I was glad that I had thought of something that could be offered to these people.

The old man came into the kitchen and I felt pride rise within me as I said to him in an offhand way, "I have made some coffee. Do have a cup."

I poured for him and felt pleasure in my accomplishment as I watched him drink the coffee that I had prepared.

"I gotta get my gun and get going," he said. "I'm gonna walk clear back to nowhere and bring us home a deer today."

I said, "You folks are staying at Brandon's for the sole purpose of nursing her and the baby. I do not see why you cannot order what you choose from the farmer who will come here this morning."

He shook his head. "Don't think I'd like Brandon feeding me."

"Well, then, be my guest. The farmer will charge to my family anything that I—"

He smiled thinly and his wind-burned face creased into a network of deep, fine wrinkles. "We didn't come here to be feasted," he said.

"No, but—"

He put down his cup and said, "It's enough I drank coffee I ain't earned." He walked out of the kitchen and I could see him striding with his amazingly youthful step toward the wilderness of the Spurney farm.

I washed his cup and saucer and I got others down from the cupboard and placed them invitingly upon the table. I was reminded of the tea parties I used to plan for my dolls and how I had loved to pretend that they were chatting with me and finding me a splendid companion. And suddenly I felt depressed for nothing had really changed. Only now I had lost the knack for believing in the pretense.

It was when I was pouring coffee for myself that I heard a

sound that was much like a groan. I walked into the parlor to investigate and found Mrs. Shieldstone and the others still asleep. Then I knew it had been Brandy and I went up the stairs to her.

She lay upon her bed breathing heavily. Her eyes were closed and knowing nothing of these things I could not tell if she had been drugged or if she were still in a coma. The groan had certainly come from her, for as I stood there she made other small sounds of distress. And I wondered if even locked within her deep unnatural slumber she felt pain. Or was it possible that she dreamed horrifying dreams, having come at last to know the meaning of fear? I looked down at her and I was provoked at how pathetic she looked as she lay there with the dreadful blue marks upon her throat. Mockingbird or the woman had braided the shining black hair and had that easily captured the effect of simplicity and innocence. Had they prepared her for her shroud they could not have sent her to judgment looking more artless. Finding no nightgown they had wrapped her in a sheet and had draped it decorously across her full breasts adding, I realized, a contributing note of angelic calm.

If she died now and was carried to the cemetery there would be nothing to pack, to save or destroy. Mockingbird had taken Brandy's clothes, even her shoes. She would have left no mark upon the room and it seemed that perhaps in this thought that had flashed into my mind there was a promise, as when a rainbow flings itself across the sky. She would leave no mark upon us when she left. And I looked down upon her silent form and in that moment I felt compassion for her and a great surge of forgiveness. It was the braided hair no doubt, or it could have been the presentiment that when she went away we would find she had done us no harm. I do not know but there it was—an undeniable feeling that the woman, Brandon, was somehow less vicious than I had thought her.

I looked about, wondering why her clothes had been taken from her. Surely Mrs. Shieldstone did not think she could keep Brandy abed so easily. Had they taken all her belongings? No, not quite all. Brandy's reticule lay on the rungs that crossed beneath the small table at the window and on the marble top of the bureau there was a slip of paper.

I need not explain why I looked at it. Explanations are no longer in order. By now my determined candor in the telling of this series of events has put me entirely at your mercy. I picked up the piece of paper and stared at my brother Brett's handwriting, his neat figures, his habit of capitalizing almost every noun. He had written as follows:

> Our Fare
> Upwards of three hundred Dollars
> Incidental Expenses one hundred Dollars
>
> My Possessions
> My Watch   50.00
> My cuff Links, Studs etc.   100.00
> My miscellaneous Belongings   25.00

I did not know about his miscellaneous belongings but I knew that his watch and his cuff links, studs, etcetera were worth more than he had listed. And it was only after a moment of thought that I realized that he had appraised them for quick sale. Our Fare. I looked back at the woman on the bed and I could no longer be fooled by the braids or the demure manner in which the sheet had been pinned about her. What of Connie who loved her?

Of what devil substance was this woman made? What did she want?

Our Fare. Brandy and Brett. And the clock had not ticked a full minute since I had stood there believing that when she went she would leave no mark upon us.

THE *Bitter Winter*

I THINK OF THAT JANUARY as I sit here remembering. It was a bad month for us all. There was no sunlight from beginning to end and that which was snow in other places was only icy rain upon the ocean front. The world outside our windows was a gray world and Aunt Laurel's knitting lay neglected in her lap and Powell could not concentrate upon the documents that were sent to him. In the evenings we sat before the blazing fire and took no comfort in it for we were a star-crossed family and had cause to remember that for us nothing ever came right. All houses but ours along the black and angry ocean stood closed. All but we were snugly wintered in the shelter of cities where no wild winds screamed in the night. We were alone save for our sorrows and disappointments that slunk in out of the stormy darkness to sit with us at our fireside. We knew no peace or contentment and whenever the wind howled or a clatter of hail beat against the shutters we stirred uneasily. We thought of Brett who should have been there with us in our warm, bright room.

And sometimes Aunt Laurel would sigh and say, "I hope the roof does not leak." And we knew she did not mean our roof but the one beneath which Brett slept in an outbuilding on the Lankton farm.

"It doesn't make any sense at all," she would say and I would stare at the glinting lights on the fireside fixtures and at the blurred reflections in red and blue that danced on the smooth brass of the bright scuttle.

"Now, Laurel, I'm sure the boy's all right," Powell would say but I knew that his red-brown beard concealed the weary sag of his mouth though there was nothing to hide the troubled look in his eyes or to soften the lines around them.

And I would think that I could give them the truth and that I had no right to hold it from them but I kept my silence. There was nothing in the truth that would hearten them. And I have said that January was bad but the weight of our depression outspanned the month at both ends and we thought of Brett working like a slave in the freezing dawn and falling wearily at dark upon his cot and we took no pleasure in our warmth and dryness.

"You could have stopped him."

"He's a grown man, Laurel."

"But his mind is such that he needs your protection. You could have stopped him."

We did not remind her that Powell had tried and failed. We did not remind her that Powell had not dared to risk an exercise of authority lest it lose him Brett forever.

"He'll die working the way he does and in this terrible weather, too."

"You must tell God, Laurel. I am helpless and He is not."

And that was January, and I have told you what it was like though I should not have done so for it has disturbed the chronological order of my narrative. Now I must retrace and fill in what I have omitted and that will take me back to the morning after my night spent in the candlelight.

McDonald called for me and drove me home. I found Aunt Laurel in the linen room. She and one of the maids were taking inventory and my aunt was busily engaged in evaluating our position in the world of linen rooms. She would turn a sharp eye

upon a sheet or a pillow slip and either banish it to the servants'
closet or nod it back to its exalted place on the main shelves. There
was also a limbo reserved for articles that required some mending,
a sliver of lace with a slight break in the pattern or perhaps a
monogram suffering from a pulled thread.

"I have been wanting to get to this ever since we arrived here,"
Aunt Laurel said, "and at last I am free to do it."

Her tone implied that the presence of Brett and Powell had
somehow hampered her in her work and I knew that in a very
peculiar, deeply feminine way she felt that only in their absence
could she operate without criticism or supervision.

And I thought of the boy who had drowned so long ago, the
boy Aunt Laurel was to have married. By now they would have
celebrated their silver anniversary had he lived, and I knew that
Aunt Laurel—an Aunt Laurel with friends and married children
—would consider herself on a happy, busy holiday when he took
himself away for a time. If told, she would not believe it but I
knew it was the truth. And as I looked at her an odd thought
came to me. Perhaps Aunt Laurel had been destined to stand in a
linen room on this day contentedly counting stacks of towels and
bed clothes and perhaps to Fate it made no difference whether
she stood in her brother's linen room or in her husband's. Somehow it was a frightening thought that only the counting of these
objects was important and that the years of Aunt Laurel's life,
full or empty, were of no consequence if only the linens were
properly counted upon this day and date.

"Did you have a nice evening with Connie's wife?"

"Yes, very nice."

"I'm glad, dear."

"Did Brett and Powell get off all right?"

She nodded and said, "Twenty-one, twenty-two, twenty-three." And she frowned slightly to indicate the depth of her concentration.

At the midday meal she was more expansive however, dwelling at great length on Brett's behavior after I had left on the preceding evening.

"He missed you. He was so restless after you had gone. He asked if you truly intended to remain all night at the Coberleys' and when I said that of course you would remain he seemed not exactly annoyed but rather downcast."

"Really?"

Aunt Laurel stared at the food upon her plate. "Brett is a lonely boy," she said. "I suggested to Powell that perhaps he could arrange to have him call on Minette while they are in the city. I have not forgiven her but I will do so if she receives Brett kindly."

"She could never be at ease with him, Aunt Laurel."

"You may be right but there has to be someone, for it is my conviction that a young man needs the companionship of a girl. A sister won't do, Liz, for there must be flirtation and romance. Do you see what I mean? The charming sort of thing one finds on a valentine."

Flirtation, romance. I thought of my brother's midnight trysts with the woman who had been well-called a slut. Lacy, pink hearts upon a valentine and my brother going to lie at night with another man's wife in the dirty, dusty house that sheltered her. The charming sort of thing, Aunt Laurel had said, and I could not laugh for I was not Brandon whose laughter came easily. I was Brett's sister and I could think only of a dying baby, the blue marks on Brandy's throat and the betrayal of men mad enough to love her. A valentine, if you will, a valentine of violence and woe.

"It could be that again Minette would do Brett a great disservice," my aunt said. "But somehow he must meet with a girl who will not run from him."

I could not say that Brett already had such. He had a girl who would not run from anything on earth, who laughed at danger and stood and fought when murder struck. I knew little of men and their reactions but I could not help thinking that Minette would seem bland indeed to one who had known Brandon.

"Do you realize, Liz, that quite awhile has passed without his suffering one of those awful spells?"

"He's doing splendidly," I said and I wondered how many nights of silence could be accounted for by my brother's absence from his bed. And I wondered, too, if lying beside Brandy in the dark he had ever startled her with a sudden shriek or fit of weeping. I thought of Fredericksburg and the bloody sights and the soul-chilling sounds of it and I thought of Brandy's red mouth and it occurred to me that God may have created the second so that a man could forget the first. I recognized the wickedness of my thought even as it came to me but I will say that it persisted even so.

When we rose from the table Aunt Laurel asked me what I would do with my afternoon. It was apparent that she was looking forward to returning to the linen room, yet loath to leave me without happy occupation of my own.

"It's almost a pity that you didn't stay till dinner time with Connie's wife," she said.

"Perhaps I will go back there later in the day."

"Oh, do," she said and laughed shamefacedly at her eagerness to be relieved of my company. "That sounded awful. I really didn't mean it that way. It's only that there's so much to do and when men are about they get underfoot so I must be industrious while they're away."

She hurried off to the linen room and I thought that I would do well to hurry after her. Perhaps it would be possible to acquire a taste for following the career of a towel from shop to servants' quarters. What would I do with the years ahead that would give me the satisfaction that Aunt Laurel found in managing our houses? I thought of the bulk of minutiae that made up her life, the elaborate details that had no importance, the painstaking check that was made on such things as preserves, spices and condiments. And I knew that this was her way of filling the barren years but it never could be mine. It would not matter to me that it was the week for polishing, waxing or oiling. I would never care that the curtains had not been starched, stretched or hung in just a certain way.

I picked up a book, holding it only till I was sure that Aunt Laurel had been thoroughly recaptured by her work. Then I went to Brett's room and opened his top drawer. Though we had not expected him to have use at the shore for a beautifully engraved gold watch or for cuff links and studs either, they had of course been brought along. One does not leave such things in an empty house. He had had them here in his bureau in a tooled leather stud case. I found the case but the valuables were gone. Had Powell suggested that they might be needed in New York? Perhaps. But I was not certain. If Brett desired to sell his belongings, obviously he would take them to the city. They could not be sold here. I searched thoroughly but all I found was a slip of paper, companion to the one I had found in Brandy's room. It was marked with figures estimating fare and incidental costs attendant upon the romantic adventure they had planned together.

I wondered what far reaches of the world Brett and Brandy dreamed about. And I thought how they had made no provision for living expenses when they arrived there. That seemed natural enough, for the plans had been drawn by an ignorant woman and a boy with a sick mind. To them it would appear that the elopement was all that might offer difficulty. It would be impossible for either of them to figure beyond the point where they had eluded all followers and were free in a new and different land.

I will tell you that I did not understand any part of this. Why did Brandon want my brother? To me it was unbelievable that Connie could be cast aside for Brett. True, no sister is able to estimate correctly the appeal her brother may have for another woman and I conceded that Brett was handsome but this woman, Brandon, had the love of Connie Coberley and I was baffled. I was certain that Brandy knew nothing of Brett's illness but still she must find him tedious company when compared to Connie. And as I say I understood no part of this though I tried to grasp its meaning, tried to guess why a woman who was deeply desired by Connie Coberley would desert him for another man. I found no answer. I found nothing but wonderment.

And I thought of Brett and what his future would be with such as Brandy. What would become of my brother? Surely he would soon be proved incapable of earning a living and she would turn to other protectors, other providers. She would abandon Brett and he would suffer, for love the woman he must. And I thought that we would never see him again and that he would die neglected and alone, and hatred for Brandon swept over me in a hot wave that set me to trembling.

"Don't be a fool. You know it is not going to happen," I said to myself and that was the truth for I would not let it happen. I would not permit the woman to ruin my brother's life. I would not permit her to break Connie Coberley's heart. She must be there waiting for Connie when he came.

I went from Brett's room to my own and I sat in the window and stared out at the ocean and I thought about Brandon and Gilly, Brandon and Connie, and Brandon and my brother. I thought that men must be great fools indeed for there was no woman alive who could not tell at a glance that Brandon was worthless and evil.

I watched the great ceaseless motion of the sea and I thought how it would still be there crashing itself against the beach long after all of us were gone. And I found no consolation in the thought. Philosophical reflections predicated upon the shortness of our life span as compared to that which mountains and oceans enjoy had no cheering message for me. I have never felt my troubles melt away as I contemplated the distance of the stars or the majesty of an oak tree. It is perhaps an exposé of my complete shallowness but my worries and perplexities have never disappeared in sudden, glad realization that Nature has devised other works more wondrous and more durable than I.

And the ocean could not hold me for long and I left the window seat and drove back to the house on the bay.

When I inquired concerning Brandon's health I was assured that she was doing well.

"She is awake," Mrs. Shieldstone said. "You may visit her if you like."

"Thank you. Is the baby responding to treatment?"

Mrs. Shieldstone said, "The baby has no more fever."

"I did not know that it had a fever."

She said, "That should surprise neither of us since you knew nothing at all concerning the baby's condition."

She left me then and I heard her voice a moment later issuing from the kitchen and it was plain that Mockingbird had in some way displeased the woman.

I stood irresolute in the hall and as I stood there I became aware of a familiar, commonplace odor that sometimes haunted my own home. It came from the parlor and I walked in there only half-believing that my nose had not tricked me. Furniture polish, I had thought, and I had not been wrong. The room had been thoroughly cleaned and looked almost as I remembered it from summers long ago. Had it not been for the burned place in the carpet one would say the room had been perfectly restored for it had been swept, dusted and polished and it gleamed with new life and beauty. It seemed strange to me that they had bothered to clean a parlor that belonged to the Coberleys, a parlor that had been misused by Brandon and would certainly be misused by her again. Was it that Mrs. Shieldstone could not bear to live with such disorder or had the cleaning been meant as a rebuke to Brandy?

The blinds were drawn and a shadowy dusk lay upon the room which led me to think myself alone but this was not so. Tippy was on the sofa and I saw him only after I had stood for some time pondering the energy that had been so lavishly expended upon the parlor. He seemed to be sleeping and I thought this must be a pleasant change for him from lying on the cold earth of the Spurney farm. There was a cushion at his head and he lay back against it, his eyes closed, his lashes dark upon his pale, thin cheeks. I had thought to withdraw so quietly that he would not awaken but his eyelids fluttered and raised.

"You're back," he said.

"Just leaving. Please go to sleep again."

He stirred restlessly upon the sofa. "I just been sleeping all day," he said. "Nothing else to do." He looked at me with something that was almost friendliness and I had the feeling that he was lonely and knew not the way to ask for company.

"Do you mind if I sit down?" I asked.

"It's not my house," he said.

I sat down and I said to him, "It's very cold out." And I can tell you that I felt a very great fool indeed to have nothing better than this to say.

"Well, course it is. It's winter, ain't it?"

"Not quite. Usually at this time of year there is a briskness in the air but not this deep, penetrating cold that goes right through one." Ah, now we were off. How gay I was, how witty to have hit upon so enlivening a topic and how brilliantly I had spiced it with original observation and sparkling comment.

"Is your name Elizabeth?"

"Yes. Why do you ask?"

"I gotta know peoples' names. I'm funny like that. I always gotta know peoples' names. I thought I heard you tell her your name was Elizabeth."

"I suppose you mean Mrs. Shieldstone."

"Sure, I mean her."

"Well, you're right. My name is Elizabeth. Elizabeth Carpenter. And by the way, I'm funny, too, about names. I like to know what people are called." When one explores in darkness one never knows what will be found nor which road will lead to the discovery. One must take advantage of opportunity and so I said to Tippy, "I know your name but not your grandfather's."

Tippy looked at me blankly. "My grandfather?"

"Yes, the old man who goes hunting and—"

"Oh, him. He's not my grandfather. He's Bellew Rankin's grandfather."

"Is he? And who is Bellew Rankin?"

Tippy frowned and rubbed his eyes. "Well, now, I just wouldn't know how to tell you that. But it don't matter nohow. Bellew Rankin's dead." Tippy caught his lip between his teeth and gnawed at it and I had not found out who Bellew Rankin was but he was dead and I had only to look at the face of Tippy to know that this mattered terribly.

I kept my silence and sat there in the shadowy room and I wished I had taken no interest in the odor of furniture polish. I wished I had stayed out of the parlor for I had brought Tippy nothing that he needed, nothing that he had not already possessed in full measure.

The room was quiet and I heard nothing, but the portieres moved and Mockingbird was there. And I had an uncanny feeling that she knew that I had hurt Tippy and had come to comfort him. I was relieved when she said, "They'd like to see you in the kitchen."

I did not know what she meant but I can tell you I was glad to go. Out in the kitchen Mr. Fort was waiting. He greeted me unsmilingly and there was deep concern in his black eyes. At a glance I could see that they had clashed, these two, Mr. Fort, the farmer, and Mrs. Shieldstone from the crumbling house on the wild Spurney land. And you may say that you would forgive me if I omitted so homely an incident as the bickering in the kitchen between a farmer and a gray-haired woman but I must tell you that in looking back I have not judged their quarrel to be unimportant or lacking in influence upon the things that happened after.

Mrs. Shieldstone paused in the business of shaking ashes from the coal stove. She said, "I've ordered a chicken which is to be used for Brandon. I assure you that none of us would touch a wing of it but the man is disturbed. Can I depend upon you to gain me a fair hearing with him?"

I said, "Mr. Fort, this is Mrs. Shieldstone and she knew young Mrs. Coberley back in North Carolina."

Mrs. Shieldstone turned her stony eyes upon me. "Only by sight," she said. "I will not get her a chicken at the cost of having this man think I was her friend. At that price I would not take a swan."

I did not blame Mr. Fort for gazing helplessly at me, for I felt helpless myself. After the woman's remark I could not continue as I had intended. Could I say now that young Mrs. Coberley had been taken ill and that her loyal fellow Carolinian was nursing her? Mr. Fort would be thoroughly confounded and I thought it likely that he would drive away without further conversation.

I said, "Mr. Fort, consider the chicken a gift from me to Mrs. Coberley. Put it on our bill. I will explain to my aunt."

How? But there was no time to think of that now.

Mr. Fort said, "Miss Liz, I wouldn't want you to have to do that and I'm sorry I started so much commotion and all but the dealings with this house nowadays are not to my liking. Mrs. Coberley—that is, young Mrs. Coberley—has been running a pretty sizable bill and I ain't like to get my money till next summer and it's going to be a considerable drain on me any way you look at it. So naturally when a strange woman starts ordering a chicken I got to think about it."

"The chicken is not for me," Mrs. Shieldstone said.

And the two stood eying each other wrathfully and you must not think that they were treating the matter with a seriousness entirely disproportionate to its true value for that which lay between them was no picayune business. The purchase represented to Mr. Fort his livelihood and to Mrs. Shieldstone her honor and these things are not without grave importance. And the kitchen throbbed with the silent enmity each felt for the other and right was on the side of both but neither could see that it was.

I said, "Mr. Fort, your point is well taken because Mrs. Shieldstone is a stranger to you. However, I ask you to please let her order as she chooses and charge her purchases to us."

Mrs. Shieldstone said, "I'll order nothing that isn't for Brandon."

"I know that," I said.

"But I want *him* to know it. I do not care who pays for Brandon's food but food she must have. Anything I buy will be for her use only and I will have no people of this insufferable Northern countryside thinking otherwise."

And she had done badly when she had mentioned that we were of the North for there was a boy dead at Gettysburg whom Mr. Fort had not forgotten.

His black eyes smoldered dangerously in his leathery face and he said to her, "Ma'am, you can starve for all of me and young Mrs. Coberley with you, for you're a pack of worthless, rebel scum not fit to eat the decent food I raise and I can tell that none of you ever saw good victuals or a good home before by the way that slattern treats this house and the way she smothers everything in grease and—"

"Please," I said. "Mr. Fort, Mrs. Shieldstone is a lady and deserves to be—"

"I apologize, Miss Liz. I went too far."

"You did," I agreed. "Will you apologize to Mrs. Shieldstone?" He shook his head. "What's the good?" he asked, wearily.

And he had done wrong but I pitied him for I knew that had I a son dead at Gettysburg I would have had no fair words for secessionists.

Mrs. Shieldstone said, "New lands, new experiences. You may take my word that never before has a fellow of mean degree dared to—"

"Mrs. Shieldstone," I said, "here in the North we have no fellows of mean degree."

And I was annoyed that sectional loyalty had flamed within me for it was ridiculous—with Appomattox eight long months in the past—still to be conscious of a schism.

Mr. Fort said, "I won't be back here. I think it is only fair to tell you that I won't be back. I want to thank you, Miss Carpenter, for trying to guarantee me my money."

Mrs. Shieldstone said, "You insulted me, farmer, but I will not hold it against you. I do not wish to be the cause of your losing an account that may be of value to you. I will be in this house but briefly and during my stay I will pay you no further heed. If you will honor me with the same treatment I do not see why you cannot continue your deliveries here."

I thought this fair enough but Mr. Fort shook his head.

"And," Mrs. Shieldstone went on, "if you wonder what motivates my pardoning of your rude behavior I will tell you. It was that your disrespect was not directed toward me at all but toward the young woman who lies sick upstairs. For weeks you have doubtless stored up within yourself resentment against her carelessness and slovenliness and today your control broke. It broke against me though it was aimed at her."

Mr. Fort gave her a startled glance and backed out of the kitchen and I knew he would not return till the Coberleys' cook ruled that region again. I thought that tonight he would have quite a scene to recount to Mrs. Fort. They would sit at the well-soaped, well-rubbed table in their kitchen and he would try to describe Mrs. Shieldstone to his wife. And most likely he would finish by saying, "There's something odd about that woman." He would never know what it was and I would never know—for sure.

I turned to her and I said, "That was all most unfortunate and I am sorry you were subjected to it. He is truly a fine man but his son was killed at Gettysburg and I am afraid he is rather bitter about the war."

Mrs. Shieldstone said, "Do not apologize for him. If his son was killed he has reason to be bitter."

And I did not answer her, for I was thinking of what I had lost that day and to me it seemed no small thing. I had walked into that kitchen as an adult and had sought to assume the responsibility of arbiter and mediator and in doing so I had forever lost my right to ride beside Mr. Fort on his wagon. He had called me Miss Carpenter and that was just another way of saying that it was time I learned my place.

I hoped Mrs. Shieldstone would not talk for awhile and I turned toward the window and gazed out at the kitchen yard.

The drying lines were heavy with towels and bed things and blankets and the garments that had been upon the baby. Brandy's most intimate underthings were there, too, her stockings and even her black dress. And when I turned back to the room I noticed for the first time that Brandy's shoes stood primly beside the stove with a new coat of black polish upon them.

"What will Brandy do now for food?" Mrs. Shieldstone asked.

"I'll make arrangements," I said. "There are other farms that will sell to her on credit. The Coberleys are well known here."

Mrs. Shieldstone brushed a patch of fine ashes from the hem of her skirt. She said, "Do you invite a farmer to be swindled when you arrange for him to serve Brandon?"

"No," I said. "For since I am the factor in the dealings my father would not permit anyone to suffer loss in the event that the senior Coberleys disclaimed responsibility for credit extended in their name."

She nodded. "I am glad that it will be so. It is splendid of you to stand as sponsor for the farmer's reimbursement and so simple, too, seeing that you have a wealthy father."

I said, "Well, Madame, I could scarcely do it with an impoverished one, so at what point do I earn the right to go my way safe from sneers?"

Her hard eyes considered me for a moment. "You have a sharp tongue," she said.

I smiled at her. "I feel like a young artist whom Rembrandt has praised."

I left her then and drove to the Farwell farm which was not far away. The Farwells served some of the ocean front homes in the summer season and I knew Mrs. Farwell slightly. She was a friendly, blonde woman married to a man twenty years her senior.

She was plump and happy and hard working and she always wore a bright ribbon around her hair and I thought that this was because, though forty now, she wished desperately to be remembered as John Farwell's young wife.

She greeted me effusively, offering doughnuts and milk, and I was forced to accept for, rightly or wrongly, I felt that I was asking a favor. And while we had our little snack I thought that I had changed considerably within a few weeks as I had no heart to play "You Amuse Me" with Mrs. Farwell, no will to search out a less obvious weakness than the bright ribbon around her hair.

I explained the situation at the Coberley house. That is to say I lied to Mrs. Farwell. I told her that Mr. Connie's wife was here, that she was ill, and that she had prevailed upon a rather eccentric but capable acquaintance from North Carolina to take charge of the house. In fact there were a few other acquaintances who just happened to be close by.

"What is Mr. Connie's wife like?"

"You haven't heard?"

"No."

"She's lovely, just lovely. You've never seen anyone so beautiful, Mrs. Farwell. You'll have to have your husband drive you over one day when he's delivering there so you can see—"

"Oh, I drive the wagon now. He's got so much to do around here, with help scarce and everything. I'll be bringing the stuff to the Coberley house. Do you mind saying why Mr. Fort quit bringing up there?"

"No, I don't mind telling you. It's just that everyone there is a Southerner, Mrs. Farwell, and Mr. Fort feels a distaste for them that he cannot help. It's on account of his boy, of course and—"

"Yes, his poor boy. Just terrible. But I feel that you have to forgive and forget. You can't live with hatred. You have to share the world with other people and give and take. Live and let live and try to love your neighbor."

I was slightly bewildered by this flow of tolerance and good will and despite its being expressed in tiresome and repetitious phrases I thought it admirable. And she looked at me with her round, bright eyes aglow and she asked, "Do you imagine we'd get the summer order, too, at the Coberleys'?"

I hadn't tried for it but there it was, my score against her, and I stooped as though retrieving something from beneath the table and I whispered, "You amuse me." And thus the score was officially recorded. When that had been attended to I asked her about a chicken.

"Yes, I'll be glad to send one. I've got a fine stewer. We were going to have it tomorrow but if I can sell it we'll get along with something else. Do you mind carrying it up today, Miss Elizabeth? I hadn't planned on going out."

"I'll carry it."

"Want some eggs, too? How about some jarred things? I got the best pickles you ever tasted."

I said, "Talk it over at the house when you start your regular deliveries. You understand now about the bill, don't you? It may be June or later before it's settled."

"That's all right. The Coberley name is good enough for me." Her smooth forehead suddenly creased in a frown of perplexity. As it turned out she had thought of something that I had never considered. And after she had spoken it seemed odd that Aunt

Laurel had not remarked upon the circumstance, that it had remained for Mrs. Farwell, a farmer's wife, to notice so peculiar a hole in the structure of Brandon's story. "Say," she demanded, "why do you suppose Mrs. Connie would come to that big house with a baby and all and no Coberley servant along to help with the work and everything?"

I said, "The Philadelphia staff was distant with Mrs. Connie because of her Southern birth and so she didn't like any of them very well."

"Oh, it's just awful how people can be. Here's a poor, lonely bride being mistreated by servants. A person can't trust anybody any more. I tell you, it's all going to lead somewhere."

"No doubt," I said, gravely and after awhile I took my leave thanking Mrs. Farwell for the chicken and for her co-operation.

"You tell Mrs. Connie she's in good hands now. And, oh, yes, I just remembered, you tell her, too, that my grandma was a Southerner. From Maryland she come."

"If I mention it I'll say Virginia. Do you mind?"

Back at the Coberley house I gave the chicken to Mrs. Shieldstone and explained the new arrangement with the Farwells.

"Order as you choose. Mrs. Farwell will be delighted to serve you."

"Please remember that she is not serving *me*."

"Very well. I only meant that there will be no more bickering for you with farm folk."

"It did not disturb me," she said. "It disturbed the farm folk."

She unwrapped the chicken and examined it carefully.

"What do they feed their fowl?" she asked.

"You will have to ask Mrs. Farwell. I have never fed fowl. Is there something wrong with the chicken?"

"It's shamefully scrawny. Does she intend charging for it?"

I turned to challenge this fault-finding and when I met her gaze I saw that she had been baiting me, that with her this was a game that she expected me to share. And I found that a sparkle of humor in those stony eyes was startlingly unnatural and she did not become more comfortably understandable for its appearance. I can only explain this by saying that a granite boulder that shook with mirth would seem more odd to you than a granite boulder that made no sound at all. And I did not smile at her or signify that I enjoyed her game and she said to me rather brusquely, "I thought you planned to visit Brandon. You'll find your friend well treated, I think."

I wished that I might disavow any friendship for Brandon, for I resented being linked with her in such a relationship as thoroughly as Mrs. Shieldstone herself, but I was helpless. I was bound to Brandy by loyalties I could not name and I would never be free to say that I despised her.

I found her propped up in bed with Mockingbird sitting beside her and it was a curious sight to behold. I will try to tell you why it was curious but I am not certain that I can paint the picture clearly. In her hand Mockingbird held a bowl of milk into which small squares of bread had been placed and Mockingbird was feeding Brandy. And this was a gentle bedside scene familiar to everyone but the thing that made it strange was the awful hatred in Mockingbird's eyes as she sat there carefully, slowly spooning the food into Brandy's mouth. No mother could have fed a well-loved child with more patience, more care, and all the while hatred blazed in Mockingbird's pale eyes though the feeding never faltered. And Brandon chewed and swallowed and watched Mockingbird with contemptuous amusement and it was a wonder to me that Mockingbird nursed a woman whose glance jeered at her and almost a greater wonder that Brandon dared accept food from one whose hatred was so strong and naked.

I said, "How are you, Brandy?" And both nurse and patient turned shocked eyes upon me and I realized that I had used the Carolinians' very own salute to her. I thought that perhaps an apology was in order but I did not know to which girl it was due nor for what I would be apologizing.

"I'm all right," Brandy said. Her voice was thickish and no doubt speech was a discomfort to her.

I stood at the foot of the bed and assumed the expression that is proper to wear in a sickroom, the conventional mingling of interest, sympathy and good cheer. I knew, too, the bland phrases that usually accompany this expression, but none that I recalled seemed anything but absurd when I considered the blue bruises on Brandy's throat.

Mockingbird said, "Sit down if you like. Visiting won't hurt her none."

I slid a chair closer to the bed.

"Bet you were real scared last night," Brandy said.

I nodded. "Weren't you?"

"Why, no, honey, I didn't know he was trying to kill me. He'd about done it before I knew what he was at. He often hit me and I just thought this was gonna be like always."

"He never hit you," Mockingbird said. "He was the softest man I ever knew."

Brandy said, "Mind your own business. Nobody asked you nothing." She swallowed and rubbed her throat. "Damn him anyway. It hurts."

"You talk too much," Mockingbird said.

They glared at each other and then the gentle feeding continued. I was reminded of a ballet I had seen in which hostile forces warred with each other in a shimmering riot of tinsel and gilt pausing between attacks to act out the dainty, precise measures of the dance.

"Last thing I heard before everything went black was you screaming, Elizabeth."

"Yes," I said. "I screamed."

"And God bless you, honey, for being able to scream so loud. Who'd think that a little dried-up body like yours would have a good yell in it?"

Mockingbird took a deep breath and her lips curled back from her sharp teeth and had she snarled I would have experienced no surprise. And I knew in that moment something of what she was like. She suffered when she witnessed cruelty and ached to strike at it and I thought of the frustrations that she must have known. Those who suffer so keenly for others are always helpless to deal punishment when the hound has become the hounded.

"Never thought you was so fond of me, honey, till I heard the way you was yelling." Brandy's eyes laughed at me and at Mockingbird.

"I would try to save any life that was in peril," I said.

"Meaning there's nothing special about me?" Brandy rubbed her throat again and waved the bowl of milk aside. "That's enough," she said. "I can't go another mouthful."

"Rest your throat for awhile," Mockingbird said.

"Oh, quit pestering me and get out of here."

Mockingbird withdrew and I said, "Brandy, I have something rather important to say to you. It's about the baby. Did you know that you were killing it?"

Her mouth curved in a scornful smile. "You just believe everything."

"I believe that. I saw its poor little body. You ought to be ashamed."

"I got nothing to be ashamed of, honey. It just took sick and it was getting better. You don't know how I worked over that child, washing her and—"

"Stop lying. The baby was dying of your laziness and stupidity and there is something I am going to tell you and you'd better listen."

She laughed. "Little old fusspot. What are you going to tell me now?" And she was remembering that she had beaten me before and had watched my tears and had felt herself strong.

I said, "If that baby dies I'll tell Connie why it died. I'll tell him you murdered it."

"He won't believe you."

"He will, Brandon," I said, quietly, "for I have witnesses."

And I do not know how the aching throat bore the strain of her laughter and water flowed from the amethyst eyes as she gave herself up to the wild merriment that had seized her.

"Oh, you little dummy," she said to me. "You have witnesses! Them rag-picking backwoods tramps! That's really good. You think Connie would believe them when they speak ill of me? You'll just kill me with laughter, Elizabeth Carpenter! You have witnesses, them ragamuffins!"

And it may be that lying had become as natural to me as the truth had once been but I could not bear her laughter and I said to her, "While you were unconscious last night I took the baby to my aunt, for it was very ill. We sent for a doctor from Seaverne and he said the child was dying of cruelty and neglect.

My aunt and that doctor are my witnesses, Brandon, and Connie
will believe them."

And I did not fear that the Carolinians would destroy my
story, for they did not respond easily to questioning and it was
with satisfaction that I saw her sink weakly against the pillows
as her laughter faded.

"I brought the baby back here to die but Mrs. Shieldstone
saved it," I added.

She said, "I never knew much about babies. I did my best
but—"

"You did your worst. If it isn't different from now on I will
see that Connie knows every detail of your guilt."

She said, "Well, I can sure see now that you ain't my friend."

And when I did not reply she turned her back upon me and
lay staring out the window. I knew that she dealt with problems
beyond her intellect. Why had I not let Gilly murder her? And
why did I keep her secret? I thought that by accident she might
some day stumble upon the truth and come to realize that I loved
Connie. I thought that if this knowledge were ever hers I could
not bear the cruel delight she would take in taunting me.

I said, "There is another matter, too, I wish to discuss with
you."

She tossed impatiently and flung the blankets aside. "I don't
have to stay here and listen." But she did not rise from the bed.

I said, "If you love Connie—"

"If? There ain't no ifs about it, and I don't gotta keep telling
you that I love him. It's his business and mine and nobody else's."

"Not my brother's business, Brandon?"

She turned back to face me and her eyes blazed angrily.
"Listen," she said, "why do you keep messing around with things

you can't nohow understand? Your brother's in love with me and I'm trying to let him down easy. What do you want me to do? Tell him straight out that he don't stand no chance?"

"Yes," I said.

"Well, I ain't that mean. If it makes him happy to think I love him, too, I don't see what harm I'm doing."

I stared at her unable to think of a single thing to say. She knew nothing of honesty or fidelity or basic principles of behavior. Where could I start to point out the fallacies of her argument?

"He's making plans, Brandon. Plans for the future and they include you," I said after a time.

"I'm making plans, too, and they don't include him, but I'm not going to tell him so. You tell him if you want. On account of you're such a loving sister you may like the job of breaking his heart."

I said, "Why did you set out to win Brett in the very beginning?"

"When you look like me," she said, "you don't set out to win a man. It just happens."

And that was another lie, for although her beauty and allure were undeniable she had made it plain to Brett that all she was could be his for the asking. And she waited for me to make the next move but I had no move that seemed worth making. As I rose from my chair she swallowed painfully and I did not wonder that she experienced great discomfort.

"Ask that damn girl to bring the cold rag for my throat, will you? And Elizabeth—"

In the doorway I turned back. "Yes?"

She was lying there looking at me with a half-smile upon her face and I hardly know how to say this after all that has gone before but I was dazzled in that moment by her beauty. And I knew that I gazed upon the face of evil for surely evil could not have so many converts if it were ugly and sour.

She said, "Don't tell your brother that I'm not going with him, it'll make him feel just awful."

I said nothing and I hoped that my cold silence did not betray the fact that I knew how right she was.

"I don't want the boy hurt, Elizabeth."

"Where were you going together?"

"Just far away. It made the planning more fun for him when it was just millions of miles somewhere far off. Let him think about it awhile. I'd hate to have him hurt."

"But you're going to hurt him eventually."

She said, "That means some day, I guess. Well, some day doesn't have to be right now, does it?"

And I walked away thinking that I must accept the counsel of wickedness, for certainly I could not speak to my brother of his affair with Brandon. And I had involved myself in matters with which I could not deal wisely and someone would suffer. In my mind I avoided calling the victim by name though it is only fair to say that this was sheer cowardice. Some time ago I had known that a sacrifice would be demanded and I had selected my brother for that role lest Fate choose Connie Coberley.

In the kitchen Mrs. Shieldstone was watching the simmering water in which the chicken had been placed. She said, "Do you care to see the baby?"

"If it is convenient."

She fixed me with her hard eyes. "I'm sure the baby is not busy," she said.

"I meant if it was convenient for *you*."

"Well, I am not expected to fetch the child, am I? It is in there." She motioned toward the servants' sitting room. "Just walk in and look."

And I would have done as I had been directed save at that moment I glanced out the window and saw the old man. He was walking wearily but determinedly toward the kitchen and across his great shoulders hung an animal which I took to be a doe for it had no horns. And the old man marched on toward us and there was no pride in his bearing but instead the matter-of-fact acceptance of one to whom a successful day's work is no novelty. He did not pause but drew ever nearer and the thought came to me that he would butcher the creature here in the Coberley kitchen and I did not wait to see the baby but fled swiftly homeward.

Brett and Powell returned from the city on Thursday. They had not been home an hour when Powell beckoned me to the den.

"I have much to report on my assignment," he said. "I went to your room as you ordered, bringing with me a small shaving of layer cake. Lemon icing, if I remember correctly. I sat quietly for over an hour and was beginning to tire when I was rewarded by the sound of a slight scratching in the vicinity of the northwest corner."

I gazed happily, a little breathlessly, at Powell as he spoke. And for the first time in my life it was a conscious effort to be artlessly delighted with the tale he brought me and I became aware of a new responsibility in the parent-child relationship. It was, I realized, my duty never to break faith with him but to permit him to speak whimsy till the day that he himself recognized that I was no longer a child.

"And I am pleased to be able to report that he gobbled up every single crumb but it was obvious that this was simply a luxury item. He seemed very plump and sleek and I rather think he dropped in only out of common courtesy."

So the mouse had not come at all.

I said, "Oh, it's good to know he's well. I got very fond of that mouse."

"I know you did, dear." And he smiled at me and patted my hand and we each felt a bright contentment at having pleasantly deceived the other.

"How was Brett?" I asked.

"On the whole, very well, I think." His brows drew together thoughtfully. "He had a nightmare, Liz, but it was different."

"How?"

"It began as usual and I hurried to his room. I spoke his name as I always do and then a peculiar thing happened." Powell paused and he was thinking back and the expression in his eyes suggested that now when he came to tell of it he himself did not believe the thing that had happened. "It was odd, Liz. As I say, I spoke his name and he sat upright in bed and he said to me, 'Did I call out?' Of course I said that he had, and he said, 'Oh, I'm sorry,' and that was the end of it."

"The end?"

"Yes, absolutely the end. It wasn't like anything we've known before. I remained in his room for a few minutes and then went back to bed. He slept the rest of the night in complete silence."

"That's wonderful," I said.

"Yes." And now that he had told it to me, had heard his own voice recounting the incident, he believed it and it did seem wonderful. "You know, Liz, anyone can awaken in the night feeling frightened and lost. Anyone at all."

"Yes, anyone at all."

And for a moment we sat quiet, pleased with the notion that all over the world people had bad dreams and awakened in terror.

"He went out by himself in the city, Liz. He said he didn't want Hendon with him. I was concerned but quite helpless. I can't give the boy a feeling that he's incompetent, can I?"

"No, indeed."

"He went to shops and I think that he must have seen articles that caught his fancy for he asked that I give him some money."

"And did you give it to him?"

Powell nodded. "I gave him a part of what he requested." Powell reached for a cigar and lighted it deliberately. "Brett was young when he went to war and had no real understanding of the value of money, therefore I do not believe that it is his illness which prompted his rather overlarge appraisal of what he needed. I believe he just doesn't know what young men usually carry about in their wallets, Liz. He asked me for five hundred dollars."

I tightened my grasp upon the small, carved lions that graced the arms of the chair on which I sat. I thought of the dreams my brother had fashioned. The faraway place to which he would journey with Brandon. And I wondered if she could be right. Were the dreams enough? Were they so full of ecstatic anticipation that they would be worth the wretched awakening? I could not tell for I plagued myself with two questions. Why is it better to be miserable tomorrow than today? And the second question was even more difficult than the first and I thought it came dangerously close to being an application of Brandy's murky thinking: Who knows for sure that there will be a tomorrow?

"I gave him a hundred dollars," Powell said. "I don't think he has any real use for it but I have a theory that it might be good for him. It might create a sense of importance, of ownership and responsibility. Do you see what I mean?"

"Yes, Powell, I see what you mean."

"I don't know what he did with the money. I don't really care if only it has no adverse effect on his well-being."

I thought I could describe exactly what would become of the money. It would be carefully tucked away in Brett's bureau, counted frequently, added to when possible, and it would lie there inspiring the dream that one day he and Brandon would run away together.

And I cannot tell you why I sat before the fire in Powell's den thinking in so trusting a manner. Surely my experiences with the woman, Brandon, should not have led me to believe a single word she breathed. I should have been aware by now that nothing she said could be accepted without close examination and wary search for underlying reasons and dangers. It seems strange now as I look back that I did not question her thoroughly uncharacteristic consideration for Brett. When had she ever considered the feelings of anyone? Never to my knowledge. Still I had not been animated with suspicion when she had asked me to spare Brett a broken heart, to keep my silence. Why was it that it had not seemed singular indeed to me that she was desirous of preserving this fool's paradise for Brett? How odd that I should not have instantly guessed that something existed here which must be to Brandy's advantage.

I will tell you that at the first opportunity I searched Brett's room to discover whether or not he had sold his valuables. I did not find them anywhere, nor did I find the hundred dollars. It was plain that he had hidden his treasure in an inaccessible location. I glanced with interest at the lofty cornices above the windows and dismissed the matter. I could search no further.

Winter came in bitter force that year and I loathed leaving the fireside but there were obligations I had imposed upon myself. And I went alone to discharge my duties, for somehow I had lost my brother and he roved the winter countryside without me. I did not know what he was about but I knew that some part of every day was spent with Brandon.

And my restlessness and worry were communicated to Powell and Aunt Laurel, for they took to standing at windows and I knew that they watched for Brett though no one ever said so.

"What does he do with himself these days, Elizabeth?"

"Oh, visits people, I suppose."

"Without you?"

"I could go if I wished."

And sometimes Powell reminded my aunt that we had moved to the shore so that Brett would be free to roam. And sometimes it was my aunt who reminded Powell why we had come. And there would be remarks such as, "He's perfectly all right. What could happen to him here?" And the other would say, "Of course, I know he's all right. I just wonder how he occupies himself."

I said to Powell, "I would not have you think that I tired of being with Brett or that I consider the cold too great a hardship. In fairness to myself I must say that he prefers to go without me."

"I know, dear, and I take it as an encouraging sign. He is

beginning to plan his own days and I believe you are wise not
to force your company upon him. I offered this morning to walk
with him and he showed clearly that it was his wish to be alone."

Aunt Laurel said, "Elizabeth says he visits. If so then it is not
his wish to be alone."

"But the visit is of his volition. Don't you see, Laurel, he needs
that freedom of decision, that feeling of not being led about by
his family."

Thus they attempted to reassure each other that all was well
but not for a moment did either think so, and I do not know
what they thought but they were troubled.

And a dreariness of spirit lay across the days and there was
only the cold and the worry. But when I called on Brandon I
saw that she had not been touched by the strange dejection that
stalked abroad. Her laughter was as easy as ever and when she
looked at me she could scarce control herself, for she had a source
of secret amusement that I did not understand.

"You don't come to see me, honey, do you? You come to make
sure the baby's all right and you ain't fooling me for one minute.
Go look at her. Clean as a pin, that child, and eating like a
horse, too."

And she was right. I never found the baby when it wasn't neat
and tidy and I could see that the small body was rounding into
pleasant chubbiness.

"You satisfied?" she would ask.

And when I said that I was she would laugh and it was plain
that she thought me disappointed, that it was my wish to find
the baby ill and badly treated. And I did not care that this was
what she thought so long as the baby prospered.

"You ain't never going to get the joy of carrying any tales

to Connie, Liz Carpenter." And it unnerved me to realize that the only pleasure she took in tending the baby properly was in the belief that it represented a triumph over me. The baby itself, its comfort, its health meant nothing to her. It was only an instrument through which she could beat me every time we met. And for her it was a series of small victories which somehow compensated for the fear of the two witnesses I could bring against her.

I do not believe she ever knew how difficult it was for me to make my calls upon her, for I lived in dread of surprising her and Brett together. The embarrassment should, in such an event, have belonged to them but it would have been mine. And I do not know to what humiliating position I would have sunk in my brother's estimation had he been able to feel that his secret was safe with me. I can believe that a woman who condones her brother's guilty love affair may have his full-hearted gratitude but I cannot imagine that she also has his respect.

So for me it was a matter of great inconvenience, as I could not drop in on Brandon when I chose. There was always the need to make quite certain where Brett was before I dared venture near the Coberley house. And all this was mean and degrading and it had its place in that hard winter in which no one but Brandon found anything at which to laugh.

And I remember a day that fitted well into the melancholy pattern. A day that I arrived at the Coberley house and found Mockingbird standing in the snow. Her face was blue with cold, and inside my fur-lined cloak I shivered as I walked toward her. She had a blanket about her and she stood where, on less bitter days, Tippy had lain, just on the other side of the Coberley property line.

Mockingbird sang as she stood there and she signaled me not to interrupt and her song was mournful of melody. Indeed I do not know how she sang at all in the bleak, icy blast of the wind.

> "Down by the river, a little bit south,
> I nearly got bit by an old cottonmouth.
> Why should I hate him? His life I won't take.
> He never pretended he wasn't a snake.
> Heart of stone, heart of stone
> I'm watching you,
> Heart of stone."

And her blue face was raised to the windows of the Coberley house and I could guess that the bitter serenade was reaching Brandon's ears.

I said, "Mockingbird, you'll die of the cold."

"A person's got things to do," she said. "Can't pay no heed to the weather."

"Why don't you go home?"

"Why don't you? Ain't you out cause you got things to do, too?"

"Yes, but I'm dressed for the weather. I'm lucky enough to have the right clothes to keep me warm."

"There ain't nothing to keep a person warm like having the right song to sing."

"That may be true but you should be beside your fire today. I'm surprised your mother would let you out."

And I had known that the old man was not Tippy's grandfather and I knew that Mrs. Shieldstone was not Mockingbird's mother but there was a compulsion within me to know how she would answer.

She said, "I ain't got no mother."

"Oh, I'm sorry. I have no mother either. I thought Mrs.
Shieldstone—"

"No. She's not my mother. She's Captain Shieldstone's
mother."

"I see. And where is he?"

Mockingbird said, "He's dead."

And I knew now that Captain Shieldstone was dead and that
Bellew Rankin was dead and I said to Mockingbird, "Have you
a father?"

She shook her head. "He's dead," she said.

I remembered from a song I had heard in the candlelight that
he had been called Samuel Moore and I placed his name on the
list with that of Captain Shieldstone and Bellew Rankin. And
the sky above us was heavy and gray and the damp cold knifed
at me and I stood trembling there for it seemed to me that the
wraithlike child could be dead, too, that none of these people
really existed but were only ghosts that haunted the wild Spurney
farm land. And I put my hand out to her, half expecting her to
disappear at my touch. But she remained and she smiled at me
and she said, "You're the one who needs a fire. You're shaking
with the cold."

I said, "It's not the cold."

Her smile disappeared. "I've talked too much," she said.
"Don't you tell nobody what I said. I talked too much."

I did not know what she had said that she should not have
said, but when I walked into the Coberley house the fire did
not put an end to my shaking and I could not bear the laughter
in Brandy's amethyst eyes, for there were too many dead and
too much grief in Mockingbird's heart.

And her high, penetrating voice came clearly into the parlor and brought her song to us and Brandy said, "What was she talking about?"

"The weather."

Brandy laughed. "Well, I hope she freezes in it," she said.

"Perhaps she will, Brandy," I said, "perhaps she will." And I looked at Brandy and I thought that the girl out there in the snow should be infinitely more dear to God than this heartless woman, but it was Brandy who had laughter on her lips and a good fire to sit beside. And I said, "But you won't freeze, will you, Brandon? You'll always be sheltered and comfortable."

She said, "Only fools freeze, honey. Only fools." And she smiled at me then and I turned from her for she must have known the men who were dead, yet she felt no kinship with Mockingbird's sorrow.

And that was the shape of the winter, the way it was till it got worse. It got worse for us when Brett moved to the Lankton farm. As I have said, Powell tried to dissuade him, but my brother grew obstinate and resentful and Powell wisely refrained from pushing the matter to a lamentable conclusion.

It was hard for Powell to explain Brett's going, for, of course, he did not understand himself.

"They're short of help there. Mr. Lankton has lung fever. The seventeen-year-old boy can take over his work with Mrs. Lankton's assistance but that leaves them with no one for—"

Aunt Laurel said, "What does Brett know about a farm? Good heavens, has no one any sense? Can Brett milk cows or doctor horses or—"

"Laurel, I've just explained that Mrs. Lankton and her son can do the specialized work. Brett is going to feed the animals and drive the wagon to the railroad and to the stores in Seaverne with the eggs and he's going to—"

"I don't want to hear any more. Brett feeding pigs and delivering eggs like a peddler. He's your son, Powell Carpenter, he's your son. What are you made of that you can permit him to work like a common farm boy? Brett has two fine homes in which to live, wardrobes bulging with expensive clothes, servants to do his bidding, everything a gentleman should have and you are willing to let him—"

"I am not willing, Laurel. I am helpless to stop him."

"Are you going to demean yourself by having him accept money for this work?"

"Would you rather he was paid in eggs?"

"I would rather we could consider he was doing a favor for the Lanktons."

Powell looked away from her and his face darkened. "I do not think we can consider it a favor, Laurel. He stated his price quite stubbornly. They haggled but he stood firm and since he is the only strong, unemployed man available I presume they were obliged to agree."

"He told you that himself?"

"Oh, no, I heard it elsewhere. Our social world, my dear, is a-buzz with the story. It's the main topic at the post office. Everybody is chuckling at the Lanktons for having to pay a city man five dollars to—"

"Five dollars," Aunt Laurel gasped. I thought she was about to faint. "He is going to slave his heart out for five dollars! Give the boy five dollars a week if that's what he wants, Powell."

Powell said, "I had been giving him ten dollars, Laurel. When I offered him fifteen he accepted graciously saying that with his farm job that would be twenty. You see the situation? If he were offered a thousand he would make it a thousand and five with the job."

"But what does he want the money for?"

Powell shook his head. "I don't know, Laurel. The human mind is a curious mechanism that only God understands. Brett is ill and what does not make sense to us can be perfect reasoning to him. We must resign ourselves."

And nothing was further from our hearts than resignation and we sat that January before our fire and we knew no contentment. And I thought how Brett's hidden riches were mounting and how the day must soon come when he would run to Brandon and fling his savings in her lap. And I wondered if she would laugh at him.

I had another duty now, for I went sometimes to the Lankton farm to see that all was well with my brother, and I did not like what I saw there. I do not think that I was ever as conscious of my situation in life as my aunt. I had never had a place in society such as she had enjoyed before tragedy struck, but I will tell you that it set poorly with me to watch my brother clean a stable. And to me he did not look well, for he was lean and his hands were red and raw and it irked me that he loaded the wagon for Seaverne without the Lankton boy offering any assistance.

And I said, "Brett, come home."

"I can't," he said. "I'm working here."

"I see you are. Let them get someone else to work."

He shook his head and when the wagon was loaded he drove away in it though the sky foretold that he would drive back in a freezing downpour.

I did not tell Powell or Aunt Laurel how things went at the

Lankton farm or how Mrs. Lankton and her boy were getting full value for their five dollars. And I did not sleep well beneath my fine blankets, for I had seen where my brother slept and I prayed that he would not die of the work and the winter.

And I will tell you of the day I met Mrs. Farwell upon the road and you may judge for yourself whether or not I slept better after that. I had intended to pass her with no more than a greeting but she asked me to stop a moment and I did so.

"I ain't see you, Miss Elizabeth, to thank you for getting me in at the Coberley house."

"Oh, you like going there?"

"Just love it." She backed her wagon slightly so that her horse could gossip with mine as we stood in the road. "Never met a nicer girl in my life than Mrs. Connie."

"Good. I'm very pleased."

"She's a real lady and nothing fancy about her either like some of the high-toned gentry that thinks themselves too good to be friends with farm people. We just have more fun together, her and I. I'm teaching her to sew."

"Indeed?" Sew? Brandy?

"Yeh, look a-here." She reached back in the wagon and brought forth a parcel. "Just came from the post office and I dassn't open this because naturally it's addressed to Mrs. Connie but if the paper's torn a little she won't mind." I waited thoroughly puzzled as the woman dug her fingernails into the wrapping paper and ripped a few inches of it loose from the contents. After a moment of digging and ripping she stepped down from her wagon and came to me. "Look. Ain't that pretty?" I stared down at a flame of scarlet that glowed hotly in the bleak, gray light.

"What is it?" I asked.

"Material. Red satin. It's a little lighter than we wanted, I think, but when you order by mail—" She shrugged. "It's right pretty anyway, ain't it?"

"Oh, yes, indeed."

"Hope they wrapped the silk thread to match and the trimming we ordered. Poor little thing, if it wasn't for me she wouldn't have known how to send to the New York stores for things nor nothing. I don't think she even knew about these new patterns that are on the market now. You know, slaves used to do all that sewing and stuff for her."

"Is that so?"

"Sure. She had one who didn't do nothing but basting all day long. She's just so sweet and funny about knowing nothing. I guess we've made about four dresses for her now. One's all over little lavender flowers and it's sure pretty with her eyes. We got shoes to go with everything, too, and, oh, I can't tell you what not all. I haven't had so much fun in years."

"Isn't that lovely."

"And generous! She don't care how she spends her money. You know what she made me do? She made me buy ten yards of stuff for myself, kind of like to show her gratitude, you know. I got green silk but I ain't cut it out yet. Too busy working on her things, but it's a real pleasure. And you should see the lace she's bought for underclothes and all that kind of stuff."

Mrs. Farwell was still chattering when I suddenly pulled away from her and drove off. And I can remember now the hurt amazement upon her face for none of this was Mrs. Farwell's fault and well I knew it, but I was seized with an anger I could not contain. I flicked at my horse with the whip and tore along those frozen roads and I must have been slightly mad, for when I reached the Lankton farm I had no civil word for Mrs. Lankton who had been my friend.

I did not reply to her pleasant good-day but instead shouted at her, "Where's my brother?"

"Is something wrong, Miss Elizabeth?"

"Of course something's wrong when a boy works from dawn to dusk, breaking his back and ruining his health and sleeping on a bed I wouldn't offer to a dog. What do you feed him? He's thin as a rail."

She stared at me and her eyes narrowed into slits and she said, "He eats what we eat and you often et it, too, and found it good. What's the matter with you? Have you gone insane?"

"No, I haven't gone insane. The boy's my brother and he—"

"I don't care whose brother he is, he's working here as a farm-hand." And she turned and walked away from me.

And I could have killed her for leaving me there to splutter my rage to the sky and the cold ground. I needed someone to blame, someone to assail for these terrible things that had happened to Brett. I hated Brandon and Mrs. Farwell and Mrs. Lankton with a black hatred that blinded me and I lumped them together in my mind and cursed them though not a one could ever have hurt him had I not loved Connie Coberley more than I loved my brother. And perhaps inside myself I was placing the responsibility squarely where it belonged, for surely I was acting wildly and I have learned that this is often the device of one who wishes to avoid a simple but unbearable truth.

I ran toward the barn shouting for Brett and when he came his eyes were frightened. "What is it, Liz?"

"Come with me. Get out of here," I begged. "You don't need

their five dollars. The money is—the money is for nothing. It will never buy you anything you want. It's no good to you."

And I saw that I had caught him at a time when his eyes were sharp with understanding. He was listening to me and I wanted to tell him all I knew and I wanted to tell him nothing that would irrevocably involve me in his intrigue and I shook in helpless, impotent rage.

He said, "You yelled so that I thought something had happened."

"You have to get out of here. Come with me now, Brett."

"I can't, Liz. I'm working here. They hired me. They need me."

"You can't like working here. You can't—"

"Yes, I kind of like it."

And I wept then for my brother who had been sold by those who wished to use his strong body and his sick mind. And he was puzzled by my tears and he said, "Liz, you aren't well. Go on home and tell Aunt Laurel to put you to bed."

He turned and went back in the barn and I knew there was nothing I could say that would save him. And it came to me that once I would have been heartened by the way he had listened and by his solicitude for me. But there was nothing to hearten me now. His power of reasoning was weaker than ever, for he obviously felt that it was his duty to remain here and had professed almost a liking for his laborious tasks. And so between his desire for Brandon and the uses to which the Lanktons had put him he was a captive, a pitiful young giant unable to think or act wisely, a victim of greedy creatures.

And I ran back to the carriage and raced my poor beast all the way to the house on the bay. I rushed past Mockingbird without a word and into the Coberley parlor. Mrs. Farwell had been there and gone but I think I would have said what I had to say even with an audience.

I found Brandy with the red satin, a great splash of color, before the mirror. It was draped experimentally about her and she turned to me, her cheeks flushed, her black, tousled hair gleaming as richly as the satin.

I said, "Is there nothing that shames you, nothing to which you will not stoop?"

She said, "Oh, for the Lord's sake, Liz Carpenter, what's bothering you now? A few yards of silk? He gave me the money. I didn't steal it from him."

"I know. He gives you twenty dollars a week on top of the original hundred and whatever he got for his watch and the other things."

"And none of it's your business," she said, sulkily.

"I think it is."

She flung the red satin aside and turned to me. "Listen," she said, "you knew I didn't have no clothes when I came here. I had to have some, didn't I? Where was I gonna get 'em?"

I stared at her. "From the first moment you saw Brett you planned—"

"Well, I knew about the Carpenters just rolling in money. I didn't think it would be anything at all for Brett to get a good-sized piece of it from his papa. When I talked about running away with him I thought he'd just go ask and get the money and then I'd find something to delay us going. Honest, I didn't know he'd have to go work like a dog just to get a few measly dollars together. Your papa must really be a tight-fisted old man."

"Brandon, you amaze me. You have no decency, no ethics, no—"

"It was the no clothes part that bothered me, honey. Hell, I wasn't going to have Connie come for me and find me looking like a draggle-tailed nigger in an old worn-out dress." And you may not believe it but, with perfect composure, she picked up the length of red satin again and tried it before the mirror, considering it one way and then another.

I said, "Don't you think Connie would rather find you in an old black dress than to know you gave yourself to Brett for a wardrobe full of new clothes?"

Those queer eyes of hers flashed anger. "Listen," she said, "you keep talking like that and I swear I'll kill you."

"But you did it. You lay with my brother and yet you will go to Connie and tell him that you love him."

"I do love him. Ain't another man in the world my old black dress wouldn't be good enough for. Yes, and with the God damned streaks on it, too, that came from the washing the witch gave it. But I ain't going to run no chance of not looking pretty to Connie Coberley. He's going to see me waiting for him in the best clothes money can buy. A woman can lose a man just by not looking pretty."

"She can lose a man by giving—"

"Who's to tell him? You? You got two witnesses for that? Besides I never went to bed with your brother, and if you say I did I'll fix him so they'll lock him up in a lunatic asylum. He's dangerous, running around scaring women, climbing in windows— I could make quite a story, Liz Carpenter, if you really want one."

And I stood there with ice in my veins and my stomach turn-

ing over with the sickness of disgust. I was not frightened by her
threats. It was something else that had roused my revulsion and
I could not look at her when I spoke.

"You knew all along that Brett was—not well."

"I found out soon that he was half-witted. Is that what you're
too delicate to say, Miss Carpenter? I knew he was touched in
the head—"

"And yet you used him to get your clothes and—"

"Why not? How did it hurt him?"

"It will hurt him when he finds out that you—"

"Crazy people don't get hurt. They forget right away."

"He's not crazy."

"Sure he is. I wasn't surprised none. Connie didn't know that
Brett was touched but he had told me about your aunt and your
papa. Her wearing her wedding dress on holidays and your papa
sitting closed up in a room talking to his books. And as for you,
Liz, you're twisted inside and outside both. Think I don't know
that you hate me just because I'm good-looking?"

I said, "Do you think that's why I hate you?"

"Why else would you?" she asked. Her eyes widened in sudden
comprehension. "Oh, you admit you hate me."

"Yes, I admit it. I think you're the most terrible woman who
ever lived."

She roared at that. Her laughter filled the room, and I knew
as I listened that after she was gone it would fill my dreams. And
I stood there watching her as she screamed with amusement, and
for the first time it came to me that I would never be free of her.
Always when a woman laughed too loudly I would remember
Brandon. And when female beauty was the topic I would remember and if talk turned to evil I would not be without thoughts on

the subject. And that is what came to me as I watched her. "I will never be able to forget her," I said to myself. "Never. No matter how hard I try."

I must have been right or I would not be sitting here now remembering all the things I have told you about the woman, Brandon.

And I will tell you, though it has no place here, that that was almost the last time I ever entered the Coberley house. Not the very last time, you understand, but almost. I went home that day determined that I would never again see Brandon, and the thought had a familiar ring to it as though once long ago I had made that same promise to myself. I sat at the fireside in my room for hours and I thought how I had moved beneath the old unlucky star of my family when I had taken Brett to the Coberley house that autumn day. Had I stayed away much would now be different. He would never have known Brandon, and that in itself would have been a blessing. We had brought him here to recover, but I had led him to the woman and his destruction. And for him the worst still waited, crouched and ready to spring. He had yet to learn that she did not love him, that she would never go away with him on the money he had worked so hard to save. And I sat there and I thought bitterly that there was nothing that could help him now. In the beginning I had failed him. Connie Coberley had meant too much to me. I had protected the woman he loved at Brett's expense and at the cost of heartache to Powell and Aunt Laurel. If, in the beginning, I had exposed the woman for what she was— But I had not and I knew that even now I would not, for Connie still came first. And I was not blind to the stupidity and cruelty of such a futile love as mine.

There was nothing on God's earth that Powell and my aunt would not suffer if in some way it benefited me. From Connie I could expect naught but a casual pleasantry, and yet he was more dear, more important, and I did not like the thing my love had done to me and mine but I could not deny its existence and its strength.

A chill passed over me as I sat by my fireside and I glanced with annoyance about the room, searching for the open door that might be causing a draught upon me. And I thought then of Mockingbird standing in the snow, her thin face raised to the windows of the Coberley house and I thought of her sleazy blanket and I grew less concerned with the small draught that had circled about my dry and well-shod feet. I walked to the window and stared out at the frozen world and at the dark, icy waters beyond the stretch of wind-swept beach and as I stood there I thought of Elizabeth Carpenter and I will tell you that I thought of her without pride or pleasure.

It was impossible to consider the bitterness, the misery of that winter, without recognizing how much I had contributed to the despair of my family and how little I had done to alleviate the suffering of the people in the crumbling farmhouse. I could not, would not, change the thing I had done to Brett and to Powell and Aunt Laurel but I could do a small thing, surely. I could help those who struggled against the cold down on the Spurney land. Why had I not done it before? And it was an easy thing to say that Mrs. Shieldstone would not let me. But why had I accepted her edicts without argument? Why had I not persisted in what I knew to be right? And the answer was simple and it was the same in both cases. It was because I was a weakling without force or courage who would permit myself to be silenced by any voice that rose against me. And I knew that I must try again or live forever with the knowledge that my tears of pity were as the crocodile's. There was something I could do against the bitter winter. Something that needed doing, and I went to my wardrobe and pulled out a heavy cape for which I had no need.

I found my aunt and I said to her, "What can you spare for a family that is freezing? What of Powell's, what of Brett's may I give them?"

She looked up brightly from some sewing and she said, "A family freezing? Here, dear? How odd. What family is it?"

And I felt a wave of weariness sweep over me, for there was too much to tell, too much I had not told in the beginning. Like a child jealously nursing a secret from the grownups I had concealed the fact that there were humans trying to live on the Spurney farm, people enduring the rigors of that bitter winter without the bare necessities that made survival possible. And it was not of my doing that they were there, not my fault that they were unprepared for the terrible cold, but I had not made a true attempt to aid them.

I said, "Aunt Laurel, I will tell you about them tonight or perhaps tomorrow, but now just help me. Please find me two warm coats that men can use and something of your own that you do not need."

She gave me a long glance then rose from her chair. "I have an old mantle," she said, "that is poor style but—"

"If it is warm, it will do."

And from my aunt I got the things for which I had asked and much besides. She piled the sofa high and when Hendon and McDonald came to carry the mountain of clothes downstairs something fell loose upon the floor. I picked it up and saw that it was one of the pair of fur-trimmed gloves that last autumn I had not dared to filch for Mockingbird.

"I'll drive you, Miss Elizabeth," McDonald said, "then I can carry—"

"They'll carry the things themselves. Just load them for me please."

And I can tell you that as I drove toward the Spurney farm I knew it to be entirely within the realm of possibility that soon I might be driving home again with my offerings rejected. But this time at least I would know I had made an earnest effort.

I drove first to the boundary line and Mockingbird was not there. The old man stood motionless in the snow and when I spoke to him he could not answer at once for the chattering of his teeth.

I said to him, "I have a warm coat for you. Would you like to come here and take it? It's the brown one right on top there."

He said, "What do I want with a coat? I got a blanket."

"It's a very poor blanket and you are going to die without this coat I have to offer. Would you rather die than—"

"Mrs. Shieldstone, she said we weren't objects of charity."

"Does she stand in the snow?"

"Sure she does. She got a blanket, too."

"Are you going to take this coat?"

"I sure can't do it, Miss. I told you—"

"Very well."

I left him then and went directly to the house. Never before had I approached it without trepidation but I felt strong now, strong in the knowledge that whatever came it would only be after I had done my best. And the door opened before I had knocked and I was in the dark, uncomfortable room of the Spurney house. And it was cold in there for there was little fire and there was a place where ceiling and wall conjoined through which I could see a streak of sullen sky. The boy, Tippy, was huddled close to the low flames and Mrs. Shieldstone sat upon a barrel and worked with stiff fingers at the business of repairing a broken shoe. Aloft on the ladder top perched Mockingbird and her banjo, and when I greeted them she responded with a polite chord.

I addressed myself to Mrs. Shieldstone. "Madame," I said, "I have brought warm clothing for all of you. I am not, believe me, interested in playing the role of village philanthropist nor do I expect thanks. It is only that I cannot see the sense of having two cloaks while another girl freezes."

"Did this other girl ask you for anything?"

"She did not."

Mrs. Shieldstone did not reply. She worked with her stiff fingers upon the broken shoe and I said, "Is it that I am a Northerner? Is that why you reject—"

"I have rejected you and your offerings for one reason only. Charity is a curious thing, young lady. It strengthens those who give and weakens those who receive."

"Not so."

"How would you know?"

"How would *you?*"

"I am older. I have observed long and well. There is no individual who does not soften and in due course rot beneath the benevolent flow of warm, sympathetic tears."

And the low flame on the hearth went black and instantly seemed to cease radiating even the faintest heat. Tippy shivered and sighed and his cold breath was visible and I said, "Mrs. Shieldstone, you must consider the boy."

She looked up from her work and smiled coolly at me. "He has been considered," she said. "Long and well before you even knew of us."

The door opened and the old man came in bearing with him an agonizing blast of the cold outside.

"Why are you here?" she asked him.

"Brandon has gone out with the farm woman. I was there when she left. I will be there when she comes back." And he took his place in the corner and sat with his chin upon his chest.

I said, "Mrs. Shieldstone, I think you should confer with your friends here regarding the warm clothes I have brought."

She looked from the corner to the fireside, to the top of the ladder and back to me. "I have done so," she said. "There is full agreement."

"That the clothes are to be refused?"

"We would rather be strong than warm," she said.

"You will be dead, all of you," I told her. "You cannot live in this weather—"

"We will try and we will succeed. Would you excuse us now?"

"No. Not quite yet," I said. "I want you to know that I think you are unbelievably selfish. You may live but you have two young people and a man for whom you are in some way responsible. The boy has been through a dreadful ordeal, the girl is not robust and the man is old. By what right do you choose illness and death for these people?"

She looked at me with her stony eyes and she said, "Do you always speak without knowing anything of what you're saying? Our road is very long, young woman. God alone knows where it will take us. We must accustom ourselves to traveling light, with no encumbrances. We must learn to live with cold and hunger. We can never spoil ourselves with comforts that will make a later plight seem unendurable."

"You will never meet anything more fearsome than this winter."

"Your prophecy is interesting but open to conjecture. As I say, only God knows what we have before us."

And I had had enough of her and her oblique references to things she wished me not to understand. I did not care if she became enraged at me. She had already asked me to leave and I had not obeyed. It surprised me how far I had come from that morning when I had been shaken by her hard eyes and stern refusal to admit me. I was not so sensitive today as I had been when three months younger.

I said, "What are you about, Mrs. Shieldstone? What leads you to send these people out to freeze? What makes you live in a hovel that rats would scorn? Why, if this is not a procedure born of pure insanity, are not all of you home where you belong?"

And a sigh seemed to shake the decaying farmhouse. Then there was silence and the cold crept closer to us and I felt it in my bones. And when I looked around me all glances were turned on Mrs. Shieldstone and she sat staring ahead of her, the stony eyes fastened upon a vista beyond the wall, beyond the farm. And I shook inside my fur-lined cloak and the cold was an agony within me. I felt the suffering of the others and I could not bear the misery that the winter had brought and I turned toward the door.

"Wait," Mrs. Shieldstone said. And the banjo sharply underscored her order and I stood where I was and waited.

"You spoke of home," Mrs. Shieldstone said. "You suggest we should go there. A nice thought. What do you imagine our homes are like, Miss? Like yours? All warm and cozy and in one fine piece? We had such homes. We have them no more. One day we will rebuild but not yet. First we have other work. First we must attend to her."

"To her?"

"Do not echo me. You know of whom I speak."

"I know of whom but not of what. Are you going to tell me?"

Again her eyes went from corner, to fireplace, to ladder top, and I followed them and saw an almost imperceptible nod from each of the three and the woman said, "Last spring, if you remember, there was still war in the land—" And suddenly the cold reached her and she could not speak but sat shivering upon the barrel and she drew her shawl tightly about her and lowered her face into its folds.

"It was spring and the war was not done yet," the old man said. "Your General Sherman was a-coming and in our town—"

The banjo sounded a crashing chord and silenced him. Mockingbird took up the story.

> "We had nothing left but young boys and old men.
> Brave Captain Shieldstone came home to us then.
> He taught them to fight so our town they could save,
> But a woman named Brandon dug each man a grave."

And after that nobody spoke for quite a time and the last sad note of the banjo haunted the room. My mouth was dry and I could hear the pounding of my heart and I will tell you that the cold and the sorrow within that farmhouse were beyond words.

It was Mrs. Shieldstone who broke the silence. "The lyric

somewhat exaggerates the tragedy," she said, bitterly. Her eyes
went from Tippy to the old man and then came to rest on me.
"There were," she said, "two survivors."

And I stood there trembling in the cold and remembering the
North Carolina I had pictured one day as I stood with Brandy
at the bayside. The cabins and the fire-bright rooms and she had
spoken of the supper-smoke rising to the sky. And I saw the
gallant little band of old men and boys going out to fight for this
town that perhaps was on no map at all and I saw them dying
for the cabins and the supper-smoke. And it may have been that
they had known all along that they could not stop Sherman
but nevertheless they had gone out to face him and I hoped that
Sherman, even while slaughtering them, had taken note of their
brave stand.

"It was the town's life at stake," Mrs. Shieldstone said. "It
was the town's plan, the town's secret. We did not know until too
late that Brandon had a lover who was an officer in the Northern
army."

And my cold hands reached for support and I leaned against
the wall. Did they wait for him? Was this an ambush into which
he was to walk? And if this was so I would betray them as Brandon had done. I who destroyed a brother was not too soft of heart
to spare them if they plotted against Connie.

I said, "Do you plan vengeance against the officer? You must
remember that it was his duty, his sworn—"

Mrs. Shieldstone said, "We hold nothing against Conrad
Coberley. From him we could expect only what we received.
From her we were entitled to loyalty."

A sigh of thanksgiving escaped me. I would not have to fight
them and I was relieved for they were people of unswerving pur-

pose. I would not have liked them dedicated to Connie's destruction.

"It pleases you that we do not hold Coberley responsible." Mrs. Shieldstone smiled thinly and I became aware that all four of them were looking at me. "So that's it, is it?" she said. "We always have felt some curiosity as to why you protected her."

And the old man stared down at the broken boards in the floor. Tippy turned toward the cold ashes and Mockingbird studied her banjo. Only Mrs. Shieldstone continued to eye me. "Poor thing," she said. "Poor little Elizabeth. It hurts, doesn't it? Well, never mind, my dear, she'll hurt, too, before we're finished with her."

THE *Woman Brandon*

I DO NOT KNOW if you will understand the things the old man told me. In all candor I must say that for me it is impossible to grasp the plan of war, be it on a scale however large or small. Only victory or defeat is clear. Tactics, strategy, these matters are far beyond me. The old man spoke of the town and where it lay and how he and his fellow townsmen had turned out to save it. Silent and concealed they had waited in a hollow for the Federal soldiers to pass. The plan had been to permit them passage and to trap them then between the town and its defenders. Everything had depended upon secrecy and surprise and for hours they had waited quiet and motionless for the enemy to come. And as the old man spoke I realized that childishly I had been picturing Sherman himself and all his mighty army bearing down upon a handful of Carolinians. It had not been so. The odds had been but three to one against Captain Shieldstone's volunteers, and had the element of surprise not been lost to them they might have prevailed and saved their town.

"Only they wasn't surprised, the Yankees wasn't," the old man ended. "They knowed where we was and they just rid right down on us from all sides. They had the numbers and the guns, so what us volunteers needed was to take 'em unawares but they'd been warned."

And Tippy said, "I wasn't no volunteer. I was a regular soldier. I come back with Captain Shieldstone to help organize our town. I hadn't been wounded yet then and I guess I helped some. But what I want to say is this: I got no love for any part of the Yankee army. They was all a thieving, murdering band of bullies but 'cause I was a soldier I gotta say what civilian fighters always forget. Them fellers was after a bridge they wanted to take. They wasn't just going for to burn our houses."

"But they burned 'em, didn't they?" the old man demanded.

"Sure. They burned every house but one," Tippy said. "Every house but hers. And they killed every man who fought against them excepting you."

"And you," Mockingbird said. "They didn't kill you, Tippy."

The boy laughed shortly. "I only count the old man as coming through alive," he said. "But what I'm getting at is this: they had a bridge to take and they was in the soldier business. I hate 'em but I ain't mad at 'em, if you see what I mean. With her, it's different. We trusted her."

And they were silent again, thinking how they had trusted her and how wrong they had been to do so.

After a time Mrs. Shieldstone spoke. She said, "We women bathed and buried our dead." Her voice was flat and cold as she added, "I will say that Brandon offered to assist us."

I could believe that she would make the offer, for there was nothing on earth that could harrow the soul of Brandon. Neither pity nor remorse could touch her. I well knew that she could have looked upon the townsmen she had murdered without suffering grief or pangs of conscience.

"Her offer was refused," Mrs. Shieldstone said.

And she told how all in the devastated town had ceased to speak to Brandon, how they had avoided her and had left her alone with the flour and rice and coffee that she had received from the Yankee commissary.

"It is a wonder that no one killed her," I said.

"There was talk of such," Mrs. Shieldstone said, "but I won my point. I was not for it."

And Brandon found no one who would say a word to her or who would perform the smallest or the greatest service for her. Her child had come with only the help of a daft, wandering Negress, and the women of the town had gathered in Brandon's yard to listen exultantly to her agonized screams. Some prayed that her fine, white breasts would produce no milk and those prayers had been answered.

"Some prayed that she would die," Mrs. Shieldstone said. "But I prayed for her to live."

"Why?" I asked.

"Why?" The stony eyes looked away from me. "When death strikes it is the end of suffering. I did not want Brandon to die. We had a meeting. It took place in the church, for with a superstitious instinct natural to savages, the Yankees had left the roof on God's house if not on mine. I told the people all that I had learned, all that I knew now of Brandon. She and Coberley had been lovers since he had first come with your General Foster in December, '62. At that time her husband was fighting in Virginia though soon he was to be made a prisoner of war. And of those who knew Gilly, this woman's husband, there was none who did not love and admire him, so my news was sorry hearing to the people."

"They would have killed her then," Mockingbird said, "only Mrs. Shieldstone talked so good they listened to her."

"It would have been stupid to kill her," the woman said. Her eyes grew thoughtful as she went back in memory to the meeting in the church. "I had a better plan. I did not know at the time that I would be chosen to administer it but I was so chosen, and these three with me, to avenge the town and our well-loved dead."

I shook my head. "It will not work," I said.

"You have guessed what my plan is?"

"I believe so."

She said, "It is of course simplicity itself but we have already proved that it will work, for soon after her child was born she tried to slip away from us. She took nothing, hoping to hide the fact that she was leaving. She did not pack but only dressed and took her infant as though it was but a day's outing she intended." Mrs. Shieldstone looked at me with her eyebrows raised quizzically. "I think you know how soon we had followed her here to New Jersey."

"Yes," I said, "and I will tell you that it is my guess that you did not vex her into leaving but that probably a shortage of flour or rice or a yearning to live in a better house was the reason she fled."

"No, she could not bear our constant presence reminding her of her crimes against us. And all her life we will pursue her and she must live and look at us forever. We will follow no matter where she goes. Always we will be where she is and never for a moment will she be allowed to forget what she did to us. And for her there will never be any peace, any tranquillity, for we will haunt her till all four of us are dead and perhaps even after that."

And the hard eyes were filled with hatred and determination and I was astonished that this woman, who had been clever enough to learn all that she needed to know for her pursuit of Brandon, had not the wisdom to understand Brandon as I understood her.

I said, "You could not be on a more futile errand if you sought a mountain made of cheese. You could not waste your time and ruin your life more completely. Your project is built upon the premise that Brandy has feeling, imagination, nerves. She has none of these things. Her heart is solid rock. She laughs at you and you will never make the slightest impression upon her though you die in the attempt."

Mrs. Shieldstone said, "She is only flesh and blood. We will wear her down and she will come to quail at sight of us and we will—"

"She is too hard. You don't understand her. You must take my word that I know her better than you do. Even in so short a time I have come to understand her well. I beg of you go home, forget her, build new lives for yourselves. Never will she feel anything so deeply that you will have your satisfaction and revenge."

And I looked from one to the other and I saw that they recognized my sincerity even as they rejected my argument.

"There is no one totally without feeling," Mrs. Shieldstone said.

"Now I am sure you do not know Brandon." I turned to them imploringly. "Think, all of you. Did you ever know her? Did you ever have dealings with her before the betrayal? What do you really know of what she is like? What does an acquaintanceship of years signify if there has never been close contact?"

I had made a point for they turned their eyes away, not one of them able to say that they had known the woman well. And this I had guessed to be a fact, for none was of an age to be a likely companion to Brandon, being both too young and too old. And there were other factors to be considered.

I said to Mrs. Shieldstone, "You once boasted that you only knew Brandon by sight. How could it be otherwise? What would you want with the company of so ignorant a person? These others here— They have known her better than you perhaps but none are of a turn of mind that would set them to analyzing the nature of the woman. I say that you are like hunters seeking a quarry without knowing its size, its habitat or whether it flies, swims or crawls."

The old man chuckled. "I'd sure hate that day's work," he said.

"Well, that's the work you've chosen," I said, "so perhaps you'd like advice from one familiar with the beast you are stalking. I assure you I am qualified to judge her. She is as hard and cold as ice. You will never inflict upon her even the smallest amount of distress or anguish. Give up the chase. Go home. Leave her alone or the result will be disastrous to you."

Mrs. Shieldstone said quietly, "Your father is Powell W. Carpenter, the famous lawyer, is he not?"

I will confess I was taken aback. The woman was a never-ending source of surprise to me. "How did you know that?" I asked. "And what has it to do with that which passes here between us?"

"Only this," she said. "You are not aspiring to follow in his footsteps, are you? You could not be advocate for the woman, Brandon, could you? If so I must warn you that your eloquence is wasted. At this bar your client has already been tried and convicted."

"I am pleading for you," I said. "You four who would be better employed in giving your energy and cleverness to the ruined town your men died to defend."

"That will come later," Mrs. Shieldstone said, "after we have settled with their murderess. She will never escape us and she will grow increasingly aware of us and it will take all the courage she has to face each new day. Finally she will find herself reaching deeper and deeper for that courage and it will not be there. And we will see her suffer. That's all we want—we want to see her suffer."

I said, "You are judging her reactions by what your own would be had you committed a foul crime. Can't you see that you are dealing with a woman who does not think or feel? A woman who cannot experience suffering?"

"None such exists," Mrs. Shieldstone said. "All women can suffer but to you I will say this: It is possible that somewhere I have erred and if my plan is not a good one I will find a better, but we are here to see the matter through even though it consumes all the years that have been allotted us."

I said, "You're mad. Give up. Go home. She will beat you, for she has no vulnerable point."

And they shook their heads for they believed that they could shatter stone, that they could visit pain upon that which had no feeling.

I had no more words and a feeling of despondency came upon me and the cold, which had been momentarily dispelled by the heat of argument, came back to settle in my bones. And it was all very dreary, for these people had much to offer their ravaged homeland. I knew that if the dead could speak they would say that North Carolina's needs were great but that revenge was not among the things she needed. I turned from them and spoke my good-bys and even in my own ears my voice sounded so small and sad that I did not wonder at Mrs. Shieldstone's words.

She said, "I believe you suffer for us, young woman."

"I do indeed."

And for a moment she said nothing. Then, "You must not think us harsh or ungrateful but we have our work to do and we must go about it in the way that seems best to us. I will make a bargain with you."

"What sort of bargain?"

"In future do not seek to weaken our firm resolve or to fill our heads with doubt of the excellence of our chosen plan. Do not dangle before our eyes the shining notion that going home would be both sensible and commendable. In short, Elizabeth Carpenter, leave us alone, for our fervency is great indeed and has naught to fear save simple logic."

And she walked toward the black, cold fireplace and stood looking down at it, her back to me. And it was only when her stony eyes were no longer visible that I could think of her as a woman who had lost her son. I remembered how she and Gilly had wept together in the candlelight and I knew now that she had been recounting to him the slaughter of Captain Shieldstone and his townsmen. In the end even Gilly had approved her plan and I marveled at the presumption of such as I telling her that she was mad to seek revenge. How glibly I had criticized and advised. But then no doubt it was always those who knew the least that were most willing to speak authoritatively. I wanted to say that I regretted my intrusion into affairs that did not concern me and I wished for words that spoken in a Yankee accent would sound neither mawkish nor offensive in conveying my sympathy for her loss of Captain Shieldstone, her son. But Mrs. Shieldstone was not as other women and I was not as other girls so no word of regret was offered her.

Instead I said, "Madame, you spoke of a bargain."

She did not turn but remained staring at the black, dead leavings of the fire. "Yes," she said. "In return for your abandoning us to our zealous onslaught upon the insensitive Brandon we will

promise to wear the warm clothing that you have brought." Then
to the old man, "Go get it."

She turned then and sought my eyes, and in all honesty I must
state that no sudden spark of kinship leaped into life. There was
no moment of startling revelation in which we realized that we
liked each other very much indeed. But there in the Spurney
farmhouse, where the cold was almost beyond endurance, I had
earned an acceptance of a kind and it was a great experience
for me.

At this point I would like to say that those who have so much
charm and grace of manner that they invariably slip into all
inner circles without even bothering to make the effort are not
expected to understand the importance of the moment.

I have little of interest to say of February. It was cold but I went
rarely into the blustering winter world. I stayed at my fire and
read one book after another and Aunt Laurel worried about my
health.

"You used to visit," she said. "Did you have a disagreement
with Connie's wife?"

"Of course not, dear. Why should I have a disagreement with
her?"

"I don't know, but you seemed so busy, you had so much to do
and now— What about that poor family? The ones to whom we
gave the clothing. They seemed so sweet when you told me of
them. Why don't you visit them? I would send a pie or perhaps
a sack of apples or—"

"They're all right, Aunt Laurel. They don't need anything
now and they don't expect me to call on them."

"No, I suppose not." She frowned thoughtfully. "It just seems you've changed your ways so completely— The farm people, Liz? What about them? You used to love visiting the different—"

"I'm fine, Aunt Laurel. Really I am. I just don't want to go out. It's too comfortable here. Please don't concern yourself about me."

I could not say to her that it was impossible for me to face Mrs. Lankton. I could not say that I had almost promised the people on the Spurney farm to bother them no more. I could not say that my flesh would crawl at sight of Brandon who had betrayed her townsmen. And I could not say that in other years it had been my game of "You Amuse Me" that had made the countryside exciting for me. And I could play that game no more, for somewhere during the winter it had lost its appeal and I could not tell just when or why.

And so I sat before the fire that February and read my books and chatted with Powell when he was idle. And in the evenings we thought of Brett as we had done in January.

"I think someone should go to the Lanktons' and make sure he's all right," Aunt Laurel said. She said it frequently. I think she said it every evening.

"Laurel, listen to me. How can I drive over there and make inquiries as though Brett were an infant or an idiot? I cannot give him the feeling that I believe him to be either of these things."

"No, of course not. I suppose if I went it would be as bad."

"Certainly it would. You never called on Mrs. Lankton socially. You could be going for no reason other than to engage in an investigation."

And I could see them trying not to look at me, trying not to say outright that I was the one whose going would seem perfectly natural. I was the one who could bring them news of Brett.

"Why doesn't he come home?" my aunt would ask, fretfully. "Surely he must get some time to himself. Where would he spend it if not with us?"

"I don't know, Laurel. As I grow older things become more difficult to understand." And I would look at him and see the haunting anxiety upon his face, and the knowledge of my guilt was a living pain within me.

"There should be some contact with Brett."

"There is, Laurel." This very dryly indeed from Powell. "I leave fifteen dollars a week in an envelope at the post office and I am assured that he does not fail to pick it up."

"Would the Lanktons let us know if something happened to Brett?"

"Of course, Laurel."

But we heard no word from him and where Brett spent his free hours was no mystery to me. And in casting my eyes back across this record I see that I have mentioned that there were times when I did go out of the house that February and this is true. I believe I went only when Aunt Laurel's questions or her puzzled eyes drove me forth. I would go without desire or destination but always my horse took me up the river road toward the bay, for he was an inquisitive beast and he had to know if the Carolinians still kept their vengeful watch. And he had lost his fear of the dismal Spurney acres and again and again he led me through them, avoiding the house but scanning the landscape for signs of the invaders. They had not gone. They were still there and close to the boundary my horse always caught sight of one or the other standing vigil. And I would wave to whoever it was we glimpsed as we passed but I did not pause, for my questions and arguments were at an end. They had answered my questions and had rejected my arguments.

At home Aunt Laurel sewed and Powell closed himself in the den and worked upon his documents and every day was as the one that had preceded it. And sometimes as I stood listening to the never-ending boom of the ocean I thought that Powell and my aunt were very much like people in a photograph, eternally in one position, never changing. And I knew that it could not last. There are always changes. Something would happen and Aunt Laurel would stop sewing and Powell would look up from his documents and perhaps after that things would never be the same again.

And I remember well the day that the letter arrived. Had nothing come of it I would still remember, for, barring the letters she had received from Brett while he had been at war, I do not think Aunt Laurel ever had another throughout my life with her. Powell brought it to her from the post office. She was as amazed as I when it was handed to her. She read it in our presence but without comment. I had certainly expected her to say at once who had written and why. She said nothing that gave us the slightest hint as to the sender or the contents of the letter and I had a suspicion that a question would gain no satisfactory reply. Any letter to Aunt Laurel would have awakened my curiosity but I must tell you that her behavior was most provocative. She was disturbed by the letter. That much was clear. Even Powell noticed and, though he politely forbore to utter a single query, his eyes searched Aunt Laurel's face, eager for a clue.

I envied him, for he was not left in suspense. When he went to the den Aunt Laurel followed and I was amused at the elabo-

rate show she made of just happening to drift in the same direc-
tion. In the corridor she managed a swift whisper to him and the
next minute they were closed in the den and a person could
scarcely understand a word they spoke.

I heard my name and I heard the town of Seaverne mentioned
and I was thoroughly perplexed. Powell's voice was low and no
word of his reached me at all but his inflections were reasonably
clear. He sounded annoyed and impatient. Aunt Laurel was
puzzled by something and more than a little upset. She mentioned
my name again but I could not establish any connection between
myself and the town of Seaverne nor could I guess in what
manner I had appeared in the letter.

Of course I made an attempt to find the answers but I was unsuccessful. Aunt Laurel's room was poor hunting ground indeed,
for she was never out of the house, thus rendering a thorough
search too dangerous to contemplate. If I had known just which
drawer, box or chest to concentrate upon there might have been
a possibility of finding the letter but as it was I had little chance
of achieving my purpose.

My next hope was Powell and I had no compunctions about
broaching the matter to him.

"That letter Aunt Laurel received. It seemed to distress her.
May I know why?"

Powell shook his head. "No, dear. She asked me not to say."

I studied him carefully for a sign that he, too, was distressed
but there was only a mild case of ill humor apparent.

"We live as such a close and loving unit, Powell, that I cannot
help but worry that—"

"Don't worry," he said. "It's a lot of damn female nonsense."

I grinned at him. "Sounds like something I should know

about," I said. "Damn female nonsense is certainly in my province."

"Liz, don't use vulgar words. I shouldn't use them myself but—"

"But you're on edge. What about, Powell? Tell me."

"No, dear. Your aunt and—and this other lady are madly in love with secrecy. I've joined their organization. I promised. I was even initiated. The initiation consists of reading the letter and trying to make sense of it while someone is babbling in your ear. What happens to women every once in awhile that makes them write those letters that are guaranteed to convey no information?"

"If I knew what was in the letter perhaps I could tell you."

"No, dear."

"Will I ever know?"

"Oh, yes. You'll know."

"When?"

"That part is a very deep secret because I've forgotten. She did mention a date but I do not remember what she said."

I accepted defeat. Now all I could do was trust that in one of my quick charges upon Aunt Laurel's room I would come across the letter.

And I often think now of the morning that I awakened knowing full well that the day would be different from others. This has happened often to me and I lay it less to prescience than to the obvious fact that the very air is freighted with expectancy and that one would be insensitive indeed to miss the eager hush that lies upon the day. True, most times the breathless waiting in which such a morning holds itself signifies no more than the arrival of another Election Day or perhaps it is Palm Sunday.

Holidays have a way of making themselves known even to those who lack a calendar. Sometimes, though, it is no holiday that produces this curious certainty that here is a new day dissimilar from all others. Sometimes it is a day neither blessed nor celebrated but still a day that is never completely forgotten. This day —it was a Friday I recall—was of that caliber, and so I was not surprised to find the servants conducting themselves in a manner that betrayed suppressed excitement. And I followed my breakfast dishes to the kitchen to discover, if I could, what this thing was that had marked the day with special color and flavor.

In the kitchen I found our staff almost too busy to take note of me. I gazed in silent wonderment at the preparations I saw here, at the bustling briskness and deep preoccupation with grating, shelling, stirring and chopping. The cook was short-tempered with her helper but it seemed to me that her frown was only a mask to conceal a rather lively pleasure, that her sharp words were meant to cover the joy she was taking in her work.

"What are you planning for dinner?" I asked.

She threw her hands in the air. "Really, Miss Elizabeth, what a question! As though Miss Carpenter and I haven't been over the dinner plan a dozen times."

"Have you? A full dozen times, you say. And what are we having?"

"Everything, Miss Elizabeth. Everything you can name. It isn't that we have guests so often that—"

"Oh, the guests," I said, loftily. "I had forgotten."

She stared at me. "Never since I've been in this family's employ have there been guests. So how could you forget?"

"Well, I did. As a matter of fact I've even forgotten their names."

She shook her head and added a spoonful of sugar to the golden cake mix in its bright blue bowl and I wondered as I always wonder about cooks. What told her that another spoonful of sugar was needed?

"I can't help you as to names. Miss Carpenter didn't mention names and I'm not interested in who's coming. I would just like to know how many."

"Don't we know how many?"

She shrugged. "Maybe one. Maybe two. Maybe three. I don't know. It doesn't make any difference really."

"Of course not," I said and left the kitchen. Thoughtfully I walked upstairs and after the conversation with the cook it was not startling to find activity in the linen room. Two of the guest rooms were being prepared.

Aunt Laurel's voice came to me remarking on the fact that she wasn't certain two rooms would be in use as her information was very incomplete.

"Still you'll have to make up two rooms just in case. Be sure now that the blue blankets aren't put on the bed in the pink room. And see that there's— Oh, good morning, Liz."

I stared at my aunt. She was wearing bonnet, cloak and gloves and was evidently in some haste. A glance out the window revealed that McDonald was waiting for her with the family carriage.

"My cleverness leads me to conclude that you are going out, Aunt Laurel."

"I won't be long," she said and she rushed away from me and I knew now how the town of Seaverne had come to figure in the letter. She was on her way to the railroad station to meet our guests. I stood at the window watching McDonald tuck the

fur robe cozily about my aunt and I did not leave that vantage
point till the carriage was out of sight. Then I made a run for
my aunt's room but I was once again repulsed by the heavy traffic
of servants up and down the corridor. The guest rooms were being furbished for the comfort of the most critical, and you may
not believe it but it is the truth that I still had no inkling of what
was afoot.

It was a morning hour and therefore sacred to Powell's work
but I knocked upon the den door and entered. I said to him,
"Now that they are practically here I suppose we can discuss the
matter."

He smiled at me. "I suppose we cannot," he said. "I promised
your aunt that—"

"But it is such nonsense," I protested. "They will be here within
two hours and if I am not told what to—"

"It seems there is nothing you need be told, my dear, except
that having people in the house is an ordeal for me. I do not wish
to sound unkind but I will give you no information, and your
prying and teasing is making me very nervous."

So I withdrew, closing the door quietly behind me. And I felt
shame that in following the dictates of my insatiable curiosity I
had not realized how disconcerting all this must be for Powell.
It was more than fifteen years since he had entertained guests in
his home and the prospect of playing host, of manufacturing
small talk for strangers must be almost terrifying to him.

I went back to the second floor and found the guest rooms in
order, the servants gone. At last it was safe to make my search.
I darted into Aunt Laurel's room and began. She had so many
pieces of furniture, each with so many drawers. The desk yielded
nothing save a heart-breaking glimpse of a package of old letters

tied with a ribbon from a long-dead bouquet. I apologized for disturbing them and moved on to the dresser. It was a tedious business for each drawer had to be put back in order after my frantic search, and I will spare you the tiresome details and tell you that I at last laid hands upon the letter. It was between the forty-second and forty-third pages of a novel that Aunt Laurel had been reading on for more than a year. As is so natural and so annoying I had not thought to look in the book until after I had exhausted myself, my patience and a great deal of time. But at last I found the letter.

My dear Laurel:

Upon our return from Europe last Thursday a singular communication was awaiting us here. It came from the farmer, Abner J. Fort, who I believe is known to your household as well as to ours. As a result of his letter I must ask your kind consideration. Would it be possible for you to meet us at Seaverne Friday morning? Also could you possibly put us up for the night? I do not like to impose upon you in this manner but, as you know, only during the summer season could we hope to find either a carriage for hire or a hotel in which to stay.

You may wonder how I know you are at the shore this winter. Well, Mr. Fort mentioned that you were, and now, my dear Laurel, I must ask another favor. This one is by far the most difficult. I must request that you do not tell your niece that we are coming. If this seems strange I do not wonder. I will explain when I see you but please remember that I am trusting you to keep our plans from Elizabeth. Thank you for this and for all the inconvenience that we are bound to cause you and your brother.

With fondest regards, I remain,

Cordially,
EVELYN COBERLEY

It is perhaps unnecessary to say that my pulse raced when I read that letter. Mrs. Coberley was coming. Who was coming

with her? Did she use the royal "we"? Or was Mr. Coberley
coming, too? Or Connie? I read the letter again trying to pierce
the ambiguity of its construction. As a matter of fact I read it
three times before I was satisfied that Connie did not even know
of Mr. Fort's letter. His mother had kept it from him and was
coming to face Brandon by herself. Of course Mr. Fort had told
her that young Mrs. Coberley's behavior was not to his liking
and Connie's mother was on her way to take care of the woman
who dared represent herself as Connie's wife. Well, there was
no possible means by which I could warn Connie of his mother's
intentions. Doubtless he was in North Carolina seeking his beloved there and I could see why he had not chosen to come first
to the house on the bay. If she had remained where he had left
her then all talk and speculation would be spared his parents in
the summer community where they had enjoyed so fine a reputation. If he came here searching, questioning, then all chance of
keeping the matter secret was lost. So he had chosen the long
way around, hoping to protect his parents and that was handsome of him, I thought. And it was handsome, too, that he had
bargained on placing their name in jeopardy only if his beloved
found life among her own people unbearable. I wished desperately however that he had told his mother how matters stood
with him and Brandon. Today Mrs. Coberley would know, must
know, and the sorry affair would have to be presented to her in
the most favorable light possible. Connie would have known how
this could best be done. I did not know but it was up to me to
try, to do what I could for Connie. And I wondered if it would
disturb him to know that that which to him was the most important matter in the world was in my keeping today.

I glanced at the clock, picked up my warm cloak and ran for

the stable. Aunt Laurel fared forth so infrequently that I had grown accustomed to McDonald being there to serve me. Now I was forced to ask Hendon's help in readying my horse and carriage. He was ruefully put out at my request, grumbling as he granted it, swearing that he would smell of horses as he served our guests, muttering that there was no need for me to tear about at just this instant. And I cannot tell you how maddeningly slow he was and how unnerving his deliberate performance.

But at length I was on my way, driving once more out the river road to the house on the bay. And I told my horse that he must hurry, for Mrs. Coberley, our antagonist, was being drawn by two fine horses and would be here shortly, and he looked around at me as though to say, "I thought we were finished with the house on the bay." And I said to him, "Almost, fellow. Almost."

And today Mrs. Shieldstone stood at the boundary line and she wore Aunt Laurel's old mantle, and even as I tore past her I gave it a second look for I had not remembered it to be so impressive a garment.

I waved and smiled at the woman but did not pause for conversation. She said, "Calm yourself, Elizabeth. It cannot be so important as your headlong haste suggests."

I did not answer. I ran up on the verandah and pushed open the door that had never been locked since Brandon had come to live in the house.

She was in the kitchen frying something strong-smelling and greasy upon the stove. She smiled at me sardonically.

"Oh, you came back? What have I done now that you don't care for, Miss Carpenter?"

I said, "The time is too short for such a list. I have come to tell you that the Coberleys are home from Europe."

"Why, they ain't no such thing," she said. "If they was, Connie would have been here in a flash."

"That's what I thought at first but it isn't so. He would go at once to North Carolina. Naturally he would expect you to be there. This house was only considered a haven in case you were unable to stay in your own place down there."

"Oh, sure enough. That's where he is then. Well, he'll be here," she said, complacently.

"Yes, but not today. Today his mother is coming."

"What!" She turned from the stove and stared at me, her eyes wide with astonishment and dismay. "His mother! Good God, what am I gonna say to her? If he ain't told her about me yet it's going to be real hard to—"

"I know. Listen to me. There's very little time. She'll be here directly. You get dressed in your nicest—and I mean your nicest not your most seductive—dress. Get the baby shining clean."

"She's clean."

"Fix your hair so it's neat. Look as ladylike as you possibly can, my friend, and don't laugh. Not even once. Do you hear me?"

"And what do I do?"

"Tell her straight out that you love Connie and Connie loves you and that only his reluctance to hurt her has delayed his telling her the whole story."

She looked at me doubtfully. "Will she listen?"

"You have to try. There's no other way. Speak quietly to her in the best English you know. Be polite. Be respectful. She's Connie's mother, remember, and she's a well-born lady and your position is such that you dare not be bold with her."

"I don't know as I—"

"You don't know anything, so the best thing you can do is

take my advice. Go on now. Get that mess off the stove and hurry up about it."

I ran to the parlor and surveyed it swiftly. It had not been cleaned since the day that Mrs. Shieldstone and Mockingbird had taken pity upon its sad condition. There was not time to prepare it for Mrs. Coberley's arrival. All I could do was to carry some unwashed dishes to the kitchen, brush up the hearth and skim a dust rag across the most eye-catching surfaces. There was no fire and I built one, though I felt foolish doing so, for I had been forced to swing one of the long windows slightly ajar. The frying that I had interrupted had wafted its pungency into the parlor, and the air was heavy with food odors, candle grease and stagnancy.

And when I had done these few small things it occurred to me that perhaps this urgency had been unwarranted. Perhaps Mrs. Coberley would rest at our house for hours before coming here. Still it was necessary to be ready, for one could not be certain. And I thought it most unlikely that Mrs. Coberley would listen with sympathy to Brandy's story or that even the sight of the baby would move her, but there was no choice. If Connie had not yet told her of his love for Brandy then it was upon Brandy to tell her. And it was upon me to see that Brandy made the best impression while pleading her case.

I looked at her critically when she came down the stairs. And I must tell you that I could not cavil at what I saw, for she wore a charming dress upon which small lavender flowers bloomed. It was girlish and appealing in design and the little flowers repeated the color of Brandy's eyes and I thought her so lovely that I stood gazing as at a work of art. And she had parted her black, shining hair in the center and had drawn it back simply into a chignon low on her neck and I thought that the sight of her would melt the heart of anyone alive with the possible exception of Evelyn Coberley.

"Do I look all right?" she asked.

I nodded. "Remember, keep your voice low. And don't laugh. That's important."

"Can I laugh now?"

"Why should you want to?"

"Because you strike me funny," she said and her laughter rolled out freely and loudly. "You hate me like poison and yet you're buzzing around here like crazy, scared that I won't please Mrs. Coberley. You know what I think?"

I held my breath. What did she think?

"I think you're just plain anxious to have Connie get me like he wants for good and all."

"And why do I want Connie to get you?" I asked, though I dreaded her answer. Did she know that I loved him so deeply that I would help him to gain anything on earth that he desired?

"So you'll be rid of me forever. That's why."

"You're right," I said. "You've guessed my secret. Now let's take a look at the baby. Is she still in the servants' sitting room?"

"Yes." Brandy followed me and I inspected the child. It was doing splendidly, I thought. Chubby, pink-cheeked, clean.

"Pick it up," I said.

"What? With this dress on? Suppose she wets me? Suppose—"

"Do as I say. I want to see if she's clean all over. Besides, if you have any sense you will let Mrs. Coberley see you with the child in your arms. She's only a woman. The sight of you holding her grandchild could be very effective."

"Especially if I'm soaked."

"Very well. Do as you wish but I urge you to consider well the emotional hold that God has given you upon Connie's mother. Connie's child. There is no greater case that you can present."

"Oh, well, maybe I'll kind of pick the baby up after I've talked awhile to her." She fell silent then, considering that talk she must to Connie's mother. "If he'd only told her about us so I wouldn't have to."

"Yes, it is unfortunate, but he no doubt had his reasons. Now you must steel yourself to face her with the entire story. You must convince her that your love has dignity and depth and that there is nothing shameful about it. And no matter what she says to you, you must not become angered. Do not lose your head and flail out at her. Do you understand?"

"I understand a lot of things," she said. "You're getting me ready to take anything she's got to throw at me. Well, I just hope she don't ride me none because I got a temper."

"Forget your temper. You must try to make Mrs. Coberley willing to forgive—"

"Why?" she asked. "Hell, you got me so worked up that I'm in a sweat over that woman coming here. It just now enters my head that I don't care whether she likes me or not. I got Connie. What do I have to please her for?"

"Oh, you fool. Whose house are you in? Don't you want to stay here till Connie finds you? Won't life be easier for him if his mother can forgive you and learn to tolerate you?"

"Yeh, but—"

"But nothing. Remember the things I've told you. Try to be intelligent. I'll leave you now."

"Stay a minute. What was that about dignity again? Should I tell her about Gilly? Or ain't he dignified enough to mention?

You tell me, Liz Carpenter, 'cause I never had to go through anything like this before."

"Tell her your love for Connie is so genuine, so true that of itself it makes nothing of other promises, of other obligations. Tell her there is nothing you would not do for Connie and that, though he search the world, he will never again find a love as selfless and deep as yours."

And she stood there in the servants' sitting room listening intently to me, her lips moving as she tried to make my words her own, testing them, striving to capture them so they would be there when needed.

I said good-by to her and walked through the kitchen to the main hall. I was approaching the door when it opened with a fierce bang and there I was confronting Mrs. Coberley.

And she said to me in a biting tone, "Oh, Elizabeth, you are here. I asked your aunt where you were and she said she had no idea."

"As indeed she had not, Mrs. Coberley," I responded, coldly. And I looked steadily into the eyes of this well-corseted fat woman and I said, "I trust your journey was a pleasant one."

If there is any joy in finding yourself an adult it comes when you see a bullying, middle-aged female suddenly realize that she must treat you in a mannerly fashion.

"Why—er—yes! It was not unpleasant. Thank you. It is nice to see you, my dear Elizabeth. How well you are looking."

"Thank you, Mrs. Coberley. May I return the compliment?"

And I wondered that Brandon had not come. She could not have failed to hear the crash of the large front door as it had been thrown open against the wall. For what was she waiting? There was no way of avoiding the encounter with Mrs. Coberley.

It occurred to me that perhaps she lingered, debating the advisability of making her entrance carrying the child in her arms.

I said to Mrs. Coberley, "Don't you want to close the door and move into your parlor?"

She did not close the door and it is no wonder that she did not close it and I, who had been poised and articulate, went into a rapid decline of tongue-tied idiocy, for Connie came. Connie with the sweet blue-gray eyes and the enchantment I had never been able to resist. Connie whom I loved beyond all others.

He said to me, "Elizabeth, my adored one, why didn't you meet us? I was pining for you." And he put his arm around me and smiled down at me. I suppose I smiled back at him. One never remembers exactly how one reacted to exquisite pain.

The front door, which had now been closed, opened once more but this time gently, quietly and we were joined by a slender young girl in a black velvet bonnet with a strip of ermine elegantly framing its edge and setting off the patrician features of her white face.

"You should have stayed in the carriage as I asked," Connie said with no severity at all in his tone.

"I couldn't," she said.

And at that moment Brandon came from the back of the house and I knew she had heard Connie's voice and had found no reason now to delay her meeting with his mother. And no one but I seemed to see Brandon as she came down that long hall toward us. Mrs. Coberley moved into the parlor and we followed her and Connie still had his arm about me and he said, "Veronica, this is Elizabeth, my own true love. She's always been my girl and you will have to share my heart with her. Elizabeth, this is Veronica, my wife."

And we were in the parlor now and on the threshold between the portieres stood Brandon, her wonderful eyes clouded with puzzlement as she looked from Connie to the girl in the black velvet bonnet.

Mrs. Coberley said, "Yes, this is Veronica, *my son's wife.*" And she fixed her glance upon Brandon and she asked, "Who are *you?*"

Connie looked then upon the face of the woman, Brandon, and he said, not with vindictiveness as is a woman's way but with stern, masculine dignity, "Yes, young woman, who are you?"

Brandon said, "Connie! Connie! Before God you must be fooling. You know who I am."

He shook his head. "Never before have I seen you," he said.

And I looked at Brandon and I saw her full, scarlet lips go pale and I saw Connie with his stern glance fixed upon a point directly above her head as though he dared not meet her eyes.

"Suppose you explain this masquerade," he said in a calm and reasonable tone. "I do not wish to be brutal to you but you have caused me great embarrassment. To begin with—who are you? And where did you get my name?"

And now her face was chalk-white and she trembled as though she stood in a great, cold wind and she said, "You know who I am, Connie Coberley, and you know why I took your name."

He said, "Have you known a man who passed himself off as Conrad Coberley? A man who perhaps resembled me somewhat? Look at me well."

She looked at him well and their eyes met and I saw his falter before her steady gaze. And Veronica, too, looked well at her husband and it seemed to me that she did not miss what passed between him and the woman Brandon. She must have seen the faltering of Connie's gaze, for her own eyes narrowed and I thought that this Veronica might not be what the little flowerlike face and the delicate fluttering gestures would lead one to believe. She seemed a woman who wanted the truth and had bravely sought it and would spend all the rest of her life learning how to live with it.

And Connie went to her and spoke softly. "Darling, you should have remained in Philadelphia or at least rested at Miss Carpenter's house. This is a sordid business."

"Of course it is," Connie's mother said. "The woman wants money. It's a trick adventuresses have used on fine families for years." She turned to Brandon. "If you will admit that you never knew my son, if you will—"

"Never knew him!" Brandon stared at Mrs. Coberley. "How can I admit a thing like that? I knew him well. You just wait a minute. I'll show you how well I knew him." She flew from the room and came back carrying the baby in her arms. "Does this look like I never knew him?" she demanded. "This here child belongs to him—to him and me."

Veronica stood stiffly, her eyes averted, her small hands tightly clasped together. And I saw that learning to live with the truth is no task for the cowardly. It was asking all that Veronica had in the way of courage.

And Connie gazed at the baby in a manner that was not unkind and he said to Brandon, "Doubtless you are married to someone, my poor young woman. Are you and I both victims of his avarice? Did he plan this attack upon my reputation?"

Brandon said, "I'm getting mighty sick of all this fine Yankee quality talk. The child is yours and you know it is."

Connie smiled sadly. "I'm trying to be patient with you. Don't test my self-control, I beg of you. Do not continue your brazen contention that you have known me in the past."

Brandy looked him full in the face and she said to him, "God Almighty, I think you ain't fooling. I think you're really set on claiming that me and this here child don't belong to you. I'd of never believed it. Never in the whole wide world. Connie, you loved me once."

And Connie, so tall, so handsome, so much the vivid representation of all that is fine in young manhood, ran his hand wearily through his shining black hair and he smiled boyishly at me and said, "What a beast I am, Elizabeth, not to have had your coachman take you home. This was no scene for a young girl to have witnessed. My apologies, my dear. Do I have your forgiveness?" And he came to me and he took my hand and he said, "I forgot your presence in the midst of this dreadful business but it is a comfort to have you here, for I know that if there is one on earth who will judge me fairly it is my own girl, Elizabeth."

He dropped my hand then and turned swiftly to his wife and mother, presenting to each the radiant, boyish smile and he said to them, "I am afraid that nothing has been proved. I can only hope that I have your full confidence."

His mother went to him then and told him that she had never known a moment's doubt, and after a time Veronica walked into Connie's arms and she smiled up at him though the smile was a trifle sad. And I thought that in the future she would learn much and would bring off very bright and flashing smiles and the very gayest of words. This after all was only her first attempt at living with the truth.

And Brandy could not take her eyes from the sight of Connie

holding tightly in his arms the girl whom he had married, but
when Veronica raised her lips for Connie's kiss Brandy looked
away. And I saw the amethyst eyes filled with pain and I saw
that which I had never expected to see—the tears of the woman
Brandon. She stood with the baby in her arms, the tears wet
upon her lovely face and she looked so helpless, so pitiful that it
was only with effort that I could remember how great her
wickedness had been. And not for a moment did she doubt the
love of Connie for his wife, for there was heartbreak in her eyes.
Connie had loved her once.

Then suddenly Veronica broke from her husband's arms and
advanced upon Brandon and I was stunned, for now I did not
know whether I had misguessed the girl or not. Had she already
learned how to outbrazen the facts or had I been mistaken and
was she after all only a sweet and stupid child whom Connie
could fool? Her velvet cloak fluttered like the black wings of the
Avenging Angel and she said, "And this is the end of the matter.
I will have no more of it and I warn you never to trouble us
again. If you have more to say, say it now, for I will not permit
you to threaten our happiness another time. If you have evidence
that you can present, present it now. Have you a keepsake his
mother would recognize? Have you a picture? Have you a letter?"

Connie's high color drained from his face and he swallowed
hard and there was a moment of terrible silence and in that
moment I said to myself, "I was wrong about her. She trusts
him fully or she would not dare to question Brandon." Yet now
that I am older I ask myself what else she could have done but
settle the matter there and then. I did not know and I do not
know what the girl Veronica thought as she faced Brandon.

And Brandon spoke. She said, "I got no proof. I got nothing—
not even a letter."

And I thought of all the times she had vowed her love for
Connie and how in all those times I had not believed her. I believed her now. I remembered well the letter he had written her,
the letter that lay upstairs. And in that letter he had left nothing
unsaid and he had called her his precious, his beloved, for it was
true that he had loved her once. Not his mother, not his wife,
could read that letter without knowing who had fathered Brandy's
baby. But she was not going to let them read it and when I
looked at her she gave me a defiant glance as though to say,
"Now do you believe I love him?" And I wanted to say, "Yes,
Brandy, I believe."

And I had not known that she and I would ever experience
a moment of sisterhood but the moment had come nevertheless.
Together we had looked upon Veronica in Connie's arms and
had known that this was his love, his chance for a lifetime of
happiness. And neither of us would say the word or perform the
deed that would rob him of Veronica. And I will tell you that
I stood there staring at the woman, Brandon, and thinking little
of my own ability to judge character. I would not have guessed
her capable of such devotion.

And Mrs. Coberley was saying to her, "We will return in the
morning and if you are still here I will have you placed under
arrest." And she said to Veronica, "Come, darling." And they
moved together toward the door.

Connie said to me, "May I walk you to your own conveyance?"

His blue-gray eyes smiled down at me and the sweetness of
his glance was a thing that could be wondered at, for this man
had renounced his flesh and blood and the woman to whom he
had promised much.

We walked across the parlor together and were almost to the
hall when he could bear no longer the pretense that he was un-

aware of Brandon's eyes upon him. He wavered and raised his glance to her.

She said, "Ain't you even gonna say good-by?"

And for him it was a difficult moment, for he had my presence to consider, and yet it was little enough she asked when one remembered all he had led her to expect of him.

He grinned and he said, "A curious request under the circumstances, isn't it, Elizabeth? But I don't suppose it would hurt to say good-by if that's what she wants." And he turned then to Brandon and he said to her, "Good-by, young woman."

And though she wept, her eyes blazed an angry fire, and I thought of lightning flashing through the rain to strike dead all who might have sinned that day. She said, "You know my name."

He shrugged and said to me, "Persistent creature, isn't she?" And I imagine that this pose of his had been difficult to sustain and that it was bound to show a weakness somewhere, for he turned to her then and he said, "Very well, if it will please you—Good-by, Brandy."

I do not think that he ever knew that he had called her by her familiar nickname. I do not think he ever knew that he had ruined a magnificent performance.

Outside the house there was Mrs. Shieldstone standing at the boundary line and it gave her no embarrassment that the Coberley women gazed at her with curiosity as they sat in Aunt Laurel's carriage. And as they drove away Mrs. Shieldstone turned her stony eyes upon me and they were alight with a strange glint that could have been triumph had the woman had aught to do with Brandy's misery.

"No feeling, eh?" she said to me. "No vulnerable point?"

She smiled grimly and turning away walked swiftly toward

the decaying farmhouse, and it was not till that moment that I remembered about the parlor window which I had opened and had forgotten to close.

I drove homeward so slowly that when I arrived our guests were already settled before the fireplace and Hendon was offering a tray of warm drinks to them. Aunt Laurel greeted me with something less than delight as I entered the room and I wondered if I had failed to properly rearrange any of her possessions through which I had pawed in search of the letter. Powell held his hand out to me and I went to sit beside him on the sofa. He looked very ill at ease indeed and I thought it an imposition that he must be burdened with the sort of thing he had for years avoided.

"I was very proud of Connie," Mrs. Coberley was saying. "Not once in dealing with the creature did he lose his temper. He was so sweet and patient. It was quite extraordinary, I thought, when one considers the outrageousness of what she did."

"If we could only forget," Veronica moaned and Aunt Laurel turned a bright smile upon her and tried to change the subject.

"When was the wedding, Veronica?" she asked. "You must tell me about it."

The wedding had taken place in Paris and had been very elegant indeed. Veronica and Connie had met on shipboard.

"Re-met really," she smiled. "We had known each other as children but didn't remember. My mother and Connie's mother were old friends and it was quite a surprise when we all discovered each other the first evening out."

Aunt Laurel said, "A wedding in Paris must be delightful and romantic. Was it more so than marrying at home where you would both be surrounded with multitudes of friends?"

Veronica pouted prettily. "Oh, I was disappointed in a way, Miss Carpenter, not to have the festive round of parties and teas and the enormous wedding that we might have had. But Father is in the diplomatic service and will not be back here for years. Mother and I were joining him when I met Connie. You see, my parents wanted to attend my wedding of course and so—"

"Of course," Aunt Laurel said.

"And," Connie's mother said, "you can imagine how shocked we all were upon arriving home to find that there was a woman here representing herself as Connie's wife."

Veronica shuddered slightly but Aunt Laurel had done her best and must now surrender to the conversational desires of her senior guest.

"I could scarcely believe Fort's note, Laurel. It stunned me so, that I had a dreadful headache for hours after. It was clear that he didn't believe for a moment that Connie would have married such a creature but he didn't actually say that. For an uneducated man I must admit his subtle implications were quite masterly. His instincts, I will say, were remarkably sound." She waved a fat finger at me in a revolting attempt at playfulness. "Aren't you ashamed, Elizabeth, that you aren't as smart as a poor old farmer? How could you bring yourself to believe that Connie would marry such as she?"

I felt no awe of Mrs. Coberley, no obligation to make myself small before her.

"Why wouldn't he?" I asked. "I firmly believe her to be the most beautiful woman alive."

"Gracious, child," Mrs. Coberley said. "Do you think Connie would choose a wife by so unthinking a standard?"

Connie laughed and said, "It makes me uncomfortable to be discussed as though I were not here. Of course I would choose a wife for her beauty. I chose Veronica, didn't I? And what about that secesh woman's looks? Are they unusual? I really did not notice."

And I said, "They are so unusual, Connie, that they would catch a man's eye even if he were on horseback riding at a good gallop past a farmyard in which she stood."

And Connie looked away from me, and Powell picked up the drink which he had not yet touched and he sat staring thoughtfully into it.

Mrs. Coberley said, "I believe you grew fond of that woman, Elizabeth. Even Mr. Fort hinted that it was deplorable the way that you—"

"I did not grow fond of her," I said, "but it seems to me that her crime against you is small and—"

"Small!" Mrs. Coberley squeaked and Aunt Laurel looked at me entreatingly.

Connie said, "Elizabeth is right, dear. After all, the woman is very probably the dupe of some unscrupulous fellow and has no real idea of the thing she did to us. She wanted money, I suppose, had heard my name somewhere and, knowing something of the value civilized people put upon reputation, she set out to pry us loose from a rather large bankroll. It's all over now so let us tell the Carpenters about Switzerland."

Veronica said, "Oh, yes, it was enchanting in Switzerland." And she held Connie's hand while he told us of the chalet they had occupied in a fairy-tale village where the air was as intoxicating as wine.

And I sat there as Connie spoke of the people they had met,

the adventures they had experienced. And though he was as gay
and amusing as a character on the stage, I could not keep my
mind within that room. I could but think of the woman, Brandon,
and I do not expect this to be anything but confusing to you,
for I cannot explain why I felt pity for her. God knows she had
pitied no one, and yet I am made of such spongy material that
I could not rejoice in her dark hour or take pleasure in her
humiliation. And I repeated to myself the story of the boys and
old men who had gone forth to defend their town and of how
Brandon had handed them over to the enemy, and I told myself
that she had destroyed my brother, Brett, and that she was an
evil thing who deserved to suffer. And I could not even then
forget her, for she loved Connie Coberley and I was not un-
acquainted with the suffering that had been visited upon her.
And he sat there with Veronica's hand tightly held in his and
they smiled those secret smiles so peculiar to newly married
couples and I said to myself, "Had Brandy willed it Veronica
would not be smiling at him now and she would not permit him
to touch her." And I trust that you will not think that Mrs.
Coberley was right and that I had truly grown fond of the
woman, Brandon. I never liked her and that is God's truth, but
I am one who can hate a dog who attacks a cat and yet weep
for the dog's scratched eyes. And nothing in life had conditioned
me for contributing any merriment to an afternoon filled with
honeymooners' memoirs and I could not sit there watching the
secret smiles and the loving handclasps of those two. It may be
that I was more at home with misery than with joy or perhaps
I was guilty of an inner conceit that led me to believe that I
could bring comfort to the sorrowing. Or it may be that I was
remembering that moment of sisterhood which I had shared

with Brandy. I could sit in that room where Connie told his
bright stories no longer and I left them and drove once more
back to the house on the bay.

I walked into the Coberley house and directly up the stairs. I
thought I knew well what she would be doing. What was there
for her to do but pack? And I wondered in what she would
carry her new finery for I was remembering that she had brought
no luggage to the house. I did not find her upstairs. Though I
called her name, she did not answer, and I went down to the
parlor and she was not there. And I found her in the kitchen.

And I must warn you that I will not tell this well and I will
not pretend that a haziness exists because of my delicacy and
my wish to spare your feelings. The truth is that I do not know
how to project to you the stark horror of what I saw. As God is
my judge I thought first of the red satin and the way she had
draped it across her lovely body trying it for style and beauty.
I actually thought that the bright red splash I saw was once
again the soft, gleaming material that had pleased her so. But
it was not.

She was there at the kitchen table. I ran to her and the large
carving knife that she had used balanced for a moment on the
table edge and clattered to the floor. I screamed as it showered
small, warm drops of Brandon's blood upon me. And I must
have been mad with shock, for I did not like the woman and
yet I could hear myself sobbing and I clasped her to me as though
I could make her live again. And she would not breathe for me,
she would not live, though the amethyst eyes never closed but
remained fixed in frozen agony. I would not believe she was dead,
for once before my screams had brought help and life to her

and I tossed aside my bloody cloak and ran once more down
the slope, across the eerie deserted land that had been a farm and
I called their names again and no one answered me. I kept
running and listening as I ran to the hysterical cries that I knew
were mine and I ran directly to the splintered door of the old
farmhouse and it stood open and I ran in screaming for the witch
and for the girl with the banjo. But they were not there. There
was no fire. No sign that there had been one for many a winter.
And the door swung squeakily upon its rusted hinges and I
screamed in terror and I called, "Mrs. Shieldstone! Mrs. Shieldstone!" But there was no reply and I was alone with my fright
and my hysteria and the blood of Brandy drying upon my weak
and skinny hands.

And I ran back to her for we were alone in a world that had
forgotten us, where there was no help, no voice to answer us,
and I thought that I would die beside her, for I could not bear
the horror and the loneliness and the dizzying pounding of my
heart. And I dragged myself back to the kitchen and I must have
been more than mad, for I called to my horse that he come help
me, and when I heard the front door open it seemed reasonable
that he had heard and was coming, and in relief I sank upon the
floor and waited for him to find me.

But it was Powell who walked into the kitchen and I looked
up at him and I do not know where I found the word, for I
had never spoken it before, but I said to him, "Papa, oh, Papa,
help me."

And he stood transfixed for a second, gazing upon the hor-
rible thing that had happened in the Coberley kitchen. Then he
picked me up and carried me to the parlor sofa.

I do not know when he left the room for I sank into nothingness and when I was again aware of him, he was bathing my face and hands and looking down at me with his kind, calm eyes.

"All right, Liz?"

"I'm all right."

He drew up a hassock and seated himself. "I'd like you to lie there for a bit if you will, dear."

"I will. I feel sort of odd."

He nodded. "Of course."

"It was awful," I said.

He glanced away from me. "Connie sold the girl out, didn't he, Liz? Or would you rather not answer that?"

I did not reply.

He said, "When it came to me that this was what he had done, I knew where you were."

"I'm so glad you knew, so glad you followed me here."

"Well, I knew that if she'd been hurt you'd want to help her and I was afraid for you. I thought that you would defend him and that she, in anger, might quite possibly—"

"No," I said. "She is the one who defended him."

Powell said, "Of course. People always defend Connie. Why do they, Liz?"

And I said, "Because they love him. You cannot imagine how much they love him."

"No, I cannot," he said, "but I have seen evidence that must convince me." And he took my hand and sighed deeply. "Liz, my baby, I would give my life if it would bring you happiness and yet I have always felt so strongly about Connie Coberley that had he asked to marry you I would have disapproved his suit."

And I thought that under the circumstances he described I

would have defied him. I would have taken Connie at any price that I was forced to pay. I buried my face in the sofa cushion and wept for the love that had filled my life with melancholy regrets and fooling imaginings.

Powell stroked my hair. "Liz, he was never worth a tear, never worth a thought."

I looked up at Powell and there were things I would have said had I believed that he would understand.

And he said to me, "You are not crying because he came with the pretty little Veronica at his side. This I know full well and you must not think me so obtuse that I misinterpret the cause of your grief. You do not weep for the dead woman. You do not weep that Connie has married another. You weep because you have seen him as he is."

I did not look at Powell or dare to answer him.

"It is the emptiness that troubles you now, Liz. The aching question of what to put in place of a dream. Shall I tell you what to put there, darling? It's very simple. Just put another dream."

"There are no other dreams," I said. "Not for me."

He smiled in a way I had not seen him smile before. "I am an authority on the subject," he said. "And I assure you there are always other dreams."

I shook my head. "For others perhaps. For me, no." I sat up and found that I could face now the ordeal of walking to the carriage. My heart no longer pounded. The dizzy, whirling world was normal again, normal and dreary. "I can go," I said. "I'm perfectly all right. Powell, will you take care of everything about —about Brandon?"

"Of course, darling. Don't think of it. I'll have everything attended to."

And at that moment Brandon's baby cried and I had not thought of her till then.

Powell said, "Oh, yes. She had a child. I'd forgotten." He walked back to the kitchen wing and found the infant and brought it to the parlor.

I looked at the little thing and I said, "This matter also you will have to attend to, for the child has no one."

And he was silent looking down upon the child of Connie Coberley and the woman, Brandon. And after a time he raised his eyes to me and put the child into my arms.

"I have attended to the matter," he said.

You will think that I forgot my brother in all that had occurred, but this is not so. I spent that night at the Robertson farm, for I could not bring my baby home while the Coberleys were there to speak of her in a manner that would anger me.

On the following morning I went to see Brett and I hoped that he had had no news of Brandon, for I thought myself best equipped to deliver it in a way that would react upon him least adversely.

It was necessary for me to approach Mrs. Lankton and I dreaded it but she was more cordial than I could have hoped.

"I wonder if I could impose upon you, Mrs. Lankton. Would you give my brother a free hour so that I can speak to him alone?"

"Heavens, you must think I'm a slave driver," she said. "What's gotten into you, Miss Elizabeth? We used to be friends."

I flushed. "I'm not going to explain," I said, "but I'm going to say that all that has happened between us is my fault. Is that enough?"

"More than enough." She held out her hand to me. "I always liked you, Miss Elizabeth, and hoped that you liked us." She left me then to summon Brett and I waited for him in the farm dining room where I had been received. And while I waited I was not at ease, for that which lay ahead of me was unpleasant business indeed. And I did not know what my tidings would do to my brother. Yet he could not be left to discover Brandon's death in any haphazard way that chance afforded.

When he came into the room he looked anxiously at me, wondering what my call might mean, but he kissed me in greeting and I realized that it was a very long while since I had seen him.

"How are you, Brett?"

"Fine, I guess. How are you?"

I assured him that I was well and Powell and Aunt Laurel, too, and then he waited for my news and, as I caught his glance, it occurred to me that I had been fortunate in all recent contacts with my brother. Never once in months had I caught him with the fearful, empty look in his eyes that told of retreat into the shadows.

"Let us sit down, Brett."

And we sat at the table and stared at Mrs. Lankton's darning basket that occupied the central position as though it were a bowl of tasty fruit.

"Brett, I must tell you something that is very sad and it will be difficult to bear. It—it concerns Brandy."

"Brandy?"

"Yes, dear. She met with an accident."

He stood up and pushed the chair back and it made a harsh, grating sound upon the well-scrubbed boards. "Where is she?"

"Brother, sit down. You cannot help her."

He looked at me and his heart was in his eyes. "Liz, you mean that—she's—dead?"

"Yes, Brett, and you must not let it hurt you too deeply. You must look upon Brandon as someone who came into our lives and was never intended to remain there."

He crossed his arms upon the table and buried his face in them and wept. And I thought that I would have to ask Mrs. Lankton for a room in which he could lie down and that I would bring Powell to him. For I remembered Brett's weeping and how it left him shattered and weak. I let him weep and I hoped that he would not drift from this grief to the older one and the memories of Fredericksburg and I sat temporizing. Should I ask the Lankton boy to go for Powell? What was best? What was sensible?

And after a time Brett raised his head and he said to me, "You knew, didn't you, that I was in love with her?" And I was astonished that the sudden sorrow had not shaken the clarity of his thinking.

"She was beautiful," I said. "A young man could not help but—"

He said, "She was my whole life, Elizabeth."

I shook my head. "No, Brett, for your life will be very long."

"But she's been all the life I've had since I first saw her. She's been all the life there was since Fredericksburg. She was always in my thoughts, in my dreams." And the tears gathered again in his eyes and he said, "God knows what would have become of

me in the end had it not been for her. She gave me something
to think about, something to want, something to work for."

And of course it was a wild exaggeration to credit her with
great good, for she herself had been evil. What he had wanted
of her was corrupting to his soul and the work he was doing was
unworthy of him. But I looked at my brother and I was sorely
perplexed, for I could not see that she had done him any harm.
How could this be when she had been so wicked and his longing
for her had been sinful and an abomination to those who cham-
pioned virtue? And at her instigation he had all but deserted his
family and had chosen a hard, mean life of back-breaking labor.
And the things into which she had led him were not things we
who loved him would have wanted for him. And I was puzzled.

He said, "What happened to her, Liz?"

"Will you let the matter rest if I say to you that it will serve
no purpose for you to know in what manner her death occurred?"

He smiled sadly at me. "I will leave it so if you wish, but I
would be able to listen, for there is something you must know,
Liz. I have not dreamed of Fredericksburg since Brandy said
she loved me."

And it seems to me that I have come to the end of the narrative. I am not certain, for I have no sure knowledge of how
these things are concluded. I do suppose however that this record
of my experiences during the winter of 1865–66 finished in the
dining room of the Lankton farm. It was there that I knew
Brett's recovery to be no longer in doubt. It was there that I knew
he would be cured, for he had not dreamed of Fredericksburg
since Brandy said she loved him. And it had been evil of her
to tell my brother such a lie but because she had told it, he could
pronounce the dreadful name of Fredericksburg in a calm and

normal tone. And I do not wish to be quoted as having said that lies can be good things but the woman Brandon lied to my brother and he fought his way back from the dark shores of madness to listen. And in the dining room of the Lankton farm I suddenly knew that my brother would take his place again among the well and strong, and so I say that this is probably the end of my narrative, for certainly if all this writing has had a main figure of interest, that figure has been my brother.

But I will write more, for I do not pretend that this is a work of art which must be laid aside just at the breathless second of completion, before the creator has the opportunity to ruin it with another stroke, another word. This has been an enjoyable pastime for me. Since I do not sew or knit it has been, I suppose, my version of fancy work and I will not leave it till I have ended it neatly, as one puts an edge of crocheting around a shawl.

I called the baby Laurel, for I never knew what name Brandon had given her. And I can tell you that my aunt instantly found a dimple in the baby's cheek and an intelligence far in advance of any child she had ever seen before. And when we moved back to the New York house small Laurel's laughter brought a color and flavor to that house that I had never known and that Powell had forgotten. And we lived through new joys and new heartaches, for when she suffered her baby ailments we suffered, too, and it was Powell who would have none but the finest doctor for her. And in passing I would like to say that the doctor had been part of Powell's old social life and after he had dined at our table Powell could not be so rude as to refuse to go to his.

And small Laurel was mine. I raised her and she calls me Mother though she knows that I did not bear her. And she told me once that had she choice of all mothers alive she would have chosen me and I have not forgotten that she said that. Would you in my place?

It is a curious thing that I—when too young to know bitterness —had dreamed of possessing one day a child of Connie Coberley's and that my dream became reality. I have had a child of his to love which is more than can be said of Veronica who has had little happiness from life.

I would like to tell you, too, of the summers at the shore and how my little girl took to Mr. Fort and liked to ride with him on his old wagon; and how Mr. Fort and I never spoke of the bitter winter but pretended that the Carpenters were like all other families and knew the ocean only when it glittered in summer sunlight. And each June we move to the shore but it is not common practice to ride up the river road, for anyone will tell you that it is more pleasant on the beach.

But there are times when I go alone to the small rise of ground and look at the house on the bay. The Coberleys have never walked into it since the day that Brandon died. The older Coberleys are gone now but Connie has his reasons for not wishing to spend his summers in that house. It has long been for sale and no one wants it. Perhaps it is the stories that have arisen. It is said that the house is haunted. I only know the house has never been sold and that Connie has done nothing to keep it in repair. The grounds are wild with weeds and rot and you can no longer tell where the Coberley property ends and the Spurney farm begins. It is all one. A weird, desolate stretch of land that frightens children and sets adults to remembering.

When I go there I think of the Carolinians and it almost seems at times that I have caught a flash of the strong old man seeking a rabbit in the underbrush or that I have seen Tippy lying beneath

the ill-fated trees. And I think of Mrs. Shieldstone and her hard
eyes and I remember how she said to me, "If my plan is not a
good one, I will find a better." But I am almost forty now and
for many a year I have been too busy to ponder much on the
existence of witchery. Most times I remember Mrs. Shieldstone
only as a remarkable woman. Most times.

And every year I sit in my carriage on that rise of ground
and I look at the deserted land and at the house in which Brandon
died and when I see Mockingbird streaking toward the crumbling farmhouse or hear her banjo strike a chord I know that it
is time for me to leave.

I go home to our house on the ocean. All summer long it is
filled with crowds of young people and it rocks with song and
laughter. Brett's wife thinks I have spoiled Laurel, for she is stern
with her children. I cannot see what she has gained. Hers are not
finer, not more loving and considerate than mine.

Powell and my aunt are aging but they enjoy the gaiety that
came along with my small daughter. Powell has had no honors
in life that brought him greater satisfaction than the child's love
which was offered simply, spontaneously, from the sincerity of her
warm little heart. For my aunt the great moment came when
Laurel was married and wore the wedding gown that had lain
so many years waiting to fulfill its destiny. It is a strange thing
that no aura of tragedy lay upon that gown, for we had known
so many years of happiness that we had forgotten how to weep.

And my Laurel wore that gown and was married last Tuesday
at the Church of St. Thomas. She married a splendid young
man, and at the reception he said to me in wonderment, "I don't
know why a beautiful girl like Laurel wanted me."

Yes, she is beautiful. She has coal black hair and her eyes are

Connie's, blue-gray and bright with warmth and laughter, but I am not frightened for Laurel. She is not like her father nor is she like the woman, Brandon. And if I were forced to give a reason as to why she differs so greatly from them I would say that it is Nature's way of striking an average. All of my Laurel's goodness and decency were needed to balance the scales.

I have written this narrative in the room that was Powell's library. He gave it to me for my use a few years ago and I have had it changed to my taste. It has crimson draperies and small furniture fitted to my comfort. As I write there are three cats roaming the room and there is another looking at me with sleepy yellow eyes from a cushion on the hearth. And it strikes me that I have been so fortunate that I have nothing of which to complain. I am like the sleepy, yellow-eyed cat, cozy and content.

But I cannot close this narrative—or bind off my crocheted edging—without wondering about it all. We were a star-crossed family and never expected joy to enter our lives, and it would indeed never have done so except that upon a windy day I met an evil woman.

And I have omitted no detail pertinent to the matters which have been set forth here with sober attention to truth and justice and I can do no more. This then must certainly be the end of the narrative. And it is just as well, for I am going to begin taking lessons in china painting next week. They say it is fascinating.

ELIZABETH GRACE CARPENTER
New York City, 1886.